Randall Stevens

HELLN, TEXAS

Randall Stevens

Torture,

Human Sacrifice,

Reincarnation,

Armageddon,

… words **in the English Dictionary;**

… events **happening in…**

HELLN, TEXAS

Randall Stevens

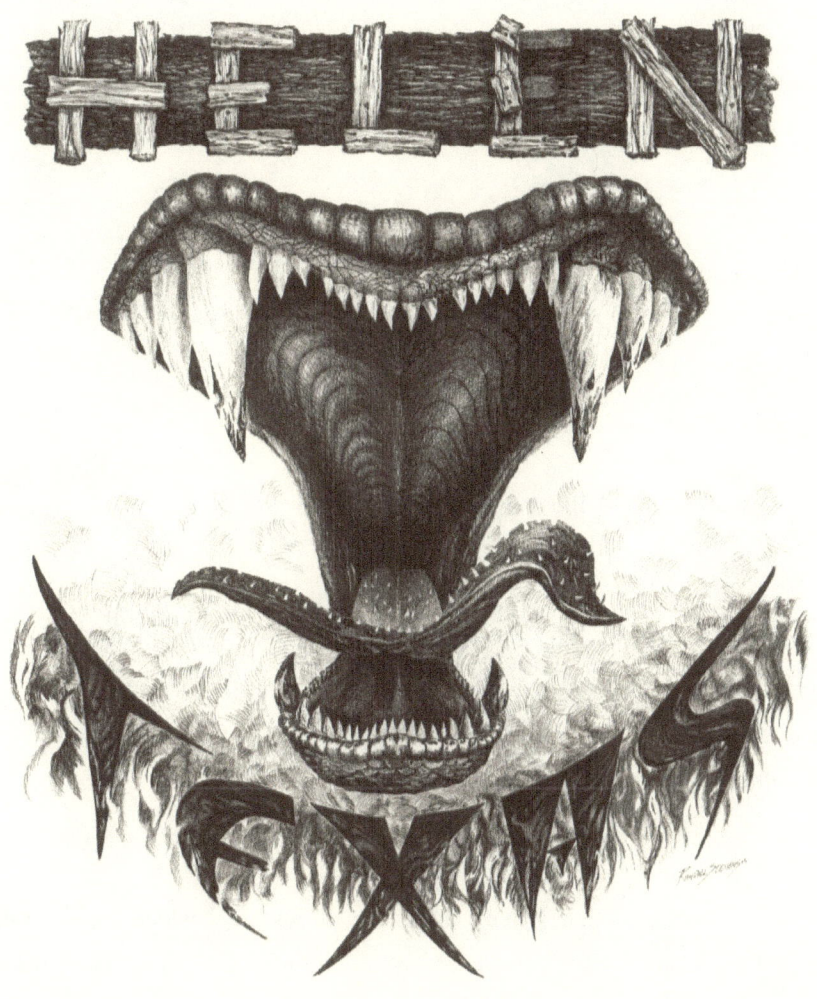

by
Randall Stevens

HELLN, TEXAS

Published by Randall Stevens

ISBN 978-0-6151-3476-5

Copyright 2006, by Randall Stevens.

All rights reserved

Illustrations by Randall Stevens.

This is a work of fiction. Names, characters, places and incidents are either the product of the author's imagination or are used fictitiously and any resemblance to actual persons, living or dead, business establishments, events or locals is entirely coincidental.

Randall Stevens

To my parents Robert and Ruth;

I love you.

HELLN, TEXAS

Randall Stevens

Acknowledgements

I would like to thank the following people, who for not their generous help and understanding this work would never have come to be. Stephen King, who's book 'On Writing' gave me the inspiration and confidence to write. To Beth Bloom, the first one to read the rough draft and do the final editing, Skip Press, Hollywood Writers Group, Siobhan Wallace and her knowledge Nordic Mythology. Special thanks to my daughter Tara Campbell and friends Martha Bush, Karen Hanahan, Donna Charles, Linda Samuels, Chris Aakhus, DuAnne Hagerty and Sandy Tischer whose comments and support I couldn't have done without.

HELLN, TEXAS

Author's Foreword

Included in this book there are several references to Norse Mythology. In development, I used 'creative license' to employ a few minor changes to some of the characters, while taking every precaution possible to stay as close as possible to the mythological stories that have been past down through the ages. I am not, nor profess to be, in any way an expert on the subject

For those that would like further education on Norse Mythology, I suggest a search on line. There are several sites that cater to the subject. The most common books to use are the Poetic Edda, a series of stories put together by an unknown author around 1250 CE. The other book is called the Prose Edda and was written by Snorri Sturluson around 1220 CE.

- Randall Stevens

Prologue

Nine-year-old Susan Waythill squirmed, trying to find a more comfortable position on the hard vinyl chair. It felt like a marble slab. The hallway outside the Initial Room was quiet. The only sound was the tick of the black wall clock, nearing four AM. She was tired and cold. She scanned the letters above the door: ICU. She didn't know what they meant, but her mother was in that room and that's all that mattered. Cancer ...a scary word, a bad word. Grown-ups always looked away when they whispered it. Her father, Professor Owen Waythill, had tried to explain the night the ambulance took her mother away, but his complex words sounded like jumble at the time. All she knew for sure was that *it* took her mother, put her in that room and there was nothing she could do about it.

The hall was empty now. She wanted to go into the room, but she'd been told to stay put while her father tended to other matters. She got up. Her stomach felt like dried mud. Tiptoeing to the door, she put her ear against it. There was a muffled beep, regular, like the heartbeat of a robot.

She inched open the door. It was dark. Silent - except for the mechanical beep -

louder now. In the middle of the room a ghost-like curtain hovered in mid-air.

"Mommy?" she whispered.

No answer.

Susan stepped inside. Colder. She moved to the curtain.

"Mommy?"

Only the sterile beep sounded.

Her trembling hands parted the curtain. There she was, lying on the bed. If it hadn't been for the tubes, wires and bandages, she would have looked just like she always did in her bedroom in the morning. Her fingers touched the only part of her mother's hand not covered with the bandages.

"Mommy?"

No movement. Tears welled and rolled down Susan's cheeks.

There were footsteps, movement of the curtain.

Susan didn't move.

"Honey, you can't be in here." It was the voice of the nurse.

"I just want to be with my Mommy," Susan said softly as she kept her eyes focused on her mother.

"I know you want to be here," the nurse consoled. "But your mother is better off if she's undisturbed."

Susan stood up on tiptoes and gently kissed her face.

"I love you, Mommy," she whispered.

The nurse gently guided her to the door. Susan didn't want to sit anymore. She walked to the end of the hall stopping in front of a floor-to ceiling window. It was raining outside. She traced a cascading droplet with her index finger as it made its way down the glass. It zigzagged - then hesitated, as if it were afraid of its final destination. She knew how it felt. Everything seemed so cold, so desolate, so empty.

Susan focused on the glass again. *'How awesome it would be if it were a magic window,'* she thought, *'a passageway opened by whispering a secret phrase or word. It would let me to go back to any time or place I wanted - back to when mommy was*

14

OK'. The thought of her mother's bond enveloped Susan. She was more than a mother – she was her big sister, her closest friend whom she could share her most treasured secrets.

Suddenly, a brilliant flash of white light filled the window.

Susan's body jolted back.

The glass began to glow with a myriad of colors. They swirled and twisted into a spiral that fused into a massive white sphere. It floated in the blackness like a luminous diamond. Inside the sphere appeared the image of a huge tree alive with animals and birds of all kinds. The four seasons blew throughout the crown. New buds and blossoms of spring, full blown greenery of summer, red and gold leaves of autumn swayed and dipped like a dancer along side the bare branches of snow that draped like white frosting. Three immense roots spread out from the base. Two encircled the white sphere and grew into misshapen dark brown masses; the third pierced it like an anchor chain. Sap secreted from the bark and turned the white sphere blue.

From the center of the tree, emerged the faint outline of a human form surrounded by a radiance of golden light. The hazy image became more defined as it grew. Susan's eyes strained to refocus. She drew a deep breath, brought her hands to her face and stepped back in shock.

It was her mother!

"Suzie it's me Mommy. Please don't be afraid."

Susan gave a hesitant smile.

"Suzie, I need to talk with you."

Susan's eyes welled with tears of joy. She stepped forward and embraced her mother's warmth. "Mommy ... I ..."

"Shhh, honey," she raised her finger to her lips. *"You just visited me in my room. I heard you. I felt you. It will be something I'll always remember."*

"You're better!" Susan exclaimed wiping her tears. "You're coming home now?!"

"Honey," her mother sighed, *"I'm sorry. I have to go to another place. It's a very nice place and I will be happy."*

"Can I come, too? Please?"

"I wish you could, but I need you to stay here and do something for me. It's very important and it's a big secret! I know you're very good at keeping secrets. It's why I want to tell it to you. Are you ready?"

Pause, then she nodded.

"What you've just seen is your heritage, your history."

Susan squinted.

"It is the beginning. And it will be up to you one day to help it survive."

"Beginning of what?"

"It's the beginning of the world honey. Remember when we talked about good and evil and how there's always been a balance between them?"

Susan nodded attentively.

"Well, sometimes evil gets stronger than good and when that happens, pain and suffering afflict every living thing in the world. Everyone gets really sad."

"But I don't understand, Mommy…"

"You will when the time comes. Trust me, sweetheart."

Susan stood silent.

"The power to defeat evil and keep the balance has been entrusted to our family for thousands of years. It's time for you to be the keeper of the power."

"Will it…hurt?" Susan's voice quavered.

"Oh, no, darling," she laughed gently, *"You won't even know you have it until the time comes for you to use it. You won't remember our talk. That way, your decision to use the power will come from your heart. Trust your heart dear. It will tell you when the time is right."*

"I'm scared…" Susan put her hands to her face.

"There's nothing to be afraid of, sweetheart. I will be with you." She paused thoughtfully. *"You can remember this."* She leaned forward and whispered into

Susan's ear.

"Trust the voice inside. It will never lie to you."

Her mother leaned back.

"I must go now. You will be a good girl and take care of your daddy for me, OK? I love you, Suzie-Q."

The image faded. Susan reached out, but found her hands pressed against cold glass. She recoiled then looked around -alone. What just happened? She looked back at the window and saw only her own reflection.

Footsteps echoed through the antiseptic air. Susan turned. Her father, a tall man with graying hair and stern features was coming towards her. Susan managed a small smile. It was not returned. Her smile quivered and fell. A brutal chill overtook her as he stopped and looked down at her.

"Daddy?" Susan whispered.

"She's … gone," he choked. As he reached out to Susan his eyes caught movement in the window. It was the reflection of the doctor entering his dead wife's room. He pulled his hand back and said, "You'd better stay here."

He turned and left.

Alone – Cold – Empty, Susan closed her eyes to shut out the pain.

Her heart began to hardened.

*****

(Twenty-five years later)

The slime thinned as the huge bark slowly split opened. It revealed the dark hollow of the tree trunk. Rancid fumes of decaying flesh surged outward. The two Elders stood still as the potent air penetrated their lungs and stung their eyes. The inside of the tree then erupted in flames illuminating a tall, gaunt figure of a man. He stepped from the fiery hollow. His eyes flashed a feral yellow as he gestured at the opening. The flames died and the raw wound in the tree closed.

"The blessings of the Savior are upon you, My Lord," The two Elders spoke in unison. He was their leader and voice from the one called Savior. They quickly removed their broad brimmed black hats and bowed - neither daring to look up.

"Rise," Lord Lokan commanded. His deep voice carried immense power and the Elders straightened. Lord Lokan raised his hands in benediction, "The time has come. In eight days, the purpose of the Savior will be fulfilled and the goddess will rise to reclaim that which is hers."

"Praised be the Savior," the Elders eyes gleamed as they gave the ritual response.

Lord Lokan's eyes shined in the torch light. "The Savior will require two sacrifices." He paused. "Before midnight proceeding the final day, there will be a sacrifice to celebrate the death of the old world of the creator. The second sacrifice will be prior to midnight on the final day, *The Evening Day.* It will open the passage for her coming. She demands that the sacrifices be female to honor her. Assemble the Legions to draw lots for the right to gather the sacrifices. Awaken the swamp and prepare the bridge. Only those with rank and privilege shall be at the ceremony. The rest shall learn of the miracle from those who witness it." His voice lowered, "Be on guard. The Savior sees with only one eye, but that eye is sharp and nothing escapes it."

"Yes my Lord."

"Let the gathering begin."

The Elders disappeared into the darkness.

Lord Lokan turned to face the huge oak tree behind him. He lifted his eyes to its enormity.

"And then my time will finally come," he whispered.

One

Susan Waythill was an attractive woman who didn't have time to notice when men stared at her. She stood one inch short of six feet and had dark auburn hair that complemented her deep emerald colored eyes. Her features resembled the actor Sigourney Weaver.

A successful attorney at a large law firm, she was more than satisfied with what she had accomplished in her life and was proud to know she'd done it on her own. Her academic record revealed that she excelled at whatever lay before her, from being valedictorian at Winston Churchill High School in her hometown of San Antonio, Texas, to being on the Dean's list at Southern Methodist University Law School where she graduated Summa Cum Laude. Susan set her goals high and expected nothing less than to exceed them.

After graduation she went to work for the largest law firm in Dallas. Many firms courted her, but the proactive attitude balanced with the steady Texas charm of Landau, Cross, Alexander and Young won out. She absorbed much in the first years of her tenure. She gained immediate respect as a force to be reckoned within a courtroom. She had a talent for anticipating and then thwarting her opponent's moves. When her firm opened an office in El Paso, she was selected to help in the transition. It was part of the firm's process of grooming her for bigger and better things.

Susan's success in her professional life didn't come without cost. To her the cost was of little consequence though. Who needs friends and relationships; her life consisted of working hard. She owned an expensive condo on the north side of the city and employed a service that came once a week to clean and keep it stocked with food and beverages. Her tastes were simple, elegant, uncluttered and were reflected in her unique décor and tailored clothes. Strength training, as well as aerobics, was at the forefront of her daily routine. She worked out at a private health club five mornings a week. An occasional movie, play or opera completed her life. For the firm's social commitments that could not be avoided, she employed a professional escort service. She liked it because she was in total control and once the event was over, so was the date. Relationships required understanding, sympathy, trust and vulnerability - traits she only allowed to flourish in her client dealings. Towers of strength stood alone and that's how she pictured herself.

*****

Susan stood in front of the Masters Gun Shop on Commerce Street, in El Paso, Texas. She couldn't fathom why, only that she had been compelled to be there by her "inside voice". She never thought it strange to be controlled by this internal guide. In fact, for a long time she thought everyone had one. As she grew older, she discovered that this was not the case and instead of feeling odd or different, she considered it an advantage. It was a strong influence in her life; always steered her in the right direction... Until now?

As the bright mid-February sun painted her shadow on the concrete below her feet, she looked at the sign above the entrance identifying it as El Paso's best place for her shooting needs.

"This is absurd," she whispered under her breath as she opened the door.

'BANG!'

The sound of a gunshot going off sent Susan into a crouched position. Hearing nothing else, she cautiously looked up and realized where the shot came from. It was a special door chime. Embarrassed, she slowly straightened.

"Stupid thing; could give someone a heart attack," She muttered under her breath as she looked around. Guns or hunting had never appealed to her; the whole idea of shooting something for sport turned her stomach. Guns, ammo and an assortment of hunting gear were on display. Adding to her perception of the male oriented ambiance was the wide assortment of animal heads adorning the walls. She wanted to leave, but her inner voice kept pushing her. She walked up to the counter and stared at the glass door of the walled rifle case.

"Hello, anyone here?" She glanced around the shop.

"How can I help you?"

Susan turned to the door behind the counter and caught her breath. A tall, well muscled, man dressed in black khaki slacks and a black turtleneck sweater was walking toward her, his stride confident and sure. He reached up and brushed back a strand of dark brown hair from his forehead. He slid behind the counter in front of her. Susan found herself held gently by his dark blue eyes that had a hint of a twinkle.

He stretched out his hand.

"I'm Sam Masters - manager and owner."

Susan laid her hand in his with a sense of familiarity. She knew this man. She didn't know how, but she knew him.

"Do I know you, Mr. Masters?" she questioned as his fingers closed over hers. Their eyes locked

He smiled. "I think I would definitely have remembered meeting you."

She smiled back.

"Now, what can I do for you?"

"Oh...uh," Susan shook herself, "I want to buy a gun."

"Are you shopping for protection or just to learn how to handle one?" Sam didn't release his hold on Susan's hand. He took in everything. Especially the green eyes that seemed to change from emerald to sea green and back as she looked at him. He felt there was a lot going on under the surface. He had to find out more about her.

"What kind of business are you in?" He asked.

"I'm an attorney," Susan replied.

"I see. You're probably looking for a handgun, I suspect? Sam took a quick look at the rifle case behind him and back. "I didn't know by the way I saw you staring at this rifle case."

Susan realized he had been watching her when she came in. It tantalized her. She could only smile in response.

There was an awkward, yet sensual, pause between them.

Sam gestured to the display counter, "Would you prefer a revolver or a pistol?

"What's the difference?" Susan asked as satisfying shot of electricity flowed through her. She liked the way he took charge of the moment.

"Well, a revolver has a revolving cylinder where the bullets are loaded one at a time. A pistol has a magazine, a clip, where the bullets..." Susan's puzzled look prompted Sam to stop and pull out both types of gun from the case. "Here. Let me show you."

The absence of the warmth of his hand was very noticeable to her.

He proceeded to load the weapons with the blanks he kept under the counter for demonstration. He slammed the Glock 9mm magazine home with the palm of his hand then loaded a .357 Magnum.

"This Glock 9mm is exceptionally well balanced, not too much of a kick."

Susan took Sam's last words as demeaning. She was very sensitive to chauvinistic

22

comments and would have normally said something, but decided on restraint. She looked at the .357 on the glass counter and shook her head.

"No, I want something…bigger." She pointed at the .357, "that one!"

"That one might be a bit too much," Sam smiled, "…it kicks like the proverbial mule. I think this one would be better for you."

Susan couldn't restrain herself and said irritably, "Well, since I'm the one buying it, I guess I should get what I want!"

She folded her arms and cocked her head to one side.

Sam smiled inwardly at the stubborn set of Susan's jaw.

"I have a shooting range in the back. Would you like to try it before you buy it, you know, just to make sure?"

Susan nodded keeping her arms folded.

"Right this way then Counselor." Sam pulled a box of shells for each weapon from the drawer and led the way.

Susan followed him through the doorway into a rectangular room lined with concrete blocks, wires and clips to hold and slide the targets.

Sam handed Susan a pair of safety glasses and padded headphones. He loaded the gun.

"Now, stand with both feet planted firmly on the ground, one slightly in front of the other." He handed her the gun, "Hold the gun in your dominant hand and brace it with the other. Raise it up to shoulder level, sight down the barrel and be sure to squeeze the trigger, don't jerk it."

Susan was surprised at how heavy the gun was, but determined to make a good showing. She planted her feet, raised the gun and aimed at the target. She pulled the trigger.

The gun fired with a tremendous roar and the kick knocked her backwards, her arms flying up above her head. She suddenly found herself in Sam's arms - the headphones knocked cockeyed off her ears. Sam's strong arms closed around her. She felt like a fish out of water as she tried to regain her balance.

"Are you all right? Are you hurt?" He asked.

Sam turned her toward him, his arms still around her body. He unconsciously pulled her closer, her supple body suddenly playing havoc with his emotions.

Susan felt an intense desire to stay and let his secure arms envelope her. A claustrophobic panic wash over her. He was too close – physically and emotionally. She pulled away.

"I think I'm OK," Susan said with a little hint of a shiver.

Sam sensed her sudden withdrawal. He took the weapon from her and smiled. He liked that she tried to fire the .357.

"Well, I admire you for trying to handle this one," He said with a gentle smile, "Not many women would have."

"You must not know many women then," she counted thinly as she straightened herself. She sensed a longing to be back in his arms, shook it off. He was wreaking havoc with her emotions.

After firing the Glock, which Susan found much easier, he led the way back into the shop.

Sam finished the paperwork and slid it across the counter. "There is a mandatory waiting period of three days." He handed Susan a pen. "If you'll sign here and here, I'll give you a call when it's ready."

"Thank you." Susan turned to leave.

"Is there anything else I can help you with…Mrs. Waythill?" Sam asked.

"That's *Ms* Waythill," Susan retorted quicker than she meant.

"Sorry." Sam grinned, "I won't make that mistake again."

"Thank you," Susan responded coldly and left the shop.

"My, oh my," Sam whistled to himself as he watched her leave the shop.

*****

Sam Masters was in his mid-thirties and a transplant from Wisconsin, or as he referred to it – 'Wis <u>Cold</u> son.' He was 6' 4" with dark brown hair and dark blue eyes, a combination that made every woman who saw him turn to take a second look. He grew up on a dairy farm and their from an early age learned the meaning of hard work. He was the second oldest of four boys. He never balked at the long hard working hours of farm life, he just knew it wasn't something that he didn't want to do for the rest of his life.

After graduating high school, Sam's restless nature sent him into the US Army's Military Police Corps. His no-nonsense approach to job performance got him noticed and he had aspirations of making it a career. During his assignment at Fort Bliss, located just outside El Paso, Texas, the idea of a career was squashed by his now ex-wife.

After nine years of service Sam embarked on a civilian path that started in sales and ended with owning the gun store that bore his last name. It was the only thing he had left after an ugly divorce six years before. The only reason he got the store was because she didn't want anything to do with it.

This was the first year the shop had actually turned a profit and Sam was looking forward to perhaps moving out of the combination storage room / bedroom / kitchen in the rear of the shop and into a real home. He was careful with his money budgeting everything almost to the penny. Toward the end of the month, dinner was sometimes cheese or peanut butter with crackers. Sam took it in stride.

Sam was occasionally saved by one of his former Army buddies, Liam, 'Jumper' Hanahan. He would treat Sam to a real dinner at their favorite Tex-Mex restaurant or barbeque hamburgers at his place in the suburbs. He got the tag 'Jumper' from Sam, for two reasons; first, he was the only MP stationed at Ft. Bliss that had attended Airborne School. Second, was that he was great with the ladies. Jumper always seemed to be *jumping* out of one woman's bed into another. Of course, his wife Molly only knew of the first reason.

*****

"How's the burger, Sarge?" Jumper, still called Sam 'Sarge' from their Army days. He chuckled as Sam chewed rapidly in order to answer. "Never mind, I'll take your silence as a good sign."

Sam wiped his mouth with a napkin and laid the rest of the huge burger on his paper plate. "It's sinful how good your burgers are."

"One of the reasons I married him was because he can cook so darn well," Molly Hanahan, said as she bounced out of the back door with a bowl of potato salad and more chips. She was a tall, perky redhead with a bust line that hadn't let her see her feet since the sixth grade, "I love a man who cooks," she added.

"I thought you loved me 'cause I'm such a stud," Jumper patted his wife on the butt.

"Well, that's just a bonus," She grabbed a plate and slid one of the burgers off the grill. Sam watched in amazement as she piled it high with onions and pickles as well as mustard and catsup and slices of chili pepper.

"I don't know how you can desecrate one of his burgers with all that stuff," Sam chuckled. "I like mine plain and unadorned."

"You haven't had a burger until you've tried it this way, Sam." Molly took a big bite and sighed, "ah, heaven."

"So, Sarge, how's life treating you?" Jumper sat down at the picnic table and grabbed a handful of chips.

"Doing better," Sam finished his burger and pulled his beer closer. "Looks like I might even make a profit this year."

"That's great, Sam," Molly said.

"Say, Jumper," Sam took a drink, "Do you know an attorney by the name of Waythill?"

"Let me think." Jumper raised his eyes. "Yeah, I think I do. Woman - Is she tall, dark red hair, real elegant?"

"That's her." Sam smiled.

"Yeah, she's done some work with the Sheriff's office on a couple of drug cases. Real pro, no bullshit type, you know what I mean?"

Sam nodded.

"I wouldn't want to get her pissed off at me. She looks like she could chew your arm off." Jumper chuckled. "Why do you ask?"

"She came into the shop the other day to buy a gun," Sam munched thoughtfully on some chips. "And I just know I know her from someplace."

"I'd say our Sam has been bitten by the love bug, baby," Molly said in between bites. The burger was almost all gone. She put it down and got up to start cleaning the table. Sam made a motion to get up.

"No, Sam, you sit down and relax. It won't take me more than a couple of minutes to get this done."

Sam sat back down as Molly cleared the table. Jumper waited until Molly went into the house and then slid closer to Sam.

"So, ah…" Jumper grinned with a tilt of his head, "…what's shakin'?"

"Get your mind out of the gutter." Sam smiled back. "She's got something about her that really draws me to her, but someone in her past hurt her, you can see it in her eyes. She's got a real solid wall there. Seemed to think she knew me, too - strange."

"Well, maybe you two have seen each other somewhere and just can't remember." Jumper stood, took off his apron and put the lid on the barbeque. "She's coming back for the gun and her license, right? That should give you another chance to talk with her."

"I'll definitely take that opportunity." Sam stood up and stretched. "Thanks for dinner, old buddy. You're the best."

"Any time, Sarge," Jumper gently punched him in the shoulder. "And you let me know how things go." He winked, "All the details, right?"

Sam smiled and looked at the back door to the house and back at Jumper, "That's the ole Jumper, never satisfied with what he has; always looking for more. My friend your eyes are bigger than your stomach."

"Yeah, but they're not bigger than ole' Wally-Wally. Know what I mean?"

"You just be careful or she'll", he pointed toward the house, "cut off your ole' Wally-Wally and hand it to you someday if she ever catches you!"

*****

"Karin, Karin!" Erik Larsen shouted as he came rushing through the front door of their log home. He scanned the empty interior of the one bedroom cabin. The flames in the fireplace danced around the black kettle hanging from the iron pot holder. He flung his hat onto the wooden table and ran to the bedroom door, "Karin!?"

"Erik?" He turned to see his wife Karin coming in the front door carrying a wash basket full of clothes.

"Karin!" he exclaimed.

"What's all the commotion?" Karin asked, not even looking at her husband. She saw his hat on the table. "Erik Larsen, what did I tell you about throwing your hat on the table?" She pushed the door closed using the basket and walked over to the table. After dropping the basket to the floor she picked up Erik's hat and hastily flung it towards him. "Hang this where it belongs, please."

Erik caught the hat and put it on his head. "It's happened!" he said with controlled excitement in his voice.

"What's happened?" Karin said as she placed a garment on the table and began folding it.

"I've been selected."

Karin looked at Erik in shock. Her face paled as she placed both her hands over her mouth.

"I've been selected to get a Blessing for the Savior." Erik said with dimming enthusiasm.

Karin's eyes widened in terror.

Two

The last three days had been frustrating for Susan. The better part of the first night was spent in aimless pacing, unruly nibbling, futile infomercials and weedy reading. When she did finally fall asleep, it was so deep that her alarm failed to wake her. She found normal, routine functions were slipping by, like forgetting to set up the coffee maker the night before and losing her keys at home and the office because she didn't place them in the hook.

And it all had to do with Sam Masters. No man had ever affected her like he did. The way he spoke, the way he carried himself and the way he made her feel so damned safe and protected. It was comforting, but frustrating. Every time she closed her eyes, all she could see was his face - those eyes. Those spellbinding cobalt eyes laid a path that allowed him to look right into her soul. Then when she fell into his arms…

The disturbing part of the experience was the compelling need to buy a gun in the first place. She had no need for one, so why was her internal voice so damned insistent? Or was it a ruse to meet Sam Masters? Her thoughts always came back to him. It seemed her comfortable lifestyle was changing.

*****

Sam folded his arms and leaned back against the counter. He shook his head as he thought about the past three days. He'd made stupid mistakes in adding the day's receipts, misplaced items in the shop, forgotten what he was talking about when showing merchandise to a customer. He'd even forgotten to lock the store and set the alarms two nights ago.

And it was all because of Susan Waythill. Who was she, this smart, strikingly beautiful woman who'd walked into his life three days ago? From the moment she'd looked up at him, he was utterly fascinated. He couldn't take his eyes off of her. She was both self- confident and at the same time vulnerable, traits that made him feel like a fifteen -year old kid in the throes of that passionate first love.

The ring of the phone brought him out of his reverie.

"Hello, Masters Weapons and Range."

"Good afternoon, Mr. Masters this is Ms. Waythill. I'm returning your call?"

"Oh, yes, Ms. Waythill, I called to let you know your purchase is ready. When would you like to pick it up?" Then, almost as if he had no control of what he was saying, he asked, "Or…?"

"Or …?"Susan's voice had a nervous tone.

"I could bring it to you… say tonight…at dinner perhaps?"

There was a long pause on the other end of the line.

"I don't think that's appropriate, Mr. Masters." Her voice was cold and impersonal. "I'll come by about five and pick it up."

"Oh …" he stuttered. Now, having total control of what he was saying, he was not sure of what to say.

There was a click on the other end.

"Ah, shit."

Jumper looked up from a gun catalog. "What?"

Sam stood looking at the phone, not hearing the question.

"Sarge?"

"Huh?" Sam came back to the moment. "Oh, she shut me down."

"You mean the lawyer lady?" Jumper salvo'd the questions. "That was her? How?"

Sam fired back, "What the hell do you mean, how? I asked her out; she blew me off, that's how!"

"Listen, Sarge, don't get your ass in a fire, man. I'll bet she didn't mean to blow you off. She was probably caught off guard and didn't know what to say. Ask her again man." He went back to looking through the gun catalog.

"Yeah, right, an attorney who couldn't think of anything to say. What've you been smokin'?"

Jumper looked up from the catalog, "Nothin', Jumper knows what Jumper knows ... that's all I'm saying ...you know?"

Sam remained silent. It was true. If there was one subject Jumper seemed to know – it was women. He just couldn't believe Susan would be the type 'caught off guard.'

At Sam's continued silence, Jumper put down the catalog and added a serious tone to his arrogance, "Look, you're a dude she met in a gun shop. Of course she'd high tail it when you asked her out." Jumper smiled a sly knowing smile. "If she hadn't, it wouldn't be any fun . . . and she wouldn't be worth it."

"I don't know," Sam said as he turned away. He walked to the cash register.

"I gotta get back to the office. I can only tell you what I'd do man. You gotta go your own way, but listen to ole' Jumper; ask again." He turned to leave.

Sam watched his friend walk to the front door. Just before he reached for the door handle he shouted, "Jumper!"

Jumper stopped and turned around, "Yeah?"

"Thanks man," Sam smiled.

"No problem," Jumper pointed his hand at Sam as if it was a handgun and brought his thumb down as if it was the hammer. At the same time he opened the door, *'BANG.'*

"Ask again," he said with a wink.

Sam nodded.

*****

Susan pulled up to the gun shop and sat for a moment. Two hours of trying to figure out why she'd responded as she did had brought no solution. She had accepted that she couldn't ignore her feelings toward Sam. He was special; special to her alone. She felt a need to have him in her life – again? Where did that word come from? To think 'Again' meant that he had been in her life before. Impossible, she had been racking her brain for the past three days trying to think of where she had met him before - but was at a loss. The only other explanation, and her practical mind scoffed at the thought, was that they had known each other in a former life. And there was that 'something else' thing inside her. Some feeling that was trying to keep her from seeing Sam again. It wasn't at all like her inner voice; this was something else that was equally as strong. It was a shield, a wall of some sort. Had she done this to herself through the years - closing off people so long that it was now a natural defense mechanism? If it was, how would she get rid of it?

Susan wanted to go home and forget about the gun, but, as before, her inner voice propelled her forward. She got out of the SUV and walked toward the door of the shop. She had a plan, a way to get her through seeing Sam again without embarrassment. Since her professional demeanor was most comfortable to her, it was the way to go. She would pick up the gun, then go home to try to sort things out. Control was paramount.

'BANG!'

Susan entered the shop, this time totally ignoring the door chime. She walked to the counter.

Sam, who was talking with a customer, spoke first, "I'll be right with you, Ma'am."

She nodded once, then looked into the glass counter display and pretended to be surveying its contents. *'Ma'am!'* she thought in disgust to herself. That tone made the likelihood of him asking her out again a definite no. But what did she really want? What was she thinking? She just wanted to get the gun - go home right? - go back to her regular life - right? – didn't she? Or did she want him to try again? Her mind kept running back and forth. *'I've got to get out of here,'* she said to herself and was about to turn to leave when Sam appeared.

"Good afternoon Ms. Waythill."

She could feel the warmth of his eyes as she desperately tried to keep her focus on a barrel of one of the rifles in the walled gun case behind him.

"I'm here to pick up my gun," she answered. "Remember, you called me?"

"Oh yes," Sam said, turning his head around and looking into the rifle case. He turned back to face Susan, "Is there something else I could help you find in the case?"

Susan lowered her eyes and then quickly snapped them back.

"No, there's nothing else."

"Oh, I was just thinking…never mind… I'll be right back." Sam disappeared into the passageway.

"That was close," she whispered.

Sam went into the backroom thinking there was no way he was going to ask that 'icy thing' out there for a date, despite what Jumper said - still ..? All she could say was no. He picked up a sliver in his finger as he slid his hand under her paperwork on the unfinished shelf. "Damn it!" he cursed. *'Well that's a sign right there,'* he thought pulling it out. *'She's nothing but trouble, nothing but pain, let her go. I'll tell Jumper she turned me down, again.'*

Sam returned with the forms and the box containing the weapon. He laid them on the counter without looking at Susan.

"This is the registration form Ms. Waythill," he said still looking down at the items.

Susan looked down at the papers.

"I'm sorry," she said. She couldn't believe she spoke the words that followed. "I'm in kind of a hurry. Can you explain all this tonight - at dinner perhaps?"

Sam looked up and tilted his head quizzically.

Susan looked directly into his eyes. The warmth in them seemed to melt away her icy resolve. She momentarily allowed herself to let go and absorb herself in it. A small shy smile played at her lips.

Sam was speechless. He managed a soft smile and nod.

The sudden ring of the store phone broke their stare.

Sam raised his hand in a halt gesture. Without taking his eyes off Susan, he picked up the receiver, paused, then set it back in the cradle without saying a word.

Susan hastily pulled one of her business cards from her bag and handed it to him. "Shall we say seven-thirty?"

Sam, still finding it hard to speak, nodded as he took the card.

"Do you know the Wineforest Condos off of De Zavalla Road?" At another nod, she continued, I'm in Unit Three 'C', my cell is on the back in case you get lost."

Sam still dumbfounded, nodded again.

Susan took one more look into his heartwarming eyes, paused and headed for the door. At the door she turned.

"Liver and anchovies are the only things I won't eat - just a heads up."

Sam again nodded, he felt like a bubble head doll.

Susan turned and darted out the door.

'BANG...!'

Three

The 1989 Ford F150 up to the gate of the condo community at 7:25 PM. Sam chuckled as he remembered Jumper's instructions. ' *"Don't let on you're nervous, man. Walk in like you own the place; chicks dig that. They want to know you're in charge. Compliment her on how she looks, just once is good, don't over do it, because then they think they have you and you don't want any of that! Even if she comes to the door in a wool bathrobe, slippers and a towel wrapped around her head, tell her she's HOT!"* '

"Hot, yeah sure," Sam whispered under his breath. He pressed the call button on the silver intercom and entered her unit number.

"Hello?" Susan's voice asked through the speaker of the intercom.

"It's Sam…Sam Masters."

"Hello?" Her voice asked again.

Sam realized he hadn't pressed the call button pressed it, "Ah, it's Sam Masters."

"Okay, drive to the second road and then turn right. I'm the third condo on the left."

*****

"Right on time," Susan glanced at the silver and jade clock displayed on the oak table in the foyer. "I like that."

She had been remarkably calm in preparation. Ever since that moment in the shop the whole matter seemed as normal to her as going to work. Even though she had no idea where Sam was taking her and therefore didn't know what to wear, she wasn't nervous. She checked herself in the antique Venetian mirror that hung over the hall table.

Her hair was down, swept back from her forehead in waves that fell to her shoulders. Last weekend on a whim, she had browsed the Neiman Marcus Last Call sale and, to her amazement, found a black cashmere Mossini v-neck sweater, which cut softly at the shoulders. The price had been reduced to such an extent that she thought it had to be a mistake. Even as a mistake, it was a small fortune, but a bargain was a bargain. Tonight, she paired it with her favorite pair of Versace jeans and black Prada knee-high boots. She enjoyed the effect. Despite her love of haute couture, she finished off the look with a silver link bracelet, matching earrings.

She walked over to the wet bar and checked the refrigerator. "Plenty of beer and ice," she said quietly. She didn't know what Sam drank, but had made sure that she had the best brands to offer him, as well as a fully stocked liquor cabinet. She glanced around the condo's great room. Everything was clean and in place. She was ready.

After taking a few moments to find a visitor parking place, Sam made it to her door and rang the chime. He had on a tan sports coat over a black shirt, pants and shoes. He eyed his reflection in the gold name plate on the door and squatted to do some final adjustments to his appearance. *'I should have done this before ringing the damn bell,'* he thought to himself. Just as he straightened back up the door opened.

36

"I thought you had gotten lost," Susan said with a smile.

"No… no," Sam stuttered as he motioned with his thumb behind him. "I couldn't find a place to park right away."

"Won't you please come in?"

'She's beautiful,' Sam thought to himself as he watched her turn to lead him in the vaulted ceiling living room.

"Close the door behind you, okay?" Susan asked without turning around. "Would you care for something to drink?"

"Yes, water if you got it. I mean bottled water," he corrected himself as he made his way through the hallway. Both walls had wildlife pictures of eagles. "I like the pictures in the…" he stopped what he was saying and stood staring at the great room. On the wall behind the dark burgundy leather sofa was a magnificent painting of a Bald Eagle perched solidly on the top of a dead tree. Its feathers were askew from an obvious wind blowing against it. The large bird appeared to have its stand firmly affixed to the limb with a look that defied anything to knock it off. In the background were several majestic mountains cutting their way through stormy amethyst clouds. The violent winds atop the mountains were swirling the snow cover in all directions. Hanging on the adjacent wall was a large dream catcher made of feathers. The main circled part was wrapped and meshed together with a wide straw material. Five beads were attached every few inches, three snowflake obsidian and two jade in different order each time. Six separated leather straps with three jade beads at the top of each one hung from the bottom of the circle. But the most stunning piece in the room was in the corner. It was a bronze eagle in a flight attack pose with its claws opened and wings flared back; the tips of which almost touched the ceiling. Its eyes pierced across the room to intimidate any visitor - this time Sam Masters. Decorative lights carefully illuminated the eagle and cast impressive shadows below it, making it appear to be actually frozen in mid air.

Sam was staring at the eagle when Susan walked in with two tall glasses filled with water and ice.

"Do you like eagles?" Susan asked.

"Yes, very much as a matter of fact, but I must say not to the degree you seem to." He answered her still looking at the bronze.

"Please sit," Susan directed as she handed him the water.

He took a seat in one of the finely crafted ochre colored leather chairs.

"I became fascinated with them soon after my mother passed away when I was nine."

"I'm sorry about that," Sam said, then asked, "Why eagles?"

"Thank you. I don't know. There's just something about them that's comforting... familiar."

"Well, I've never seen anything like that, ever," Sam said taking a drink. "I was under the impression that you didn't like the outdoors, you know wildlife and such."

"I love wildlife and nature. I just don't like killing it for sport." Susan said in a stern voice.

The tone shot through Sam and he turned to her and said, "Sorry. I didn't mean anything by that."

"I know." Susan said without apologizing. "I hope this doesn't scare you in any way. I'm not possessed or crazy, or anything like that. In fact, I have very few guests and really don't even notice the décor when I'm here. Not until I see that." She moved her head towards Sam.

Sam looking quickly behind him and turning back, "See what?"

"That look on your face," Susan grinned.

Sam chuckled softly at the joke and Susan stretched a wide grin.

"I thought maybe you were a superhero or something, you know Eagle Woman," Sam stood and raised his arms mimicking the eagle in the corner.

Susan joined in by raising her arms and trying to screech. They both laughed.

*****

After Susan locked the door she took hold of Sam's offered hand and they walked to the parking lot. Their demeanor was light.

"So sir, where are we going tonight?" Susan asked with a smile.

"We're going to…" Sam was saying as he reached for his keys and suddenly stopped.

"What's wrong?" Susan asked.

Sam stood there looking totally embarrassed. They were no more than ten feet from his truck when he suddenly realized it was a *truck!* He had been driving it so long that it never occurred to him that he should have borrowed Jumper's car.

"Sam?" Susan asked again then followed his eyes to the truck. She suddenly realized what was going on. "Sam," she jerked on his arm.

"What," Sam answered a bit uncertain.

 "I was wondering if you could help me with something on my SUV before we go. It's new and everything, but it's making a cha-chinging noise that I don't think I'm supposed to be hearing. Could we drive it so you can listen?"

Sam looked at her, at first not knowing what was going on, but soon realized what she was doing. "Sure," he smiled.

*****

Erik moved to Karin and wrapped his arms around her. She burst into tears.

"Shhh now, Honey. It's going to be all right."

She shook her head and pushed out of Erik's arms. "How can you say that!?" she said. "You know what will happen if you don't… "

"Karin, you knew I had to put my name in the lottery. We talked about this. It's the only way I can exact any kind of revenge for what happened to my mother. Once I do that I can, we can I mean, put a stop to all this insanity and death."

Erik Larsen didn't really believe what he was saying. It was true he wanted to exact revenge against his father, High Elder Larsen, for sacrificing his mother to the Savior in order to gain his position. But the matter of wanting to end all this craziness was just to appease his young wife. He couldn't tell her about his aspirations in the coming time, the new order. He loved her dearly, but there were some things she just didn't understand. Once he gained prominence, she would see and be grateful for his vision.

Karin Larsen had always hated all that was going on in the town of Helen and wanted to put an end to it. She thought about the dreams she'd had, dreams that at first, she'd kept to herself. But when Erik told of his idea to seek revenge she told him of the prophetic dreams, dreams about someone who would come to destroy the evil that gripped their lives.

"Karin, listen," Erik said as he grabbed her by the arms and looked her in the eye. "I've brought them in before. I've never failed yet, have I?"

"But this is the final one Erik, the one that will put you on level with your father. What if something happens and you don't return or come back in time? Then I will have to... I will be the sacrifice."

"I swear; nothing will go wrong. I would never let anything happen to you. I love you."

"I love you, too." Karin melted back into Eric's arms, safe for the moment.

Four

The Saturday morning following their first date, Sam showed up at Susan's office bearing Danish and hot coffee, along with the new weapon and paperwork which he had forgotten to bring with him the night before. Susan was pleasantly surprised. She accepted the continental breakfast even though she already had her two cups of coffee and never touched pastry. Sam was surprised to see it was typical attorney's office, cold and professional. The only concession to her passion was a smaller version of the bronze eagle in her condo.

"Are you going to work the entire day?" Sam asked while sitting in one of the comfortable chairs in front of Susan's desk and taking a sip of coffee.

She paused, put her hand on the stack of paperwork. "These need to be gone over. I have to make notes on them in case anything comes up while I'm gone next week. Why?"

"I think you need some more time on the range. I'd like for you to have some experience firing your gun with your non-dominant hand."

"I don't know," came out of her mouth before she even knew it, then, "I have some running around to do this afternoon – things I need to get for the trip," followed.

"We can do that after."

"Susan looked at her watch. "Don't you have a store to run today?"

"I have a friend who helps out on the weekends. He enjoys playing store manager once in awhile when I need a break."

Susan sat silent.

"I wouldn't bring it up if I didn't feel it was important. It's imperative to have that ability in case your dominant hand gets injured." Sam's father taught him and his brothers that when he was growing up, ' *"The Lord gave you two good hands; learn to use them both with equal proficiency,"'* he would say. He and his brothers could shoot a weapon, write and play sports with either hand.

Susan looked at the paperwork, her watch and then back at Sam. She knew she didn't have that much to do. She'd be done in less than an hour and that's if she took her time. And what was all this errands stuff she was saying? *Errands,* she needed a toothbrush for Christ's sake! Susan was confused. Why was she throwing all these obstacles in front of him? She wanted to be with him. It was that 'something else' feeling again. The one she had had before. It never bothered her before, but now it was becoming a nuisance. She would have to figure a way to get rid of it.

"How about I meet you there at one?" Susan smiled.

"It's a date," Sam said, "I'll have everything set up."

*****

"Don't worry Sarge, I'll be cool," Jumper said as he moved to the cash register and rang up the sale.

"There you go sir," he handed the customer the change and receipt, "thanks for your business."

42

Jumper turned to Sam, "She probably won't even recognize me."

Sam was behind him getting some rounds for Susan's gun.

Jumper was about to say something else when Susan came through the door, "Wow," he said just above a whisper. "Sarge, she's hotter than I remember."

Sam turned around and smiled. He leaned closer to Jumper's ear, "behave yourself."

Jumper just smiled as he watched Susan come towards him.

Susan walked up to the counter and said, "You're Detective Liam Hanahan aren't you - Hanahan Detective Agency?"

Jumper was pleasantly surprised that Susan recognized him, "guilty as charged counselor."

"You two know each other?" Sam said politely.

"Yes," Susan thought for a second. "That was the Rodriguez case wasn't it, detective?"

"You've got a great memory counselor."

"Call me Susan?"

"Call me Jumper."

"Sam I didn't know you knew.....wait, is this...he's the man that helps you around here?"

"We're old Army buddies," Jumper answered before Sam could say anything.

"Yes, well," Sam interjected as he put his arm around Jumper's shoulder, "Jumper has some work to do," Sam looked at Susan, "so if you'll just step around the counter we'll get to your lesson."

They spent early afternoon firing the weapon with Susan's non-dominant hand. She caught on quickly and was so pleased she told Sam she would treat him to a special dinner that evening.

*****

"This is a nice SUV," Sam said, "I should have told you the other night."

"I think you had a little more on your mind." Susan said with a smile.

"You're right," Sam agreed.

"I'm glad I bought it. I like the color too," Susan responded. "It's called Breakwater Blue."

"What kind of car did you have before?"

"A red Miata."

"Wow a small convertible to a Lexus RX330, that's quite a difference."

"Well, here we are," Susan announced as she pulled the SUV into the parking lot of a small, rather seedy looking strip mall. She glanced over at Sam. "I know it doesn't look like much, but looks can be deceiving."

Sam hoped she was right as he got out of his side of the car and went around to open her door.

Susan smiled as he reached in to help her out. She really liked that about him. Not only was he good looking, but he was a real gentleman to boot.

"So what is this place?" Sam asked as they walked toward the building.

"Castelano's, I hope you like Italian." Susan slid her hand into Sam's. "It's been here for years. The owners are from northern Italy. It's a family affair. When I first came here, Momma and Papa were chief cooks, waiters and clean-up. Now the kids have taken over. We regulars try not to let anyone know about it to keep it from being overrun."

Sam opened the door for Susan and stepped inside after her. He was pleasantly surprised to see a well laid out, village inn style restaurant. The tables were covered with dazzling white linen tablecloths and a live grapevine weaved its way up one wall and across the ceiling. Susan indicated that the maitre d' was new, but he was very cordial as he led the way to the patio.

The restaurant had large open bay windows that were heavily tinted to keep out the hot Texas sun most of the year. But this time of year the outside eating area was a favorite of the patrons. During the day two big oak trees provided just the right amount of shade and now in the early evening, the tables were perfect.

"Your waiter will be right with you sir," the maitre d' said.

"Thank you," Sam said as he slid Susan's chair forward.

"Humpf," Susan muttered.

"What's the matter?" Sam asked as he took his seat.

"Oh nothing," she answered as she picked up the menu.

"Now don't do that please, my ex used to do that and it drove me crazy.'

"I'm sorry, it's really nothing."

"… but."

"Well, am I not here or what?"

"What do you mean?"

"He said, *"The waiter will be right with you, Sir,"* like I wasn't even here. I hate it when they automatically assume that the man is in charge."

"I perfectly agree with you. I'll mention it to him on the way out."

"Sam," she placed her hand on his, "It's kind of silly, I know, but it really bothers me. I'm sorry."

"It's OK, I understand." He softly placed his other hand on hers and leaned over and kissed her. They backed away, looked at each other and kissed gently again with the hesitancy and excitement of new love.

They were enjoying the moment when the waiter came to the table. He was a young man that looked like he just graduated from high school. His light colored hair was cut short and he had a blonde mustache that was barley noticeable. He also had tattoos on both forearms that were barely covered by his white shirt.

"Good evening," the waiter said, looking directly at Sam. "My name is Jake and I will be your server tonight." It was obvious that he was new at this. He smiled nervously to himself, proud that he didn't slip up the introductory line. He looked at Sam and asked, "Would you care for anything to drink?"

"I'll take a lite beer," Sam answered.

Jake wrote the order on his pad. Without looking at Susan, he turned back to

Sam again and said, "And what would the little lady want?"

"Excuse me?!" Susan barked at the waiter.

'Oh shit,' Sam closed his eyes a second.

"Excuse me!" She slammed her menu on the table for further emphasis.

"What?" Jake barked back, nervously trying to figure out what he had done wrong.

"Am I not here?"

The waiter didn't know what was going on and he leaned back a little looking at Sam and then back at Susan. He shrugged his shoulders. "What....Lady?"

Susan pointed to Sam and firmly said, "I'm not his or anyone else's, 'Little Lady!' Is that perfectly clear?" Susan stared at the waiter for a few more seconds and then relaxed her eye contact. She decided to calm down and give the guy a break. He was obviously new. She picked up her menu again to decide between the Fettuccini with Clam Sauce or the Rigatoni with Marinara and Mushrooms.

There was a sneer at the corner of the waiter's mouth. It was obvious to Sam that 'Jake the waiter' didn't like women who stood up for themselves.

"I give you a few moments," he turned away. "Bitch," he muttered under his breath, but loud enough for Sam to hear.

Sam shot to his feet. "Hold it right there!" Jake stopped in his tracks. "You get the manager here right now!" Sam stared at him until Jake turned and walked toward the front of the restaurant.

Susan looked at the disappearing waiter and back at Sam.

"There's no need for that; let's just go."

Sam sat back down and coupled his hands around hers, leaned over to kiss her cheek and said, "Would you please go on to the car and let me handle this?"

Susan nodded reluctantly and left.

A few moments later Sam got into the SUV. Susan was in the passenger's seat with her seatbelt fastened. "Everything's taken care of," he said. "I talked with the manager. "He apologized and said we could come back and the meal would be on him, but I told him I didn't think it would be a good idea."

Susan looked straight ahead and didn't say a word.

Sam started the SUV and drove. He felt bad that he hadn't tried to fix the situation before it escalated. He didn't want to see anything like this get in the way of what he knew could be a lasting relationship.

Susan knew Sam had said something when he got back in the SUV, but hadn't really been listening. She was lost in her own world of turmoil. *'What's the matter with me? I didn't have to bark like that and spoil the evening. I don't want to be like this anymore, short fused and alone. He probably wants to end the evening as fast as possible and never see me again.'* That thought sent a chill down her spine. Only that morning she had thought to ask him to come with her next week to San Antonio and meet her dad. Now she thought she'd be lucky to ever see him again. She felt sick to her stomach.

Sam thought he'd drive back to her condo and maybe just call it the night. Then he thought that maybe he should say something – but what? *'She's got to be feeling bad.'* The farther he drove, the more he knew silence wasn't the way to go. *'No! We have to talk. We have to resolve this before it comes between us.'* Sam pulled the SUV into the nearest parking lot, stopped, looked straight ahead and said, "Well?"

"Well, what?" Susan answered after a moment's pause.

Sam turned to her and smiled, "What *did* the 'Little Lady' want to drink?"

Susan looked at him like he was crazy and then began to laugh. Sam's chuckles grew until they were both roaring with laughter.

"You still hungry?" Sam smiled.

"You bet." Susan grinned back.

"You up for pizza and a beer?" Sam took her hand and kissed it.

"Sure, but no…"

"I know … No anchovies."

.

*****

Lord Lokan crossed his legs and steepled his fingers in front of his face as he looked at the tall Elder sitting before him.

"There's still time to switch the legions, High Elder Larsen," Lord Lokan said.

"My Lord, it is right that my son be allowed to bring the final Blessing," he replied.

"You are aware of his motivations for becoming a High Elder?" Lord Lokan tilted his head to one side, "You are aware of his transgressions?"

"Yes, My Lord." His jaw tightened. "It is the fault of the woman he calls his wife. She has corrupted him."

"And yet you wish to give him the ultimate privilege of providing the Savior with the final offering? You have no fear he will turn against all he has been taught?"

"I believe that once he has become my equal, he will realize his errors and remember his loyalty to you and the Savior."

"This is a dangerous path you tread, High Elder Larsen. If he should turn, it will be your responsibility to destroy him. And you will bear the blame if he should cause the failure of the ceremony." Lord Lokan smiled, "She who comes will not condone failure."

"I understand, My Lord," his face paled. Then he caught himself, raised up and proudly set his jaw. "I will make sure nothing goes wrong!"

"Very well then. Inform Legion Larsen that he will seek the Blessing on Monday and will make sure that his wife remains in the Blessing Room at the Inn during his absence".

"Yes My Lord."

"You may go."

"As you command My Lord," he bowed and walked down the aisle toward the door of the temple. *'Nothing must stop the coming'.* He meant to make sure of that, no matter what.

Five

'Now who could that be at this time on a Sunday morning?' Susan thought as she walked to her condo door. She looked through the peep hole, "Oh, my God!"

Sam stood on the landing with a big grin on his face holding two coffees and a grocery bag. "Breakfast, my lady," He said in a loud voice after seeing the shadow in the doors eyehole.

Susan was in her bathrobe and slippers. *'He'll wake up the neighbors,'* she thought to herself. *'No time to dress.'* She made a panicked moved to the hall mirror; hand brushed her hair, wiped the sleep from her eyes, made a few bathrobe adjustments and then opened the door.

"Good morning little lady," Sam said, raising the bag, "Breakfast?"

"Get in here," Susan blushed as she opened the door wider.

"You look lovely this morning." He kissed her on the cheek as he walked by her heading for the kitchen.

She threw a glance right and left, then closed the door and watched him walk through the living room. It gave her a little thrill to see him like this. She folded her arms in front of her and smiled to herself. She started walking and caught a reminder glimpse of herself in the mirror.

"Oh ..!" She ran for the bedroom.

A little later she sat back in her chair in the kitchen and reached for her cup as Sam finished off the bacon on his plate.

"I could get used to you making my breakfast," Susan said as she took another sip of her coffee. "Only you have to start letting me know in advance so I could at least get dressed."

"That wouldn't be any fun," Sam said. He slid his chair back and picked up his plate. "Besides I wanted to see what you looked like before you got all dolled up." He smiled, "Want any more?"

"No, this is more than enough. You're a pretty good cook," Susan smiled as she ate the last bit of her western omelet.

"Thanks. I like to cook, but it's no fun doing it just for one. Where do you want these?" Sam asked, raising the plate and glass, "sink or dishwasher?"

Susan swallowed. "You don't have to do that." She got up and grabbed her plate. "You've done enough. I'll clean up." She walked up to Sam, "So, what's the verdict?"

He looked deep into her eyes and said, "If you'd been holding eleven roses when you opened that door, I would have been looking at the twelve most beautiful things in the world."

With plates and glasses in hand they kissed softly. She smiled into his lips, "Nothing like being swept off my feet holding dirty breakfast dishes."

Sam leaned back to smile into her eyes. They held for a moment.

Susan turned away to tidy. "What do you think we should ...?"

Sam reached out to her, the dishes missing the counter as he had hastily cast them aside. They crashed to the floor as he wrapped his arms around her, brought her to him and kissed her with a deep, hot, passionate kiss that sealed their destiny.

Susan's head was spinning from the heat. Her dishes fell as she wrapped her arms around his muscle hardened shoulders. Her body was thawing from nearly a lifetime of iced feelings. This was it. This was the fire that ignited in her soul from the time she first saw him. Their lips parted and they laced their passion together. He moaned as he felt her surrender to him.

Suddenly an iced fear washed through her and Susan regretfully pushed out of Sam's embrace. She quickly turned and walked away from him, her arms wrapped tightly around her body.

Sam stared at her back. Did he do something wrong? The kiss; the embrace; he'd felt her melting against him. What the hell was wrong? He looked down. *'Letting the dishes fall. That was pretty damned stupid.'*

"I'm sorry about the dishes, I'll pick them ---" He started to kneel.

Susan sighed and ran out of the kitchen without looking back.

Sam caught up with her in the living room and turned her to face him. With his hand under her chin, he raised her face to look into her tear-filled eyes.

"The last thing in the world I want to do is upset you. I'm sorry about the dishes."

"Oh, you silly, considerate man, it's not about the stupid dishes," Susan tried to blink back the tears, but it was too late and they poured out of her forest colored eyes.

"What is it then?" Sam asked as her as he wiped her tears from her soft cheeks with the back of his forefinger

"I don't know," she responded. She tried to gather her composure as she looked away at the bronzed eagle. She took a deep breath and stepped toward it. Her eyes closed and she softly said, "I just have this… this problem."

Sam sat down on the sofa. He sensed her difficulty and patiently watched - waiting.

Susan could feel his eyes on her – their warmth penetrated her soul. "I want to be close to you." She paused not knowing if she could continue to tell Sam what she desperately wanted to. She opened her eyes. The probing eyes of the statue met hers and she sensed a comfort that told her it was right to bear her soul to this man. She turned to face him. She took a deep calming breath, "There's something inside me, something that's intent not allowing you in. It's protecting me … protecting me from pain." Susan sat down in the chair.

Sam remained silent.

"This goes way back, back to when my mom died."

Sam nodded.

"I was nine when she left me …nine and all alone. She was always there for me. She was my best friend. I was devastated. I didn't understand why she had to die. And the pain; *it* was enormous."

"What about your dad?" Sam leaned forward.

"I saw even less of him than I did when my mom was alive. She said with bitterness in her voice. "They had been together for a long time. He was a professor and was always working. Even when he was home he was always in his study with books and papers and things."

Sam wanted to interject a reason, but decided to maintain his silence.

She looked down at her lap. "In my rational moments, I feel sorry for him. He was left with a nine year old daughter he didn't really know what to do with."

"So you were left all alone, emotionally." Sam settled back into the sofa.

"Yes." Susan closed her eyes and leaned her head back against the chair.

Sam felt her retreating back into herself – he needed to bring her back, "You're not alone anymore."

"But don't you see that I still am?" Susan opened her eyes – beseeching him to understand. "Obviously, I am not alone physically – you're sitting here. But something wants me to stay alone inside." There was a pause. "Do you know that I haven't even seen my dad for ten years? He always asks me to come down to San Antonio and I always make excuses. What kind of daughter does that?" Her voice cracked and she burst into tears. Sam got up and pulled Susan into his arms. She leaned into his embrace and sobbed against his chest. "I just don't want to be alone anymore."

They sat together on the sofa. He stroked her hair and let her cry. It was a deep, gut wrenching cry -- a grieving and a release. When it turned to weeping and the occasional hiccup, he started, "You don't have to be alone anymore. I'm here. I can't promise that you're never going to get hurt again. No one can. But I can promise you that I will always wipe away the tears."

Susan choked out through her present tears, "I'd . . . like . . . that."

"Susan, I think you'll find that if you open yourself up – some may hurt you," he felt her stiffen, "but some may help you. And in those some, you'll find friendship, love and safety. You just have to learn to trust."

Susan let out a little whimper and whispered against his now wet shirt, "I want to."

Sam continued to stroke her hair – he wanted to protect her, wanted to make her pain go away. He knew all he *could* do was sit there and hold her and assure her that he wasn't going anywhere. He realized that her breathing had changed and heard soft little snores coming from her as her head lay against him.

He smiled; she had worn herself out and was asleep.

He slid down on the sofa holding her close. He would be there when she woke up

*****

Sam and Susan had spent Sunday together. Susan couldn't remember ever feeling so alive. Her life was definitely changing for the better.

Now the only obstacle she faced was to fix the relationship with her father. Tomorrow was February 29th, Leap Day, and she thought it was a good omen to leap into a new relationship with him.

Before Susan closed her suitcase she made a final review of her checklist. All the items where packed away. She was carrying it to the SUV when a UPS truck pulled up.

The driver got out and started walking toward her.

"Is that for Three C?" Susan asked.

"Yes," the driver responded after double checking.

"That's me."

Susan signed for the package and carried it with the suitcase to her vehicle. She looked closer at the package. It had a return address she didn't recognize. Inside the box was a beautifully wrapped gift. She slowly untied the ribbon and ripped the paper to reveal a white box with a small envelope taped to it. The card inside read, to a real Lady! - Sam.

A smile crossed her lips and she excitedly opened the box. Inside was a leather carrying case for her handgun with an inscription that read *"Little Lady"*

Six

Erik saw the fear in Karin's tear-filled eyes as he backed away from what might be their final kiss. He held her hands confidently, trying to mask his own fears.

"I have to go," he whispered softly.

She nodded. He gently raised her chin with a cupped hand. Their eyes locked.

"I'll be back before midnight," he said reassuringly. "I will bring the Blessing back, I promise."

She raised the corners of her mouth trying to show her faith and trust in him.

"Enough! It's time," Erik's father said in a stern voice from the room's entranceway.

The couple continued staring at each other.

"Son!" his father commanded.

Erik squeezed Karin's hands and moved to the doorway. He stopped as he came shoulder to shoulder with his father.

"Don't call me son," Erik spat under his breath. He stared at his father's profile that was shadowed by his wide brimmed hat.

The High Elder remained looking forward with his hands clasped in front of him.

"Erik," Karin quickly moved to him, "Be careful."

Erik broke off his stare and looked back at Karin.

"I'll come back in time. I promise. I love you."

"I love you."

Erik brushed past his father into the hallway.

High Elder Larsen turned to Karin.

"I hope your soft ways have not weakened his resolve, woman." He turned to leave, adding, "For you shall pay the price if he fails."

He stalked down the hall toward the door and stepped onto the porch, slamming the door behind him.

Erik stood silently waiting on the porch of the Helen Inn. He didn't look at his father.

A white Chevy Blazer pulled up in front of them, out of place among the rough hewn wooden buildings that bordered the cobblestone street. It had belonged to another Blessing who had been bought to the town the day before. The two men climbed into the back seat.

"Lord Lokan granted you the power?" The High Elder asked without looking at his son.

Erik nodded.

"And you understand the Blessing must come of its own free will? There can be no coercion on your part. There must be no hesitation…"

"I know what to do!" Erik snapped.

"DRIVER, STOP!" The High Elder shouted.

The driver stopped the truck abruptly. Eric threw his hand up to keep from slamming into the front seat. High Elder Larsen didn't move.

"Leave us," he grated.

The driver scrambled out of the truck, only too glad to be away from what was

56

coming.

As soon as the door closed, the High Elder grabbed Erik's forearm.

"You will not speak to me that way, Legion Larsen!" He looked directly into Erik's eyes. "I told you when you married that woman that you must not become attached. That there might come a time when you would have to make choices…"

"Drawing from personal experience?" Erik replied bitterly as he jerked his arm away.

The High Elder retaliated by slamming his forearm across Erik's neck, pushing him against the door.

"You will not speak of her in my presence," The older man snarled through clenched teeth. "She knew her duty; you know the law. If you bring no Blessing by midnight, your wife will be sacrificed to The Savior, it's that simple." He eased back on the pressure. "I suggest you control your emotions and concentrate on the task at hand." He released Erik, sat back and tapped the window to get the driver's attention.

Erik righted himself, his eyes fixed on the road. He knew his mother had not gone to The Savior of her own free will. He knew that his father had given his mother in sacrifice in order to become High Elder, one step below Lord Lokan in the town's hierarchy. And he *knew* that one day he would make his father pay. He closed his eyes, remembering his mothers' soft hands and gentle ways, so much like Karin, so much alike. He dug his fingernails into his palms as he clenched his fists. He opened his eyes. He had to control his rage. The time for revenge would come if he was patient. He took a deep breath.

"I forgot myself," he said, turning to his father. "This is no ordinary Blessing I must bring back. I ask your forgiveness."

High Elder Larsen was silent as the driver climbed back into the truck and headed back down the road. There was a long moment of silence.

"Father?" Erik managed to sound differential and choke back the venom he felt.

Another moment passed.

"Forgiven," his father whispered, continuing to look straight ahead. "Prepare yourself."

*****

Susan took out her weapon from the secret compartment Sam had installed the day before in the dash and put in the carrying case. She placed the gun case back in the compartment. It fit perfectly – '*just like him*,' she thought with a smile. She popped open her cell phone as she started on her trip.

"Masters' guns and range."

"Jumper?" Susan questioned.

"Yes, who's this?"

"This is Ms…it's Susan. Is Sam available?"

"Well hello there, counselor, No, Sam's not here right now. He had to go to court, that fencing case."

"Oh that's right," Susan remembered. "Could you tell him I called?"

"Sure, no problem - you at the office or…" Jumper stopped what he was saying when he remembered that Sam told him Susan was starting her trip to San Antonio that morning.

"I'm on my cell, he knows the number."

"I'm sure he knows all *your* numbers, Susan," Jumper offered with a chuckle.

"Yes, I'm sure," Susan answered with a smile. "Well, have a good day."

"You too, have a safe trip."

"Thanks."

Later, as Susan slowed down for the traffic jam ahead, she dialed her father's phone. Her schedule was going to be off now, due to the gridlock on the freeway.

"This is Dr. Owen Waythill. I'm not able to take your call right now. Please leave your name and number and I'll get back to you as soon as I can. Thanks."

There was a short pause and then a beep.

"Hi Dad it's Susan. I'm going to be a little late, got stuck in traffic and there's a storm building to the west. I'll see you soon. You have my number if you want to call me." Susan snapped the phone shut and turned on the CD player. The strains of Vivaldi's "Four Seasons" filled the SUV as she settled back.

The road sign read San Antonio 539 on the outskirts of town. She could see the dark clouds off in the distance to her right. The Touch Screen Navigation Display showed that it wasn't too far to the town of Fort Hancock. Soon after, highway 10 laid in a more easterly direction and she could then put some distance between her and the storm.

After she passed through Fort Hancock the threat of the storm was out of her mind. At the town of Van Horn, she stopped for gas and a stretch of the legs. She'd been on the road about three hours and everything was going smoothly. As she got back in the SUV, she glanced at the storm that was still growing behind her.

"I should be able stay in front of it," she said quietly. She placed her Diet Coke in the holder, put the vehicle in gear and continued her journey.

Susan passed through Fort Stockton, Bakersfield and Sheffield without incident. The trip was going smoothly. It was getting dark. She was humming with the music as she drove, thinking about her life; it *was* getting better. She was thinking of the future, envisioning her and Sam. She was thinking of Sam when her cell phone suddenly rang.

"What perfect timing, this is the Little Lady's Mother," Susan answered with a smile in her voice.

"Ah... Susan?" Her father's deep, resonant voice came through the phone.

"Oh, sorry Dad," she paused. "I was expecting someone else."

"Should I call back?"

"No, no, I was just thinking... well never mind... I see you got my message."

"Yes, don't push it, OK? How's traffic?"

"Traffic's been surprisingly light. I just passed Ozona a minute ago and am approaching Gondolba and … "Susan glanced in her rearview mirror, surprised to see that the storm was moving much faster. Against the blackness of the clouds, swirling rings of amethyst hauntingly reflected the lights of Ozona. Lightning shot jagged white streaks through the storm clouds. It seemed to be growing more intense with every passing minute.

That storm I mentioned is coming on faster than I thought," Susan said focusing on driving.

The landscape suddenly burst hot white from a gigantic flash of lighting. She jumped in surprise.

"Maybe you should pull over somewhere." Her dad's voice sounded concerned.

"If it gets much worse, I will." Susan could see the rain beginning to fall behind her.

A thunderous explosion shook and rattled the vehicle.

"What was that?" her father asked.

"Just thunder, Dad - gotta go, OK? Talk with you later."

Susan tossed the phone on the passenger seat and concentrated on keeping the SUV on the road.

A violent wind abruptly slapped against the rear of her SUV, sending it fishtailing down the highway.

Susan regained control.

"Shit. I should have seen this coming. Dumb broad," She cursed herself for being so empty-headed as to let the storm surprise her like this. She always prided herself on being the kind of person who knew what was going on around her.

The cell phone rang and lightning struck at the same time. She screamed and stiffened in her seat as a strong blast of wind pushed the SUV toward the shoulder of the road. The phone made another appeal.

White flashes accompanied by loud explosions bombarded the surrounding landscape as the rain began to fall in sheets so hard she could barely see in front of the hood. The phone was insistent, ringing again. Stones hitting the underside of the vehicle's wheel wells alerted her that she was heading onto the shoulder. She turned back. The tires gripped the asphalt and sent the SUV sailing across the roadway. The vehicle shot over the passing lane into a guardrail. It banged its left front fender against the steel rail. The vehicle snapped upward and back across the roadway.

Susan instinctively turned the wheel hard and slammed on the brakes. The anti-lock mechanism employed just before the SUV went onto the shoulder. The tires crunched the stones and finally brought the vehicle to a halt. Thrashing rain poured down the sides of the car and blew forward as it was caught in the turbulent wind.

Susan leaned her head against the steering wheel as the rain pelted down on the SUV. Suddenly, the storm changed tactics, replacing rain with hail. The hail was so thick she couldn't see beyond the wiper blades. The sound echoed inside like a thousand hammers beating on trashcans. The wipers were bending from the force of the stones and she shut them off. She looked around in a panic not knowing what to do. At first she thought she would just sit and wait it out, but the hailstones increased in size, making small star breaks in the windshield. She had to make a decision... fast.

Peering through the falling hail, she saw what looked like an overpass in the far reaches of her headlights. She hoped she didn't imagine it. Trusting what her eyes told her, Susan moved the vehicle forward as fast as she dared, remaining on the shoulder she nudged the tire against the rise in the road to keep her direction straight.

The hailstones increased to the size of golf balls. The glass was glazing with cracks. It couldn't take much more. It was going to collapse in on her. Her fingers were clenched white on the wheel. Susan took a deep breath, and floored it.

She reached the overpass and as fast as it started, the beating stopped. Susan slammed on the brakes.

Her entire body was shaking. She felt as though she had just run three marathons. Dizziness and nausea churned within her. Susan knew what was about to happen. The one thing she hated most in the world, more than anything else was to vomit.

'I'm not going to do it,' she thought to herself in an attempt to ward off the inevitable. *'No, stop it!'* she commanded, *'I'm not going to do it!'* The muscles in her throat tightened as the top stomach muscles revolted. Susan could feel the hopelessness of her efforts. She slammed the gearshift in park and threw open the door. She leaned out and vomited on the highway.

"Damn it," she choked after the final spew.

Wiping her mouth, she took a swig of her Diet Coke. She swished it around in her mouth and spit it outside. Susan looked for the cell phone. It wasn't on the seat. She turned on the interior lights and looked on the floor, but saw nothing. *'It's probably between the seat and the door,'* she thought. She got out of the vehicle. Sheets of driving rain were now callously spanking the hailstones, some of which had gained the size of baseballs. She looked around. Suddenly, she was overwhelmed with a feeling of isolation. She hadn't seen a car since before the accident. Where was everyone.

Seven

Susan's feeling of isolation changed from disbelief to anger as she surveyed the damage to the SUV. There was gash in the front fender. The windshield had different sized circles of smashed glass. The hood sustained massive hail indentations. The grill, halogen headlights and bumper were cracked and damaged as well.

Susan found the phone under the passenger seat. The caller ID revealed the last caller had been Sam. She stood away from the SUV as she pressed the call back button. The phone lit up briefly and then went black.

"Well that's just fucking great!" she cursed, turned and was about to throw the phone into the SUV when she noticed it had gone dark inside. "What the …?" she leaned into the cabin, letting the phone fall to the floorboard. She tapped on the display screen, and then reached over to flip the interior light switch. Everything stayed black. She backed out frustrated and kicked the door shut. "Terrific, as if it couldn't get any worse!"

"It never gets any better, does it?" a distant voice shouted from behind her.

Susan quickly turned in the direction of the voice. She stood very still, peering into the dark night shadow created by the bridge girders. She couldn't see or hear anything. She was beginning to think she'd imagined the voice when suddenly, something moved. Terror shot through her like a bolt of electricity. She swung the passenger door open, jumped in and slammed it shut.

She pressed the power door lock button. There was no *click!* She looked at the button with panic and pressed it again repeatedly …nothing. She reached across to the driver's door and pressed the main button … nothing. Then she pushed each doors manual lock. *'I have to calm down,'* she thought. *I should have done that first!* Susan took a deep breath and closed her eyes, then opened them. The headlights were on. Susan knew that was making everything to the sides of the SUV darker. By turning them off, she leveled the darkness and looked through the side window again. Scarcely visible, and only because he moved slowly as he descended the slope, was a young man dressed in patched jeans, a letterman's jacket and baseball cap. Just before he reached the bottom, gravity took over and he ran the last few steps to keep from falling.

Susan watched his every move, as the hairs stood straight on the back of her neck. She looked around to see if any cars were coming. *'Wait a minute…'* she thought, *'Little Lady,'* and leaned over and tapped the compartment. It didn't open. Pulling the edges with her fingertips didn't do it either. "Damn it!" she cursed, "What is wrong with this thing?"

Sam hadn't mentioned that the compartment would only open if there was someone sitting in the driver's seat.

Susan turned to the window and jumped. The boy's face was near the glass and his hands cupped around his eyes.

"Ma'am?"

She could barely hear him over the sound of the rain, which had picked up again.

"Ma'am?"

She held her breath.

The boy tapped on the window, "Ma'am, my name is Larsen, Erik Larsen. I don't mean you no harm. I'm awfully sorry if I scared you." He tapped the window again.

Susan was frozen with fear. She looked inside herself and realized she was *alone!* Her inner voice was not guiding her. For the first time in her life she was scared, really scared - and totally alone.

She looked through the other windows to see if there was anyone else outside, any other cars. *'How could there not be any other cars? This is an interstate highway for Christ's sake!'*

"I broke down on this road here," he pointed to the bridge above them. "I started walkin' and saw that big storm comin', so I thought I'd better git in here."

His voice sounded young and innocent. *'Yeah and women thought Ted Bundy was a real nice and innocent guy with a broken arm.'*

Erik straightened and stood motionless. He stepped back, pulled off his baseball cap and ducked his head.

When Susan saw him step back, she leaned toward the glass to get a better look. He looked like he was just out of high school, with farm boy innocence and long light colored hair parted on the side. His clothes looked worn, but clean.

'"People are good deep down,"' Sam had said, *'"and all you have to do is give them a chance to show it."'* She'd promised him she would try to do just that, but was this really the time and place to be experimenting with good will and trust?

She was on her own and was going to have to do something because it was apparent the boy wasn't going to leave. Susan looked him up and down. He wasn't much bigger than her, and she figured she could handle him if it came down to it. He was close enough to the door that she could knock him backwards if she had to. She cautiously opened the door, keeping both hands tightly grasped on the door handle.

"Erik, is it?"

"Yes, ma'am, Erik Larsen," Erik nodded. "Ag'n, I'm really sorry if I scared you."

"This storm…" She tilted her head towards the rear of the SUV. "It's got me a little shaky. I had an accident back there and then the hail… well, you can see the results."

"Yes ma'am. Looks like you had a bit of trouble."

Susan replayed her actions in her mind and decided that she may have over reacted to the situation. She took a deep breath, opened the door and exited the SUV.

Erik stepped back.

"Let's start over," she said. "My name's Susan, Susan Waythill. I was driving from El Paso and because of the accident, I don't know if I should drive, especially in this storm."

Erik went to the front and then to the driver's side. He squatted, disappearing from Susan's view. After a moment he stood up and returned. "I think it's still drivable. I didn't see anythin' underneath to fret about none."

Susan nodded in relief as she looked away to the rear of the SUV. She didn't have her jacket on and suddenly felt the cold. She folded her arms in front of her. When she looked back Erik was staring at her.

Erik reacted as if he got caught doing something wrong, shook his head and looked down at the SUV.

"I'm sorry ma'am," he looked back at her with puppy dog eyes. "I shouldn't have been starin'." He walked toward her. "It's just that you look… just that the way you were standin … you kinda reminded me of someone I know."

Susan kept the opened door between them.

"Yes…well," Susan said coldly, not knowing what to think. "Thank you for your help. I think I'll be going." She closed the passenger door and retreated around the rear of the SUV.

"OK ma'am, but do you really think you should be driving this in this condition?"

Susan stopped and came back to the rear corner of the vehicle. With a stern look she challenged, "I thought you said there wasn't anything wrong?"

"I said I didn't see nothin' wrong. It's dark under there…ain't no tellin' without gettin' it up in the air and takin' a good look." He looked to both sides of the underpass. "With this storm it'll be chancy goin' alone. I just wouldn't want you to get stuck further down the road on my say so, ma'am. The town of Helen ain't that far away and I know we could get someone to take a look, a professional, I mean."

Susan looked back at the road. There hadn't been any cars, trucks or anything by in either direction since she stopped – since before she stopped, since *before* the storm hit, as a matter of fact.

"I noticed your cell phone didn't work. You could make a call from the Helen Inn and get someone to come and get you… and call a tow truck if you need one."

She looked at him. *'What's this guy up to?'* Susan thought suspiciously. *'First he tells me it's all right; then when I want to leave he questions his diagnosis. Is he for real, or am I being my old untrusting self?'* What were her options? Stay and hope for someone to come by or go to his town and call someone. *'What if he leaves and no one shows up? Or worse what if some crazies show up? I can't get to the gun. At least I know I could handle myself against him. Maybe I'm reading too much into this? The fact is, I'm in trouble and this boy is offering to get me help. Dad will really be worried when I don't show and haven't even called.'* She resolved. *'I have to get to a phone, that's number one priority.'*

Susan looked up at the overpass then back at Erik. She still wasn't sure about him, still didn't feel she could completely trust him.

"That's the road to your town?"

"That road empties on this highway's side road and that leads to the road to Helen." He pointed toward the direction Susan was traveling. "Heck, we ain't big enough to have our own highway bridge road. That highway side road up there leads to an entrance to the highway about six or seven miles down that way. That side hill along this highway stays like that almost as far."

Susan decided to make a suggestion. If Erik persisted in his suggestion, it would be a good indicator that something was wrong.

"I think I will just wait out the storm. Maybe someone will come by and offer help…highway patrol or something." She looked quickly in both directions then turned and looked at Erik.

"Well, you do whatever you think is best, ma'am; Best of luck to you."

Erik stood with his hands in his pockets.

Susan paused and then walked to the driver's door and opened it. She stepped up on the rocker panel and looked at him.

"What are you going to do?" she asked.

"Well, I guess I'll walk back down the road a bit and see if I can flag somebody down."

Erik touched his cap, turned up the collar of his jacket and walked toward the road.

Susan said nothing.

Erik turned and waved at her.

Susan waved hesitantly back.

'OK, If he were going to try anything, the last thing he would do is walk away and wave.' "You're welcome to sit in here and warm up if you'd like, before you leave." Susan called.

"Thanks ma'am." Erik grinned and sprinted back to the SUV.

Susan was relieved when the engine started and the interior lights came back on.

Erik jumped in.

Susan wanted desperately to try the compartment again to see if she could get to her weapon, but didn't want to do it in front of Erik.

She looked out the windshield, "Hmm?"

Erik looked at her, "Somethin wrong?"

68

It looks like one of the headlights is out, the right one." She turned to him. "Would you mind looking at it?"

"Heck no," Erik said as he got out.

Susan tapped the compartment; it opened! She quickly took the gun out of the box and slid it between the seat and the console.

Erik startled her as he pounded on the hood signaling that the light was OK.

Susan nodded and shoved the empty box back in the compartment.

"Good as new," Erik said as he climbed back in the cabin. "I don't mind tellin' you I was gettin' pretty cold. Thanks a lot." He rubbed his hands together in front of the heater. "Sure is one fine car. I wouldn't mind havin' somethin' like this m'self."

"What kind is yours?" Susan asked, as she reached in the back seat for her jacket.

"Mine?" Erik seemed to be caught off guard by the question. "ah...mine's...a," he stammered, "...old a... For...Ford. I guess that's why she broke down...old and a Ford." He chuckled, and then added, "You know... Found On Road Dead."

"What?"

"That's what Ford stands for," Erik raised his hand, printing the letters in the air, "Found... ON...Road...Dead!"

"I never heard that before." She smiled and thought she would use that one on Sam. '*Sam!*' She suddenly remembered him. How could he have slipped her mind during all this? He probably called Dad when she hadn't answered his call. She wished he was here. She would have to call him too. There was a long pause.

"Helen, that's an unusual name for a town. Is it named after one of the town's discoverers or something?" Susan broke the silence.

"Nah, the name's been shortened through the years," Erik answered. "It was originally named Hallindal!"

"That's in Norway, isn't it?"

"Yes 'um. The town was settled by our ancestors, who were all Norwegian. Over the years the town's name went from that to Hallin then to Helen."

"I didn't know any people from there ever settled in this part of the state."

"They weren't many to start with, nine or ten families at the most. They all came over to America as bond servants and when their service was finished they all got together and went west to start their own settlement." Erik pulled off his cap and ran his fingers through his hair.

"When did this all take place?"

"Mid-seventeen hundreds, according to my dad."

"Seventeen hundreds! And the town survived all that time; that's truly amazing." Susan shook her head.

"Yep, like I said there weren't many of them. They was close though, kept to themselves and grew and made everything from the land. No one ever bothered them."

Susan looked away and shook her head mildly in disbelief. Her eyes suddenly fell on the radio. She reached over excitedly, "The radio. Why didn't I think of it before? We can find out how long this storm is going to last." She pressed the on button, but nothing happened. She pressed the other buttons and got nothing. She looked at her watch and was surprised to see that it was almost eleven o'clock.

"What time's it getting to be?" Erik asked.

"It's almost eleven."

"That late, huh?"

"Your family must be getting worried."

"Yeah, they'll be pretty upset. I better be on my way." He put his cap back on and began to button his coat.

To Susan, it was another sign that Erik was harmless and she could trust him. She paused a moment and looked around again. '*Unbelievable,*' she thought, '*we're here all this time and absolutely no one has come by. Where are all the cars?*'

Susan got out of the SUV and walked to the edge of the overpass. She looked to her right.

"Is...?" Erik asked.

Susan jumped. Erik was right behind her. She hadn't heard him get out of the vehicle. "You scared the *Hell* out of me, Erik!" Susan exclaimed as she caught her breath.

"Sorry. Well, I'm pretty warm, so I guess I'll be going. Good luck, ma'am."

"No, hold on," she said turning back to face the rain. *'He's going to leave. I can't wait all night. I have to get to a phone.'*

"It looks like the rain is letting up a little," she said cautiously as she looked up and down the roadway. She paused, looked at Erik again. *'I'm going to have to trust him.'*

"I think …" she said turning away. "I think if I drive my vehicle partway up that cement incline, avoiding all that water in the ditch there, and then turn right when I hit the tall grass I could make it up on top." She pointed to her SUV. "This is an off-road vehicle; you know…all wheel drive. It should be no problem. I'll tell you what. Since you know the way to the nearest phone, what do you say we drive this thing up that hill and get on that road that leads to your town?"

"I was hopin' you'd be suggestin' somthin' like that." Erik said with a smile. "I sure do appreciate it."

Eight

Erik grabbed the handle above the door with both hands as Susan headed the vehicle up the cement rise then turned onto the grassy slope.

The torrential rain hit the hood like an automatic car wash. The SUV struggled at the angle and began to slide sideways.

"This may have been a big mistake!" Susan cried, "We should go back!"

"Turn the wheels all the way to the right and floor it!" Erik directed.

Without hesitation Susan followed the instructions. The vehicle straightened and climbed the hill.

"Ease up on the gas and let the tires do their job," Erik instructed again.

When they reached the summit Susan stopped the vehicle and took a moment to regain her composure.

"Whew," Erik said, "That was excitin', don't you think?"

Susan rested her arms on the steering wheel and suddenly shot a glance at him.

Erik was afraid he'd blown the whole deal. He knew he'd dropped the country boy drawl as they began to slide. Keeping the illusion in Susan's mind was harder than he thought. The power was there, he just wasn't used to having to maintain such a complex facade. He had known that presenting himself with that the black duster and hat wouldn't cut it, so the high school kid illusion was the best one to use. He smiled at Susan.

The headlights reflected a three stringed barbed-wire fence guarding the access road.

"You didn't tell me about that." Susan indicted with her head.

"What that? Shew, that ain't no probl'm." Erik responded, "You just wait right here."

A sudden blast of cold rushed in the cabin as he exited. Erik moved away from the vehicle. As soon as he was out of the headlights glare, he let the power relax. His familiar coat and hat shimmered into view. He faced the fence and closed his eyes. He straightened his hands out in front of him and concentrated. The fence post began to shake. Erik focused harder. The fence post rose steadily out of the ground and then fell flat. The groundwater splashed and the dormant hailstones jumped like popcorn.

Erik renewed his appearance as walked back to the SUV.

Susan jumped as Erik suddenly rapped on the window and signaled for her to roll her window down.

"You can go over the fence now!" He shouted above the storm's tantrum, "I'll replace the post after."

"What about the tires?" Susan shouted. "Won't they go flat going over the barbs?"

"Ground's soft enough. They'll mash the barbs in the mud...Go ahead."

He signaled her forward.

The vehicle went over the fence with no problem. When the SUV reached the access road, Susan stopped. Erik pulled his watch from his pocket. It was getting late. He hastily replaced the fence post and ran to the SUV.

Erik opened the passenger door and jumped in, sending Susan off her seat again. She grabbed the steering wheel harder.

"Jesus Christ, Erik, stop doing that!" She yelped.

"What?"

"Appearing out of nowhere. It's scaring the *Hell* out of me."

"Shew…I'm awfully sorry 'bout that…" He closed the door. "I didn't mean nothin' by it."

"And you can stop that phony hillbilly drawl of yours. I'm not a bit taken with it."

Erik quickly looked at her, paused, "What do you mean?"

"… Oh, never mind." Susan mumbled "…which way?"

"Straight ahead," Erik jerked his head forward.

The only sound made as they drove was that of the wipers as they methodically slapped at the rain. The hailstones on the road, now only the size of small ball bearings, were getting flushed away.

Erik was deep in thought. Things seemed to be going smoothly, but the Blessing was getting jumpy. He had to put her fears to rest.

"That fence came down easy," Susan said.

"Yeah, it was pretty loose," He smiled.

"Could you do me a favor Erik?" Susan glanced in his direction as she drove through the darkness.

"Sure, anything you want, ma'am."

"I'm a little jumpy right now, so if you could not appear out of nowhere I would appreciate it."

"Yeah, I'll try to be a bit more noisy, how's that Ma'am?"

"Fine and call me Susan… how much further?"

"We're almost to the turnoff. It's just passed the next little hill yonder… Miss Susan," Erik grinned. The Blessing was calming down and they were almost to the beginning of the road.

"There, see the sign?" Erik said pointing off the side of the road.

Susan slowed the SUV to a crawl. She suddenly stopped. There it was. A board about two feet long, attached to what looked like a crooked branch sticking out of the ground. On it was the word HELEN.

Just beyond the sign was a small, muddy, two rutted road that led into thick woods. It was barely noticeable. Two large live-oak trees bordered the entrance. The limbs of the old trees grew over the road forming a cathedral entrance and the lower limbs extended horizontally to the service road, creating a thick, impassable wall.

"This is it?" she asked as she leaned for a better look through Erik's window.

"I admit it doesn't look too invitin', but it does lead to town."

Susan leaned back into her seat and looked at Erik. "If you think I'm going down there you're nuts." She turned away and looked straight ahead.

"Miss Susan, it ain't nothin' to fret over, it's just a road. It just looks spooky, because of the storm and all. In the daylight it's as invitin' as a warm potbelly stove." Erik focused his mind on making Susan feel protected.

"I don't want to go down that road Erik. Maybe I'll just let you off here and try my luck back on the highway." Susan murmured, her eyes searching the darkness ahead.

"There's nothin' to be a feared of, Miss Susan. This road don't get much travel 'cause it's a short cut. The main road is clear on the other side." Karin's face floated up from the darkness of his mind. He had to increase the power.

"I still think it's better if I was on my way." Susan said as she placed her hand on the console.

Erik leaned toward her and put his hand on hers.

"Please, Miss Susan." Erik whispered with his face close to hers, "I can tell you're scared about takin' me on this road. I understand."

Susan was silent; her eyelids drooped slightly as Erik pushed the power a little harder.

"This is the shortest way to Helen, and it's *really* safe. The people are friendly and they'll welcome you with opened arms. You'll be on your way in no time at all."

Susan's eyes were closed, her breathing steady. Erik leaned closer.

"You can trust me."

There was a long moment of silence and then Susan let out a deep breath.

"I guess it would be wrong to come all this way and just dump you at the side of the road." She opened her eyes as Erik sat back in his seat. He wiped his forearm across his brow.

Erik smiled, "Thank you Miss Susan, you have no idea what this means to me." He grinned.

"Maybe one day you can tell me."

She put the vehicle in gear and drove onto the muddy road.

*****

As the taillights disappeared around the first turn, a tall, shadowy figure emerged from behind the trunk of one of the large trees. He stepped quickly through the tall grass, picking up the wooden sign and went to the middle of the entrance. He looked at the road ruts and followed them visually to the turn. The rainwater streamed down his wide brimmed hat; thunder shook the trees as a crash of lightning spanked its cold white light on his old, cracked, leathery face. A sinister smile broke across his lips. He raised his right arm at the elbow, extended his fingers skyward. As he lowered them, the road disappeared as the tree branches came together like fingers clasped in prayer.

Nine

Lightning and thunder exploded simultaneously across the night sky after they made the first turn. Suddenly, like someone turned off a giant water spigot, the rain stopped. The air filled with thick fog. Susan could barely see five feet in front of the hood.

The close growing vegetation dragged against the side of the SUV, like moist appendages of blind creatures desperately clutching at the object moving amongst them.

Erik was silent.

Susan regretted her decision with each rotation of the tires. *'Why did I agree to do this?'* she thought. *'It felt right, like the right thing to do back there.'*

Beads of perspiration formed on her brow as her chest tightened. Her breath became shallow. Her fingers were wrapped tight around the steering wheel.

Susan abruptly stopped the vehicle and slammed the gearshift in park.

"Where the *Hell* are we going?" she demanded.

Erik jumped back in his seat. He turned to her, "To…to Helen, Miss Susan."

"I should never have driven down this road. I don't know what I was thinking!" Susan turned to Erik, "This is nuts! This road scares me, Erik." She leaned towards him putting her hand close to the gun.

"I know the road don't look too invitin' but look at it for what it is. He lowered his voice and looked her in the eyes. "I mean, it's night time, the rain created the fog, and we're goin' through the swampy part. Hellfire, it looks scary to me, too, and I've been down it a thousand times."

Erik put his hand on hers.

Susan felt the feeling of *it being right to do* coming back. It did make sense now that she looked at it more clearly. It was just a forest; scary to look at, what with it being night and all, but just a bunch of trees, nothing to be really scared of, right?

"Please Miss Susan; it ain't much further 'til we come on the bridge… really. Tell you what," Erik said softly. "Just git me to the bridge. There's room up there to turn around just on the other side. I'll get out and you can go back the way we came."

"How much further?" she asked.

"The bridge is just around the next turn," Erik pointed.

Susan put the SUV in drive and continued through the darkness. She glanced at the trees along the road. '*They were actually kind of nice to look at, beckoning her with their branches. Nice to be so welcome in a place*' she thought as she smiled to herself.

After the turn, a darkened structure appeared over the middle of the road. It was an entranceway in front of the gated bridge. It had a large horizontal log about ten feet above it supported by two vertical logs of the same girth. Large capital letters; made of flat boards, nailed into the log, spelling the town's name, HELEN, except the top two horizontal boards on the second 'E' were missing; making the sign spell out HELLN. Susan brought the SUV to a stop.

"Your sign needs fixing." Susan said as she shook her head. *'Something's wrong, I feel like my eyes are tracking seconds behind my movements. It's like I'm on some drug or something.'* She bowed her head and closed her eyes for a moment.

"Huh?"

"Your sign," Susan pointed keeping her head down. What was wrong with her?

Erik looked at it. "Oh yeah, it's been like that awhile. Suppose we should get it fixed."

Susan regained her presence enough to inch the vehicle closer. She stopped about three feet from the gate and put the vehicle in park.

"I'll open the gate," Erik said as he got out of the SUV and walked toward the bridge.

As Erik moved away from the SUV, Susan realized her mind was clearing, and she questioned why she was there. This was stupid. She needed to leave. Every time she'd decided to leave, she gave in to Erik. Something was going on and she didn't like it. She remembered 'Little Lady' and reached down near the console. The gun wasn't there! *'It must have fallen below the seat.'* She was brought back to the moment when Erik pounded on the hood to get her attention.

"What?" she cried out.

Erik said something, but she could not hear it.

"I've got a bad feeling about this whole thing. I'm getting out now," She reached to shift the SUV into reverse.

Suddenly, her car door was wrenched open and two large powerful hands grabbed her forearm.

Susan screamed as she looked at the man, who was cloaked by darkness. She held onto the steering wheel with a death grip.

"HELP!" she screamed. It felt as if her left arm was being pulled off her body.

The front passenger door flew opened and Erik quickly climbed in beside her.

"HELP!" Susan screamed again. "ERIK, HELP ME!"

Susan felt a second of relief and then helpless horror as Erik unclipped her seat belt and grabbed her wrist, trying to peel her hand off the steering wheel.

Susan kneed out at him, catching him in the gut. He doubled over, but bent her fingers back, breaking her hold on the steering wheel. She was pulled out of the SUV. She landed on the muddy road and was abruptly jerked through the brush into the swamp. She tried to get her feet under her, but was being dragged too fast. Branches from the low bushes scraped against her neck, face, and forearms. Before she knew it, she was thrown in the cold swamp-water. Her involuntary intake of air at the coldness of the water left little in her lungs as she was held under the water by her assailant. She tore at her attacker's arms trying to scratch, pull and hit them. She struggled to maintain the last gasp of air she had in her aching lungs. Her strength weakened and life's last air bubbled out of her mouth and nose and rose to the surface. She was blacking out, spiraling down into darkness when she was suddenly pulled out of the water and her reflexes sucked the night air into her lungs.

"We can handle her now, she's weak as a kitten," Susan vaguely heard her assailant speak as she was dragged across the muddy road and then thrown onto her stomach. Her hands were wrenched behind her.

The last thing she remembered before she passed out was the empty feeling of betrayal as Erik said, "Bring her here… let's do it."

Ten

The door to the Helen Inn slowly opened. Three dark figures stood motionless in the doorway. The night rain trickled from their black, wide brimmed hats. Their long black dusters hung heavily across their shoulders. The amber glow from the street's torchlight threw their elongated shadows on the entranceway floor. The tallest of the three entered first, the other two following at a discreet distance. The tall man removed his hat, shaking rainwater on the oak floor.

"High Elder Larsen," he handed the hat over his shoulder and released it, confident it would not fall - it didn't. He took off his black duster and held it out. "Elder Ivarsson."

Both items were hung on a hook on the deacon's bench to the side of the door. Larsen and Ivarsson did not remove their gear.

Mrs. Crowley, the elderly innkeeper, appeared from the doorway down the hall. Crippled and bent, she recognized the men and immediately shuffled toward them. She stopped in front of the tall man and made a slow curtsy.

"Good evening, My Lord," she said. She raised cautious eyes and nodded to the two Elders behind him.

"We've come for the Blessing."

"Yes, My Lord," she flinched, took one step back and shuffled to the counter at far end of the hallway.

The walls stretched to a high ceiling, adding to the hallway's narrow appearance. It was adorned with one brass chandelier that hung from a long chain. Five brass spill plates held small candles that strained to light the way for visitors.

At the counter, Mrs. Crowley retrieved a key from peg number seven. She turned to hand the key to Lord Lokan and fear stretched across her features as she realized she'd forgotten to curtsy. Elder Ivarsson gasped. She tried to step back, but found she could not move. Lord Lokan fixed his feral yellow eyes on hers and then grabbed her wrist and twisted it downward.

"Ahhh!" she shrieked as the key fell onto the counter top.

"Shut your mouth, woman!" Lord Lokan whispered as his grip grew tighter.

Mrs. Crowley tasted blood as she bit down to remain silent. Her stomach heaved as Lord Lokan's breath cascaded over her with the stench of rotting flesh.

"Don't forget the respect you owe, woman," he whispered, "Or you will be taken to the bridge."

"Ye…yes, My Lord," she whimpered, tears of pain on her pale cheeks, "I'm sorry My Lord, I'm sorry."

He released her.

Using her good hand, she offered the key to him again with a curtsy, saying humbly, "Lord, may I offer you the key?"

Lord Lokan made no gesture to accept it. He raised his right hand, bending the arm at the elbow. He pointed with his fore- and middle fingers at the key. Instantly it became red hot.

"Aaiiieee…!" Her hand released the searing metal.

The key did not fall; instead it returned to its brass color and levitated in front of Lord Lokan.

Seizing this moment, Mrs. Crowley backed away into the key board. She massaged her painful wrist.

With all watching intently, the key floated into Lord Lokan's palm.

"Has Legion Larsen returned yet?" he asked.

"No My Lord," Mrs. Crowley replied.

"Bring the Blessing," directed Lord Lokan, handing the key over his shoulder.

The two men climbed up the staircase.

Lord Lokan walked down the hallway, giving Mrs. Crowley the opportunity to scuttle away unnoticed. He stopped and peered into the dimly lit dining room. Karin Larsen sat at a table, staring silently out the window into the darkness.

"Karin, my dear," Lord Lokan said.

Karin shot to her feet, bumping the back of her knees hard against the chair, sending it backwards into the next table. She grabbed the chair and put it back into place. Her eyes widened with fright as she straightened up and then curtsied.

"Please forgive my clumsiness, My Lord." She stammered.

"There's no need to apologize," Lord Lokan purred as he moved toward her. "I startled you. I understand Legion Larsen has not returned," he offered his hand.

Karin hesitated only a moment and then placed her soft hand obediently in his, cringing slightly at his cold touch.

"Do not fret, my dear; I am sure he will make it with plenty of time to spare."

"That is very kind of you to say, My Lord. I have faith that The Savior will watch over and guide him back to me." Karin wanted more than anything to pull away from Lokan's algid, dry touch, but she didn't dare anger him.

"What you have said is good - never lose that faith. The Savior protects, provides and pacifies us all. The Blessing your husband brings us will be special. For it will be the final sacrifice prior to 'The Coming.' Those who serve will reap eternal rewards." Lord Lokan moved closer, his yellow eyes glowing as he took in her features, the contours of her slim body under the skirt, apron and blouse, "And there are special ecstasies for those who serve the Savior's voice." He took a strand of her hair in his fingers. "You would feel things you could never feel as the wife of an Elder." He moved closer, his breath caressing her ear, "Passions unspoken…"

The sound of nearing footsteps interrupted the moment. The Elders stood in the doorway of the dining room, supporting a young woman between them. She was in a trancelike state, her head slowly swayed from side to side, while her half-closed eyelids fluttered.

Karin responded with a gasp. She jerked her hand away.

Lord Lokan frowned and then turned to the Elders.

"My Lord, the Blessing is emerging from its trance," said High Elder Larsen.

Karin knew what this innocent woman, who they called 'the Blessing,' had endured. The woman had fallen into a trance-like state by being force-fed secretions of The Savior Tree. She would be given to the Savior's Serpent that very night. Erik had revealed this ritual to Karin one evening and swore her to secrecy, saying that they would both be taken to the bridge if she ever spoke of it to anyone.

"Wait at the front door," Lord Lokan snapped. He turned back to Karin and took her hand. "That was not meant for your gentle eyes." He brushed his lips across the top of her hand and released it. "Your husband will return. Do not fear."

Lord Lokan moved out of the room, as quick and silent as a panther - and just as deadly.

Karin tried to calm herself. Thoughts of what midnight might bring conjured up images too frightening to consider. Clutching her fists hard against her chest, Karin prayed she would be spared such a death. She shot a glance at the clock; it was 25 minutes to 12.

Karin sat and stared out the window, hoping for any sign of Erik. She met her reflection in the glass and did a double take. She wiped at the pane, cocked her head quizzically and leaned closer. She saw an older woman's face in the glass where hers should have been. The face was aged with deep furrows and crinkly leathered skin. The eyes were worn and faded and almost colorless. The mouth had craggy, dry lips, which turned down and held a few discolored uneven teeth. Frightened but fascinated, Karin watched as the face lifted away from the glass and floated toward her. She couldn't move. The face paused in front of her. Karin could smell the rankness of its old, decaying breath.

"Nasus eno eht evas," the low, gravely voice whispered urgently, "Nasus eno eht evas."

Karin remained still, as the face tilted forward then seemingly liquefied into hers, pushing her head back. There was a quick moment of panic. Her breath stopped. She quickly looked behind her to see if the face had continued past her - it had not. She turned back to the window; to her amazement and relief, her *own* face, returned her gaze.

Eleven

Susan slowly regained consciousness. She was lying on her side in the back of the SUV. Her hands and feet were tied together with a noose fitted around her neck. There was a piece of material around her mouth as a gag. She moved her hands slightly and stopped as she felt the noose tighten. Someone was pushing against the small of her back. She strained to look over her shoulder…it was Erik. He was pushing her farther into the back of the SUV. She tried to scream, but could only make a deep moan. Erik paused when he saw she was awake. He stood under the raised tailgate with his hand on its lid preparing to pull it shut.

"I'm awful sorry about this, Ma'am," He stared at her. "It'll all be over soon."

Susan's eyes narrowed as she looked at him. She ferociously shook her head.

"Don't try and fight Miss Susan, you'll only make it hurt more." He stood motionless as his clothes changed to his black broad brimmed hat and black duster. He leaned in closer to her with a sad smile, "You should have trusted your first instinct."

Susan's head fell back and she rolled her eyes in total frustration.

Erik backed away and closed the tailgate. He walked along side the SUV and got in the passenger seat.

"Why did you have to drag her into the water like that?" Erik asked. "She's soaked."

"She's strong… needed some of the fight taken out of her," an older voice responded.

Susan breathed hard and fast as the SUV moved over the wooden bridge. Her mind was racing. She knew she had to calm down. *'If they were going to kill you they would have already done it.'* Her mind began to conjure images of what they might do to her. *'Ok, stop that! Calm down, calm, calm, breath slow, relax and don't tighten up. Think of the music,'* The opening bars of Vivaldi's 'Four Seasons' began to play in her mind. The sharp, distasteful odor of the fetid swamp water invaded her nostrils. Her clothes were sticking to her skin like thick paste. She tried to move her head, but the noose around her neck tightened. Susan could feel the shock of the road bumps in her side and shoulder as the vehicle moved down the road.

"What time is it?" Erik asked.

"Twenty minutes to spare."

An amber orange reflective glow sheeted across the glass, then another, then another. *'Streetlights',* she thought. They were nearing civilization.

The vehicle came to a stop and the men got out. Susan expected them to get her.

Nothing.

'Where'd they go? What was happening? What are they doing?!' Thoughts of torture, rape and death flared across her mind. Her primal fight or flight instinct took over. Her breathing became erratic and shallow; nausea and dizziness were swirling within her. Bile and digestive juices were hurling into her throat. All she could think of was getting the gag off so she could breath. She lowered her chin against the floor, careful not to strain the rope around her neck. Suddenly, the fear

of choking overwhelmed her and she jerked her head forward. The rope tightened. She moved her head back, but the rope didn't loosen. She was choking on the rope. Her eyes widened, throat constricted; she couldn't swallow. She moved her chin against the floor. The rope tightened… choking… couldn't move… couldn't breathe… she was going to die!

Twelve

Dr. Owen Waythill laid down the brief summary he was holding and rubbed his eyes.' *Law students are getting better at bull shit spreading,'* he smiled to himself as he stood up wearily and walked over to the bar in his office. He poured a scotch and soda and then turned to glance out the window.

"She should have been here by now," he looked up and down the street. There was no traffic. He glanced at his watch. Almost eleven o'clock. The phone interrupted the thought.

"Hello, may I please speak with Susan?" A deep, masculine voice sounded on the other end.

"May I ask who's calling?" Dr. Waythill replied, on guard for a moment.

"My name is Sam Masters, from El Paso? I am a friend of Susan's and I was wondering if she was there yet. Is this her father?"

"Yes, I'm Dr. Waythill." He sat down in the old leather wingback chair. "And you're the friend she mentioned when she called earlier."

"Yes, I guess. Call me Sam."

"Well Sam, I haven't heard from her in quite awhile. In fact, I thought this was her calling. She called about an hour ago and said she was in a storm and may find a hotel for the night. She said she'd call if she decided to stay somewhere."

"I've tried calling her, but there's no answer," Sam sounded worried.

"Perhaps she turned it off," Dr. Waythill answered. "Or perhaps she's still trying to find a place to stop for the night."

"Sure, that's probably it. Will you have her call me when she arrives?"

"Absolutely, good night," Dr. Waythill hung up. He tried to get back to reviewing the papers, but something was nagging him about Susan's overdue call. She had always been punctual, always followed through on everything she said she would do. Dr. Waythill picked up the phone and called Susan's cell number. There was no response. *'I'll give her until one, if she doesn't show by then I'll call the police.'*

*****

After hanging up Sam stared at the phone with an empty feeling in his gut. One thing Sam knew about Susan in the short time they've been together was that she didn't do stupid things like turning off her phone during a road trip. He went to the front of the store for his map. He spread it out over the countertop and began to trace his finger along the route she took, but there was really no way of telling where she was when she last talked to her dad. *'Well, maybe her dad is right. She's still looking for someplace to stop and then she'll call.'*

Sam returned to his room, made some coffee, and turned on the TV to watch the news. He awoke latter to the ringing of his phone.

"Susan?!" Sam blurted into the phone's mike.

"No, Sam, this is Dr. Waythill."

Sam's heart jumped into his throat.

"She never showed up. I'm worried."

90

Sam took a big swallow of his coffee; it was cold. He looked at the alarm clock and saw that it was midnight

"Sir, have you called anyone else?" Sam asked.

"I've called the authorities and they're doing what they can at this point. She's not really classified as a missing person until twenty-four hours have passed, which I find absurd."

"Did Susan mention where she was when you last talked to her?" Sam asked.

"Yes...yes...she did. What was the name of that town? I can't think..."

"Wait a minute." Sam ran to the front of the store and got his map. He unfolded it on his bed and looked at the towns listed on Highway 10.

"Sir, I'm going to read off the names of some towns. Maybe that will jog your memory. Kent, Toyahvale, Karintoga, Ft. Stockton...? Any of those ring a bell?"

"No."

Sam continued, "Bakersfield, Sheffield, Ozona, Gondolba..."

"That's it!" cried Dr. Waythill.

"Are you sure?"

"Yes, I remember now. Yes, it's Gondolba." Dr. Waythill said, "I'll call the police in that area and see if they've heard anything."

"Sir, could you keep me posted? I'm going to drive there." Sam folded up the map.

"Perhaps I should also."

"Maybe that would help. What's your cell phone number?"

"I... I don't have one."

Sam thought for a moment. "Well then, sir, I think it would be better if you stayed there in case she calls. I'll keep you posted on what I find out, OK?"

"That sounds like a good idea. Can I get your cell number?"

*****

The cell phone rang loudly on the night stand next to Jumper.

"This better be important," he said groggily.

"Jumper? It's Sam."

"Sam...? What time is it?"

"It's after midnight. I need your help. Can you watch the store for the next couple of days?"

Jumper sat up and wiped the sleep from his eyes, then turned on the lamp. "Sure. What happened?"

"Susan never arrived in San Antonio." Sam said. "I talked with her dad. She's disappeared. I'm driving out to see if I can find her."

"Where was that?" Jumper carried the phone into the hallway so as not to disturb Molly.

"A town called Gondolba."

Gondolba!?"

"Yeah, you know it?"

"I know the sheriff there, Sheriff Justin T. Earlee. He knows everything that goes on around his and the surrounding counties. He'll be able to help you. And don't worry about the store. I'll take care of everything."

Sam wrote down the name. He relayed some pertinent information about the store.

"Thanks Jumper, I appreciate it," Sam hung up.

"Something wrong?" Molly asked as Jumper came back in the room. She cuddled up close to him.

"Sam's new girl seems to have disappeared," he cradled her head against his shoulder. "I'm sure everything will be OK, but Sam's doomed." Jumper chuckled. "He's got it bad for this one."

"About time," Molly murmured. "He deserves to find a good woman."

Thirteen

Susan tried desperately to pull air through her nostrils. She violently rubbed the side of her face on the floor, trying to dislodge the gag. Her lungs felt as if they were going to explode in her chest. Her eyes began to darken.

The tailgate lifted to reveal the shadows of three men. Susan moaned weakly. Erik looked at her face and immediately dove in beside her. He jerked the gag off. Susan gulped in air. She coughed up a small amount of yellowish-brown vomit and it hit Erik in the face and shoulders. Susan saw it land on him as she choked and gagged; it gave her a perverse degree of satisfaction.

"Shit," Erik swore and pulled back, wiping his face with his sleeve.

Unaffected by the event Lord Lokan spiked, "Let's see this Blessing you have brought to us,"

"Yes, My Lord."

Erik and the other man grabbed Susan's legs and pulled her onto the tailgate opening.

Susan, still pulling air into her lungs in great gasps, looked at the three men with all the contempt she could summon.

"You bastards!" she spit out, "You almost killed me!"

"Silence!" Lord Lokan moved closer.

Susan looked up and was stunned momentarily at the pallid yellow color of his eyes. Then she hissed, "You sons-of-a-bitches, I'll....!"

He raised his right hand and Susan started to choke again. Her eyes widened in panic as she felt her windpipe close.

"You will not speak!" He spoke growled as he bent closer to her. "Do you understand?"

Susan lay gagging and choking.

"Do you understand?" he menaced.

Susan moved her head up and down as much as she could, all the time struggling against the increasing pressure in her throat.

He lowered his hand and the pressure was released.

Susan gulped the air.

His eyes narrowed then he grabbed her chin and turned her face back into the limited light.

"What is your name?" he whispered.

"Sus..." she choked, "Susan ... Waythill."

He drew in a sharp breath. Then with a recognized nod he smiled. "Perfect." He straightened and turned to Erik, "You were correct in your assumptions, Legion Larson," he looked back at Susan. "This one is very special. Untie her legs and bring her to the ceremonial ground. She shall witness the glory for herself. And you will be silent, do you understand?"

"Yes..." she choked out just above a whisper.

He again growled, "When you answer me, you will answer with respect, or suffer grave consequences!"

"My Lord, we have not had time to instruct her in the ways and laws," Erik intervened.

"See to it immediately." He continued to stare at her, paused, and then gave a sinister smile to Susan. "Yes, perfect." He then turned and walked away.

The two men untied Susan's legs and sat her upright in the tailgate opening.

"If he ever speaks to you again, you must answer with 'My Lord,'" Erik said. "Do you understand that? You'll wish for death if you anger him."

Susan nodded as she watched the man's back as he walked away. "Who is he?"

"He is Lord Lokan, the voice of the Savior." Erik responded.

"Lord Lokan," Susan repeated quietly as she watched him walk away. It was weird. As he disappeared an inner pang of recognition sparked. She knew him from somewhere, sometime, and she knew it wasn't a pleasant association.

Erik grabbed her arm which brought her back to the moment.

She turned to him and directed "You better hope I never get free, you bastard."

"That's not likely to happen," Erik scoffed.

They stood her up. Susan's legs were unstable. They supported her arms as they followed in the direction of their leader.

There were wooden buildings on both sides with a covered walkway in front of them. It was like an old western town minus the hitching post and water troughs. The streetlights were torches attached to the porch supports. The puddled cobblestone street they were on had sparse grass growing between the cracks.

Susan looked at the buildings on both sides of the road, "So this is Helen – real friendly looking," she said sarcastically.

Erik squeezed her arm so hard she squinted in pain.

"Enough. Be quiet or I'll gag you again." Erik said between clenched teeth.

Susan defiantly looked back at Erik. *'You fucking bastard. I should have shot you when I had the chance,'* she thought.

"Let's go,' the other man said, pulling her forward.

Susan stared at Erik until he looked away.

Her breath misted in the cold night air. A drying chill formed goose flesh on her legs and arms. She looked to the sky. Foggy clouds reflected an orange glow that came from over the horizon in the direction they were headed.

Moving slowly up an inclined road, they passed the last building, moved through a clear area, and then into the woods. Large oak trees stood next to the road as if sentinels to a holy palace. The limbs did not stretch over the road, but grew skyward and sideways into each other, forming a high wall. Halfway to the top, on her right, was an opening that revealed a small chapel.

When they reached the top of the rise, Susan was stunned at the sight before her. A huge crater descended thirty to forty feet into the earth. In the middle of the crater was the largest oak tree she had ever seen. The trunk had to be at least forty feet in diameter. Fifteen feet from the base, three huge trunks separated. The center one grew straight and sprouted smaller limbs in all directions. The other two limbs spread to the side like enormous arms. There was an opening where the limbs separated filled with a steamy, yellowish-orange, lava-like substance. The tree's trunk was covered in dinner plate sized scales that secreted a milky, gelled substance from the bottom edges. Around the bottom was a gutter-like trough that caught the gel and funneled it into a large bucket.

Erik shoved Susan forward and she stumbled forward. When they got within thirty feet of the tree they stopped.

"The Savior," Erik raised his arm proudly.

Around the massive tree were many other oak trees, spaced in a hedge-style circle. Within the circle and to the side of the Savior Tree, was a large circular building made up of intertwined tree limbs. It had a domed roof with two spiraled staircases that rose fifteen feet from the ground and formed a porched front entrance. In front of the Savior Tree was a large platform about ten feet high. Off to the right, a tall lectern, made from an existing tree trunk, the same height as the porched entrance of the domed building.

Lord Lokan was on the lectern like a preacher facing a congregation. Men stood in formations on either side of the lectern facing the Savior Tree. All were

Randall Stevens

dressed in wide brim hats, long black overcoats and tempered leather boots. Their warm breath clouded the front of their faces, as they sounded a deep constant chant.

Suddenly, a terrifying scream came from atop the platform in front of the tree. Susan could not see who made the scream. The men turned her away and they moved to higher ground. When they turned back, Susan saw that the platform was a sacrificial altar. Centered on the top was a post, about the same circumference as a telephone pole. Attached to the pole, with a large chain wrapped around her waist, was a young woman. Her arms and legs were not bound. She kicked fervently at the air and, with her hands, tried to break the chain that held her in place.

"LECTUM AVARVEAL SOMTOM!" (Beckon the Savior onto us!) Lord Lokan shouted in a loud voice.

An Elder moved from the formation and climbed the steps to the top of the altar.

"Please... Please... No!" the young woman screamed as the Elder appeared. "Why are you doing this to me!"

The Elder approached the young woman.

"Please; I beg you. Please...**LET ME GO!!!"**

Lord Lokan raised his right hand and the young woman froze like stone.

The Elder went to one knee and removed the woman's shoes. He then pulled a sharp knife from his pocket and sliced deeply across the bottom of the woman's feet. The blood spurted down. He held the shoes so that the blood filled them. When drenched he stood, turned and faced the tree.

"HOVALL THIN BLANT YON SAVAL!" (This Blessing we offer to you!") The Elder shouted raising the bloody shoes above his head.

A sudden pumping sound, like the pulse beat of a heart, emanated from the trunk.

The Elder lowered the shoes and descended the steps.

Lord Lokan lowered his hand and the woman regained her presence with violent screams of pain. She reached down and grabbed her bloody feet. Her

97

screams stopped when she heard loud crunching noises coming from the tree. She looked up and saw the side tree limbs change into giant arms. Her eyes widened and mouth opened in motionless horror - then her realization screams resumed.

The Elder moved to the front of Lord Lokan and raised the shoes. Lord Lokan nodded. The Elder turned and walked to the front of the tree. The bushes at the base separated to reveal a large black hole. A rancid odor escaped and filled the air with a stench so strong it made Susan turn her head and hold her breath. The Elder dropped the shoes into the hole and returned to the formation.

The rotted air became a furious wind blowing around the site while the tree's pulsating became more pronounced. The two limbed arms twisted upwards and stretched out, as if awakening from an elongated hibernation. The smaller branches wound themselves around the arms and melted into them like frying butter. On the ends of the hulking arms sprouted four, finger-like spikes that grew to five feet in length.

Hot liquid sparks shot out of the hollow pit. They formed curling, hissing streams of smoke when they landed on the wet scales. The tree continued a loud rhythmic pounding.

Suddenly, the third limb straightened and unfurled like a long leaf spreading itself open to absorb the morning's sunrays. From its base, just above the boiling pit, a giant snakehead began to loom. It had two, football-shaped, eyeless holes that opened and closed with horizontal side lids. Centered between was one large eye. The pupil had a greenish hue with jagged red lines. The black center dilated expansively. The nose was wet with slime and a spitting forked tongue lashed out from a slitted mouth.

It cautiously looked from side to side. It fixed a knowing stare at Lord Lokan and then focused its interest on the woman. Bubbling lava from the pit raged as if about to erupt. The rhythmic breathing became faster, louder. Terrifying cries for help continued to come from the woman.

"WHAT KIND OF PEOPLE ARE YOU?" Susan screamed as she began

twisting her body from side to side.

Everything stopped, the wind, the beating sound, the chanting, even the woman's screams – all froze in time.

The snakehead suspiciously turned its attention towards Susan and her captors.

Susan looked at Erik when everything stopped. Erik looked in the direction of the tree and the strain of fear festered across his face.

"Shut up," Erik whispered.

Susan turned and saw that the snake's eye was looking directly at her. She turned a pale white as she realized it was leaning towards them. Her throat went dry with fear. Her heart started pounding like it was going to burst out of her chest. Nerves throughout her body fired all at once; she shook uncontrollably. The men at her sides held her tighter. All at once she became still. She fixed her attention on the eye of the serpent. The exact recognition pang she felt before rose in her again; She knew it; she had always known it; it was part of her and yet, like with Lord Lokan, she could not place from where!

"GAG IT!" commanded Lord Lokan.

"Hold her," Erik said to the other man.

He retrieved the gag and placed it firmly in Susan's mouth.

The snake stopped its advance. It turned to face Lord Lokan and then refocused its attention on the sacrifice.

The tree's arms bent toward the altar. Its spiny fingers opened and closed in anxiousness. The woman frantically screamed in horror. She made feeble attempts to escape. The hands moved closer. Its fingers grabbed at the woman as she hit and kicked her blood spewing feet. Each hand grabbed at the woman. The fingers of one hand snatched the woman's head and the other her legs.

At that moment, Lord Lokan raised his right hand and the chain around the woman's waist came undone - it fell. The tree arms lifted the woman horizontally. She was bending at the waist, trying desperately to escape its hold. She beat her hands against the hard digits that held her head. The hands stretched and twisted the body in opposite directions. The woman became silent as her torso snapped. Her arms fell listlessly. The tree brought the corpse to its center and held the body over the hot pit – it frenzied in anticipation. The arms pulled and twisted the woman until the body broke open at the waist. Glossy intestines spilled downward like packed spaghetti being released from a can. A fiery splash leapt skyward and spilled over the side scales of the tree trunk. The upper and lower halves of the woman's lifeless body dangled as the serpent's tongue lashed forward. The tip of each prong wrapped around the pieces and pulled them into its mouth.

The serpent looked at Lord Lokan as the congregation bowed and fell to their knees. Lord Lokan raised both of his arms and began to pray in a language agreeable to the tree. The snake retreated into the form of the center limb. The arms positioned themselves back to their original poses and retook the shape of limbs. When all were back in place the tree ceased pulsating and the wind subsided. The skin stilled and the pit covered over with bark.

The congregation of men stood. Lord Lokan looked down and blessed them. The ceremony was over. Lord Lokan looked over at Susan and her escorts and signaled them to approach.

Susan's guards pulled and she tentatively walked with them. Susan looked at the tree with unbelievable horror. Her stare broke when they passed the rear of the altar. She looked over at the domed building, then at the pulpit when they stopped.

"Remove the gag," Lord Lokan directed.

"YOU BASTA..." Susan shouted, but could not get it all out before Lord Lokan froze her.

"The Savior was incensed by your disruption, but once I told him who you were, he became pleased. He is more than anxious to receive you."

Susan scowled and then her eyes went to fear when she realized what he had just said.

Their eyes locked. Lord Lokan made a satisfying sneer at her reaction.

'You know me then; don't you, you-son-of-a-bitch,' she thought. *'I now all of*

this. You...that serpent thing...all of this. But how...Goddammit... HOW?!'

The thought must have gotten through, because he looked away for a second then caught himself and returned his stare. Only this time...

Susan recognized the flaw. She's seen it a hundred times in court. A witness on the stand suddenly realizes their caught in a lie; they get scared. That's the look she was seeing now. *'You know who I am, don't you? And it scares you, doesn't it? It scares the Hell right out of you!'*

He shouted, "Take her to seven! Tell the old woman to clean and robe her." He made a sinister laugh. "We wouldn't want her to catch her death." He lowered his right hand and released his control.

Susan's mouth gradually smiled and she gave a triumphant nod.

"Gag her!" Lord Lokan commanded.

"Who am I?"

She shook her head resisting Erik's attempts with the gag.

"YOU KNOW; WHO AM ...?"

Erik slammed the gag to her mouth.

Susan fought desperately as they turned and moved away. She turned her head and tried desperately to scream the question again through the gag.

Lord Lokan watched them go with a thoughtful gaze.

"She seems confused my Lord," High Elder Larsen said as Lord Lokan came off the pulpit.

"The creator has sent her to prevent the coming." Lord Lokan said as the other Elder approached them. "Only she has been kept from knowing it - a simple ruse. I would've expected a more complex plan. We were fortunate to have captured her. It is for sure that others may search for her. Alert and prepare the Fenfir Bridge immediately."

Fourteen

Sam had been on the road about an hour when his cell phone rang.

"Have you seen anything yet? Where are you? Have you heard anything?" Dr. Waythill's voice sounded tired.

"Sir, I'm just about ten minutes outside Ozona…" Sam took a deep breath, "What did you hear from the police?"

"Nothing yet. They put an ATL message, which means Attempt to Locate, out over the Tele-type to other stations in between El Paso and San Antonio. How soon before you get to Gondolba?"

"About a half hour. I'll keep you posted on anything I find out, OK?"

"Yes …oh …OK."

"We'll find her, don't worry."

Sam hung up, feeling not at all as confident as he sounded. He hoped that the sheriff in Gondolba would be able to help. He had a feeling that they were going to need it.

In Gondolba, Sam found the Sheriff's office behind courthouse. The building was very old. It had a portico in back there with large double doors which were boarded up. There was a faded sign directing visitors to the Sheriff's Office/Jail down a flight of stairs adjacent to the back entrance. The solid gray steel door at the bottom opened into a small foyer and another door which opened to the police desk behind a thick Plexiglas partition.

"Is sheriff Earlee in, Sgt. Diaz?" Sam asked, eyeing the desk sergeant's name tag.

Rustling through paperwork, Sgt. Diaz replied, "He doesn't come in for another hour yet." At Sam's huff of frustration he looked up, "Is that a problem?"

Sam caught himself and said, "No. Sorry, I've been driving all night and the nerves are a bit on end." He made a gesture with his hand as if holding a coffee cup, "Caffeine express."

Sgt Diaz smiled, "You can wait over there." He pointed to a small wooden bench along the far wall that had seen better days.

Sam looked at it and said, "Thanks, but I think I'll wait in my truck."

"I don't blame you."

"An hour, you said?"

"Uh huh." Sergeant Diaz went back to his paperwork.

"Thanks." Sam left the office as the Sergeant turned to answer an incoming call on the radio.

Sam's call was answered midway through the first ring.

"Hello?" Dr. Waythill sounded anxious.

"Sir, this is Sam. I'm at the Sheriff's office in Gondolba. The sheriff's supposed to be here in an hour."

"Did you see anything on the road?"

"I haven't been east of here yet, but while I'm waiting I'll take a trip back to Ozona and check there. Have you heard anything?"

"Not a thing. How could she just disappear like that? It's insane."

"I don't know, sir. I'll call you after I talk to the sheriff."

"Thanks, I'll be here." Dr. Waythill hung up.

Sam leaned his head back against the cab's rear window, let out a large exhale and closed his eyes. He could only hope that his next call to Dr. Waythill would be more encouraging.

Fifteen

Susan was dreaming. She was flying. She wanted to fly over the bright horizon in the distance, but was being held in the air, gliding in a circular pattern. Below was a circular hole, the circumference outlined by a stone wall. It was a well. She focused on the water. As she descended the water sparkles turned to tiny pieces of triangular mirrors. There were thousands of them and all held the same image. It was her face - *on the body of an eagle!*

The shock woke her. For a moment she thought it had *all* been a dream and she was waking up in her own bedroom. The thought vanished quickly when she realized she couldn't move her arms or legs. She was upright, tied to a four poster bed. She was dressed in a white robe just like the one she'd seen on the woman from the night before. She surveyed the room. Hanging from the center of the high ceiling was an old brass candle lamp. There was a smaller empty bed, a tall dresser with a large mirror. An old stuffed chair with a faded blue material stood in one corner and a small wooden bench sat between the two beds. The walls were covered with old striped wallpaper. There was a stale, musty odor in the air.

"No windows," Susan whispered hoarsely; her throat dry and sore. Fear took heed as the door knob suddenly turned. Her pounding heart quieted when an older woman entered in the room. She carried a tray covered with a white cloth. Someone closed the door behind her.

"Morning Missy," Mrs. Crowley said. "How are you this morning?" she asked in a kindly voice.

Susan didn't answer. She watched the woman place the tray on top of the dresser. The aroma of coffee, mixed with another scent Susan couldn't identify filled the room.

"Are you hungry, dear?" she asked.

Susan lay quietly watching the woman.

"Would you like water first? I'll bet you do," Mrs. Crowley poured some in a cup.

"Yes," Susan choked.

"I filled it too much, I'm afraid," she said as a few drops fell into her callused palm. Mrs. Crowley supported Susan's head as she drank.

"Slowly now," she said with a soothing, motherly voice.

The water coursed over Susan's dry lips and down her sore throat.

"Thank you," Susan gasped.

"I think that's enough for now. We have to get some food down you, too."

She brought a bowl and sat on the bench between the beds.

"What's this?" Susan asked suspiciously.

"It's merely oatmeal, dear… to get your strength back."

"I could eat it myself if you untie me."

"Now, now," with a chuckle, "I can't do that… here." She placed the full spoon in front of Susan's face.

Susan looked at it, then back at the old woman without opening her mouth.

"If I was going to poison you, I would have done it with the water."

Susan took the spoonful of oatmeal. It did taste good, but had an unusual texture.

When she finished, the Mrs. Crowley got up without saying anything and walked back to the dresser. She came back with more water, and Susan drank it all.

"I have to go to the bathroom," Susan said, and then sarcastically added, "...or am I supposed to go here?"

"You will be allowed the necessary time soon."

Susan suddenly realized she could not remember being brought into the room, "Well, could you tell me how I got here?" She looked at the robe, "and who put me in this... I mean, changed my clothes? And where are my clothes by the way?"

"You were carried in here last night. You were unconscious...the men said you fell and hit your head. That's why you have the bandage on your forehead."

Susan hadn't noticed the linen bandage wrapped around her forehead. Her mind raced back to the night before.

She had struggled with Erik and the other man as they walked, almost dragging her away from Lord Lokan. The thought came to her of tripping one of them and escaping. She regained her pace with the men as she thought it out. She would trip Erik, the smaller of the two. They went up the hill and started back down toward the town. Susan adjusted her stride to match Erik's gait. She leaned her body to the left and swung her right leg out and rear with all the strength she had. She struck Erik's shin as he was taking it backward. She then leaned back by bouncing off the other man's shoulder. The movement surprised the man and he released her arm. Erik went tumbling forward. He released his hold to brace his fall. She landed on top of him and remembered a feeling of satisfaction and relief...then...she could not remember anything after that.

Coming back to the moment, she stared at the old woman.

"I cleaned you up and got you out of your damp clothes." The old woman cast her eyes to the foot of the bed, "They're on the chair."

Having her clothes nearby was a comforting thought somehow. Susan decided to try another tactic.

"I guess I'm just confused. Why am I tied up like this if you're supposed to be caring for me? I mean, can't you untie my hands at least? Can you give me a drink of that coffee?"

"Be sensible Missy, I can't untie you. My place is to see you don't...well deprive...well let's just leave it at that." She poured a little coffee in the cup and brought it over to her. "Here, it's cooled off enough now."

It was very bitter. Susan spit it back into the cup.

Mrs. Crowley pulled the cup away. "As you wish, I must go now. You'll be released soon and allowed to relieve yourself." She placed the cup on the tray -went to the door, knocked lightly. The door opened.

Susan watched, with growing anger in her eyes.

"You rest now."

"How am I SUPPOSED TO DO THAT, YOU BITCH!" Susan screamed at the top of her lungs as the door closed.

"GODDAMN IT, YOU GET BACK IN HERE AND UNTIE ME, YOU FUCKING BASTARDS!!!"

Susan thrashed from side to side as she screamed. The bed squeaked, the posts on the head of the bed banged on the walls and the wooden couplings crackled. *'Why am I here? What the hell did I do that got me in this...'* She began to think about her dad and what he was going through. Surely, he was missing her by now. She thought of Sam...*'maybe he'd come*?' She started to feel hope again and then thought, *'why would he come? He probably thinks I just forgot about him with visiting my dad and will call him later.'*

Susan's mind took her on an emotional roller coaster. She had to mentally grab onto something positive. She thought back to her dad. Through her childhood he was always the level headed one. Even when her mother got sick with cancer, he never broke down, nor did he blame anyone or anything. He methodically combated it, fighting every inch of the way. He was a rock; he had to be. *'I never called him. He wouldn't accept that. I know he wouldn't. He'll call someone...maybe the police...the highway patrol. Surely they're out looking for me right now.'*

Susan took this thought and held onto it like a mother would hold her child in a windstorm – the feeling relaxed her. '*He will come*,' she thought. She relaxed some more. '*He will come...*' a small smile appeared on her lips. She took a deep breath and relaxed a little more. Her eyes were getting heavy. Her arms and legs became weighted. She felt like she was floating on a soft puff of air. She was drifting away. She realized that the old woman must have given her something; instead of panicking, she didn't care...she hadn't a care in the world. Slowly, deeply, softly she drifted away into a profound restful sleep.

Sixteen

Karin was seated in her rocker staring out the side window of their cabin. The blanket of light gray frost vanished slowly from the roof tops, tree limbs and ground leaving a moist covering in its place.

"Good morning," Erik said as he came shuffling out of the bedroom.

Karin, lost in her world of reflection, remained silently staring out the window.

Erik stopped, "Karin?"

Silence.

Erik approached and put his hand on her shoulder repeating her name at the same time.

"Ahhh!" Karin jumped back to reality.

"I'm sorry," Erik chuckled as he came around to her front and knelt down.

"You scared me," Karin said with her hands on her chest.

"I didn't mean to. It's just I thought something was wrong when you didn't answer me."

"Answer?"

"I said good morning. Didn't you hear me?"

"I… I'm sorry. I must have been daydreaming. Do you want me to make you some breakfast?"

Erik slid a chair over to Karin, sat and placed his hands on hers.

Karin continued to stare out the window.

"What's the matter? You haven't been yourself since I came back last night."

Karin didn't answer.

"Karin!" Erik said as he squeezed her hands.

Her empty eyes looked to Erik's. She scanned his face then back at his eyes.

"What?" Erik asked.

"It came to me."

"What came? The dreams?"

"No, I didn't sleep very well. I've been out here most of the night." Karin's eyes filled with tears as she reached out to him. "Oh Erik!"

They held onto each other.

After several moments Erik pulled back and looked at her. "What is it? What happened?

She remained silent.

"Karin, please tell me. What's wrong?"

"I… I… had a… vision." Karin said and bowed her head.

"A vision..? What kind of vision? When? Where..?"

Karin slowly looked up. "At the Inn - last night - just before you came back to town."

His quiet eye's begged for more information.

She explained what had happened.

"Oh Erik, what should we do?"

Erik stood up and turned away in thought. Karin watched him nervously as he paced a few steps. He stopped and then came back and sat in front of her enfolding her hands in her lap.

With tears streaming down her face she said "Erik I...."

"Shhh... we must keep this quiet, like the dreams, until I can figure something out."

*****

"Come in," Lord Lokan commanded.

Erik opened the door, bowed and said, "You sent for me My Lord."

"Yes," Lord Lokan said without looking up from the opened book on his desk.

Erik moved to the front of the desk. He was beaming with the confidence a man has when he knows he did well and is about to be lauded and rewarded. He stared straight forward careful not to look down. *He's probably reviewing protocol for promotion to Eldership with special circumstance,* Erik pleasantly thought to himself. *"I will become close to equal with my dad and be able to work my plan to avenge in the new order.*

Lord Lokan looked up at Erik and commanded, "Take a seat."

Erik sat as the door to the office opened and his father came in and sat in the chair beside him. Erik was confused. '*What's going on?* ' he thought to himself. Suddenly Erik felt a chill surround him.

Lord Lokan placed his elbows on his desk, tented his hands together, the tips of his forefingers resting on the bridge of his nose. He silently stared at Erik.

Erik wanted to ask what was going on, but knew better than ever to question Lord Lokan. He did not look away.

"His wife is a subversive!" his father accused.

Erik's jaw dropped. He looked with shock at his father then back at Lord Lokan.

"I... I..." Erik wanted to defend the accusation, but was lost for words.

Lord Lokan turned his right hand and Erik became still and silent.

His father continued to tell what he had heard and surmised. "She is possessed with an evil, and it will intervene and try to prevent the coming. She must be eliminated. It is the only way to destroy the demon that lay within. I recommend she be taken to the bridge immediately. "

Lord Lokan leaned back in his chair. Not taking his eyes off Erik. The three sat silent while he digested his second in command's accusations and advice.

Erik was devastated by what his father had just suggested. His father had always disliked Karin, and now he found a way to get rid of her. *'With her gone he thinks I will become one with him in the new order. He's wrong. I will become more set on revenge than he could possibly know.'*

"It disturbs me greatly that you had no faith than not to trust me with this information," Lord Lokan said to Erik, who still could not move or speak. "My initial thought is to follow your father's advice and destroy your wife."

Erik's eyes were moist with rage, his skin turned red.

"However, I think this could be handled best by an exorcism. I have the guidelines here in this book," he turned to Erik's father. "Have her brought here before me."

"Yes My Lord," High Elder Larsen said as he rose, bowed and left the office.

Lord Lokan waited. Once they were alone he turned to Erik. "I see that you are filled with rage at what your father advised. Be reminded it is his duty to suggest such things with no matter of thought given to his feelings. You need to calm yourself." He leaned towards Erik. "From what I have read I think I can help. It can be all handled quite easily right here."

Erik began to relax.

"Of course you understand there is a chance she cannot be excised. If that is the case she will be classified as a subversive and dealt with by law. I will add that because your loyalty to The Savior, until this instance, has been performed without question, leniency is not out of the question."

Erik's eyes signaled that he understood and got hold of his anger.

"Before I release, these instructions you will follow. You will go directly to the

Inn and wait. You are not to talk to anyone. You are not to see Karin again without my permission."

Seventeen

A hard rapping noise hit Sam's ears. He opened his eyes slowly and then lifted his hand against the light. He turned to his left and saw a man wearing a beige colored western hat rapping his knuckles against the glass.

"Hey, you awake?" the man in the hat said.

Sam rolled the window down.

"Sorry, I…I must have dozed off." He had a sudden subconscious burn in his stomach when he realized he wasted valuable time sleeping. Still a little asleep and befuddled, Sam said, "Am I parked in the wrong spot? I'll move." He didn't wait for an answer as he reached for the ignition.

"Whoa, man. You're OK. I'm Sheriff Earlee. I was told you wanted to talk to me about someone that was missing – a friend of yours?"

"Yes…" Sam faced forward and rubbed his eyes. "Give me a moment, I…I drove from El Paso last night. My friend's father called from San Antonio and gave the desk officer all the information."

"Come on in. You can fill in the blanks."

As Sam got out and closed the door, the sheriff stood with his hand out. Sam shook it.

"Let's do this again; I'm Sheriff Earlee, with two E's, Justin T. Earlee."

"I'm Sam Masters."

Sheriff Earlee was well built, with a neatly trimmed black mustache. He stood a few inches over six feet tall, so he was on eye level with Sam.

"A mutual friend of ours told me about you," Sam said as they walked toward the jail.

"Oh, who'd that be?" the sheriff asked.

"Hanahan," Sam said.

The sheriff stopped in his tracks, "Hanahan? You mean Liam Hanahan?"

"Yeah, I gave him the name Jumper."

"Listen, he ain't no friend of mine and you can tell him I ever run across his sorry ass, I'm going to make him my personal hand puppet!"

Sam, shocked by the sheriff's response tried to think of a way out, "Well he's not actually a friend," Sam smiled nervously. "I knew him in the Army years ago. I just remember him bringing up your name one time."

The sheriff paused a minute in thought, "Well, just don't bring up his name again, OK?"

Sam raised his hands in surrender, "OK, no problem."

They silently turned and walked to the jail house. Sam wondered what Jumper did in the past to piss off the one guy that can help him. *He should have told me not to bring up his name.'*

"I'll get the sheet on last night's call and the ATL message," the sheriff said as they entered. "My office is over there." He pointed to a door just inside the steel mesh partition that separated visitors from the waiting area. The sheriff opened it with his passkey and led Sam to his office. "You're welcome to a cup of 'motion lotion '- it's on the bookshelf - I'll be right in. Make yourself to home."

"Thanks, but I need a latrine before that."

Sheriff pointed the way.

Afterwards, Sam chuckled as he entered the office. He just remembered what the sheriff had said. He hadn't heard the term for coffee referred to as 'motion lotion' since his Army days.

The office was small with no windows. In the center was a medium sized wooden desk with a matching swivel chair. There were two vinyl chairs in front of the desk. On the walls there were a few pictures of the sheriff posing with town officials and some framed training certificates. One larger frame especially caught his eye. It displayed a front page headline from the local paper.

SHERIFF EARLEE IS 'JUST IN TIME!'

Gondolba's own Sheriff *'Justin Tyme'* Earlee lived up to his name yesterday when he responded to a car fire call on Hwy 10 near the town's exit ramp and pulled a two year old boy from his car seat just before the car exploded.

The car was upside down, tipped on the hood, the flames blazing from the engine when Sheriff Earlee arrived on the scene. The car's driver, Mrs. Darlene Newberry of Fort Stockton, was desperately trying to get to her two year old son, who was trapped in his car seat in the back.

"The lady was lying on the ground, trying to get her son through the rear side window. The fire was getting bigger and I knew it was gonna blow any minute, so I pulled her away from the car and made her stay by my cruiser. I went back to the car and tried to get the boy free, but the belt was jammed. So I took out my knife and cut the straps and pulled him out. We got about fifteen feet before the car exploded and the blast blew us both down. That's about all there was to it. Nobody got hurt, that's the main thing."

Sheriff Earlee entered the office. Sam turned away from the article.

"I was just reading about your heroic deed," Sam said pointing at the framed front page.

"All in a day's work," Sheriff Earlee responded as he made his way to the coffee pot and poured himself a cup. "Just glad I was there to help."

The sheriff looked up at Sam, "Get yourself a cup pard, and let's get to your problem," he said as he walked to his desk. He tossed the papers on the desk and sat down, the chair squeaking ominously as he leaned back.

Sam got a cup of coffee and sat down.

"Excuse the accommodations, but I find if I have an office I'm really comfortable in, I spend more time *in* it than where I am supposed to be…out there." He nodded towards the office door.

Sam smiled in agreement. He looked at the Sheriff's name plaque on his desk and then turned to the head line on the wall. He looked at the sheriff, "That's quite an interesting name you have."

Sheriff Earlee picked up a pencil and the forms. He gave Sam a questioned look, "Oh, that's right, you're not from here. Everybody in the county knows the story of my name. I was born one minute before midnight on the Thirty-first of December, 1964. My dad was thrilled."

Sam arched an eyebrow in question. Sheriff Earlee grinned widely.

"My dad could use me as a deduction for the whole year! So I was born *Just In Time.*"

Sam chuckled.

"Now let's see what we have here, Name; Susan Waythill, Age;" Sheriff Earlee paused and looked up. "Is she a special friend of yours?"

"You could say that," Sam said, smiling.

The sheriff looked back at the form, "mid thirties," he looked up again with only his eyes, "Not polite to give their age. Traveling on Highway 10 from El Paso to San Antonio in her car alone; last known contact eight to ten last night. Auburn hair, green eyes, five eleven, One thirty…oops," he raised his eyes quickly and returned them to the form, "driving a 1988 red Miata…"

"Wait!" Sam exclaimed. "That's wrong. She has a SUV. She bought it last week. Damn!" Sam said, "I didn't tell him that."

"OK, what kind of vehicle does she have now… color… model?

"A Lexus SUV, ah… what did she call it?" Sam thought for a moment and then snapped his fingers. "A RX330!" he exclaimed. "Light blue, I don't know any more than that."

The sheriff wrote down the changes and then pressed a button on the intercom, "Sergeant, Diaz get in here. He looked at Sam; we'll get a new ATL out for her."

Officer Diaz came through the door, "Yes sir?"

"This ATL Tele-type needs to be updated with these changes. Get it out immediately."

"Yes sir." Sergeant Diaz grabbed the Tele-type and quickly disappeared.

"Is there anything else you can think of that would help us?" Sheriff Earlee put the pencil behind his ear.

"No," Sam shook his head. "I think that's pretty much it."

"Storm blew through here about that time last night. I got called out on road 1834. I had to help a guy get out of his truck." Earlee smiled.

Sam looked at the sheriff quizzically.

"He thought his truck was a boat." Earlee grinned bigger.

"Get him out?" Sam smiled back.

"Yeah, but it's going to be hell trying to get his truck out today. I have to get back out there after this." Both men chuckled for a moment and then Sam sobered.

"How bad was the storm? Was it bad enough that Susan might have gotten caught up in it – an accident maybe?"

"It's possible, but we check all the hospitals and the like when we send out Tele-type. If anything like that would have happened, we would have been notified, besides there's Smokies cruising 10 all the time."

"I see."

"Mr. Masters..," Earlee toyed with his pencil.

"Sam."

"Sam that's about all we can do for now," the sheriff raised the bottom sheet from his desk top and glanced at it. "This other sheet is last night's log…same info. We have all the agencies between El Paso and San Antonio on the look out. If she's still out there, we'll find her."

"I think I'll drive on the 10 for awhile; see if I can find anything. If I need anything, how do I get a hold of you?"

Sheriff Earlee opened his desk drawer and after scrounging around for a couple of minutes came up with a business card that he handed to Sam.

"Official number's on the front; cell's on the back."

"Thank you. I really appreciate it."

Sam was about to get up when the sheriff shook his head and let out an exaggerated breath.

"Sam, stay seated a moment. I need to tell you something."

Eighteen

Karin Larsen sat still and rigid on the wooden chair that was placed in front of Lord Lokan's massive desk. The two elders, who had taken from her home without explanation, stood silently on either side of her - motionless as statues. Fear looked out from her eyes as she glanced around the room. She stared blindly at her blood starved white knuckles and grimaced as her fingernails pierced the skin of her palms. Her arms and knees shook as if chilled to the bone.

The door opened and Lord Lokan walked silently into the room. "Leave us," he commanded. The elders bowed and left, glancing only once at Karin with unexpected pity.

Karin did not look up as Lord Lokan sat down behind his desk.

Karin felt his eyes on her as she waited for him to speak. After long moments, he spoke. "A serious charge has been lodged against you, my dear."

Karin's head came up. She suspected her father-in-law had done it - but what kind of charge?

"Your... husband has charged you with heresy."

Karin's eyes widened. She shook her head, "No, I, I, I don't believe it. He would never do such a thing, My Lord." She drew in a ragged breath as she tried to keep from crying.

Lord Lokan moved in front of her and leaned against his desk. He folded his hands in front and looked down at her with a sorrowful expression. "I'm afraid he accused you of plotting a disruption of tonight's ceremony."

Karin was stunned and looked downward in thought. *'Could it be true? Could he really have come here and turned me in? Why would he do that?'*

"He told me about the dreams and the vision." Lord Lokan said in an understanding voice. "It must be hard to think you've been betrayed, especially by one so close to you."

"My Lord," she looked back at him. "It's true I… I have been having dreams, but…"

"I understand," he nodded his head as he walked around behind her.

"My Lord nothing could be further from the…" she stopped as she felt his hands come to rest on her shoulders. She could feel the coldness of his long fingers through the thin material of her blouse.

"It is obvious that you are a good woman, and have always done what is right according to our Savior's dictates." Karin tried not to move as Lokan's hands slid down her shoulders, taking the fabric with them. He leaned closer and she could feel his breath on her bare neck. The hair on her arms stood on end as his long fingers wound their way around her neck, caressing lower and lower as he spoke. "There is something inside you that has caused this lapse in judgment, some evil thing that has taken away your sensibility."

Karin, frightened beyond words, listened.

"I must make the effort to withdraw this evil from your body," his voice purred in her ear as Karin's eyes began to slide shut. "I would be remiss if I did not tell you that it can be quite painful, but there is an ecstasy to be found in pain." He slightly raised the corners of his mouth as she leaned back against him. "Your husband has abandoned you. He threw you away like yesterday's garbage. Erik has aspirations beyond you in the new order and this was his first step in achieving it."

"I… I don't believe it." Karin whispered sleepily, unaware as Lord Lokan picked her up from the chair and laid her on the desk.

"I must exorcise the evil from you, my dear," he whispered. Karin shook her head, but was unable to move. She felt his cold hand move up her thigh under her dress and gasped as he pulled it up and cupped her breast in his hand.

"No, stop…" She gasped for breath as he lay across her body and kissed her hard. His probing tongue forced her lips apart. Once in her mouth, it changed into a forked entity that danced along the inner walls of Karin's cheeks like spidery tentacles. Her tongue lay paralyzed as his penetrated deep into her throat. She moaned with pain and pleasure as his tongue darted deeper and deeper and his hands slid up her thighs, spreading them apart.

Suddenly the image of Erik's smiling face broke through her mind and she screamed, kneeing Lord Lokan in the groin. He grunted and slid off the desk as Karin sat up, pulling her dress around her.

"I'm not possessed!" She screamed as she climbed off the desk and backed away from the groaning Lord. "You are damned. One is coming who will overthrow you. I have seen it and I know it is true."

"You will regret this," He gasped as he slowly straightened up and moved and crunched in behind his desk.

"You could have been a goddess in the new order. ELDERS!"

The two Elders entered the room as Lord Lokan flopped down into his chair.

"Take her to room seven while I decide what is to be done."

The Elders grabbed Karin and walked to the door.

"She is to have no outside contact with anyone, especially her husband. And beware of listening to her. She may try to infect you with her heresy."

Nineteen

"What?" Sam asked sitting back in his chair.

"Your friend isn't the first one."

"The first one what?"

The sheriff looked down then back to Sam, "I mean, this has happened before...several times, in fact." The sheriff jerked his thumb to his right, "People have disappeared from that stretch of highway out there and have never been found."

"I still don't understand...you mean in the past or recently?"

"It just happened day before yesterday as a matter of fact. Girl, nineteen years of age, traveling from Fort Stockton to San Antonio in a White Chevy Blazer, she never arrived. Her folks said she took off early in the morning, before sunup... no one's seen or heard from her since. Car, everything, vanished." Sheriff Earlee sat back in his chair and sighed. "Sam, this has been going on since the early 1900s, way before they built that highway. Unexplained disappearances have occurred all over this county. It's not all the time, mind you. It only seems to happen every four

124

to five years. At least one person goes missing. The law community calls this section of Texas "The Bermuda Rectangle." He got up from behind his desk and walked over to the wall map.

"See, this is my county," he pointed to a red dotted line on the map. "This," pointing to a lightly drawn rectangle, "is the outer boundaries of the last known locations of the people that have disappeared in the last fifty years, before that information is sketchy. It begins at the northwest corner, town of Barnhart, south to Juno, west to Fredericksburg, and north to Richland Springs."

"How come no one's ever made this known…I mean people disappearing like that…there's got to be questions, people wanting answers." Sam shook his head.

"Well, if they were disappearing every month, I guess, yeah you would have a lot of attention. But since it only seems to happen in the timeframe I mentioned people lose interest. Some folks think these people have run away, others think aliens…, and then others think it has something to do with the swamp southeast of here. No one knows anything really, just that once they're gone, they stay gone."

"So there are no further investigations? Nothing?"

"Look, every time someone goes missing, we all do what we can. Law Enforcement agencies are notified with APB's and flyers are produced and distributed."

"And?"

The sheriff walked back to his desk and sat down. He put his fist on the desk in front of him and looked at Sam. "Sam, the people around here have some strange beliefs. Don't get me wrong, they're all good God fearin' people. They just have these additional ideas that have developed through the years, one of which is they think…" The Sheriff paused, "I don't know. Well, they think there's some kind of monster, something from Hell that takes the people as some kind of sacrifice so the rest of us are left in peace."

"Sacrifice!?" Sam shook his head in disbelief. "You've got to be kidding."

"I wish I was. I was brought up here and trust me it's what they believe."

Sam ran his fingers through his hair as he leaned forward.

"Do you believe it?"

"Sam, I think it's pretty much crazy talk, Hell monsters and all. But the point is that disappearances are accepted around here and the only help you're gonna get is gonna be lip service at best."

Sam's shoulders slumped as he looked down at his hands. He was having a hard time rationalizing what he had just heard, but the expression on the sheriff's face was sincere and Sam believed him.

"Listen, thanks for being so candid, but I think I'm still going to search around."

"I'd do the same thing," he stood. "When I'm through with this mess out on the farm road I'll lend a hand, OK?" He got up and went to the door with Sam. "But I'm thinking you need to get some grub in you before you fall over. Especially if all you've had so far is my coffee."

Sam noticed the time was past nine.

"Yeah, you're right. Thanks for all your help."

"You keep in touch; hear?" Sheriff Earlee opened the outside door for Sam.

"You bet."

Sam walked out of the office to his truck.

*****

It was getting to be late afternoon. Sam had talked to Dr. Waythill and Jumper earlier. Jumper explained the acquaintance with Sheriff Earlee, actually Sheriff Earlee's wife, years ago, but reminded Sam that he never told him to use his name.

Sam had spent all day driving to twenty miles either side of Sonora and Ozona - twice. Sam felt sure that Susan's disappearance happened somewhere in the area of Gondolba. He couldn't put his finger on just how he knew; he just did.

Sam decided to concentrate his search efforts on the highway a few miles either side of Gondolba. He was traveling east in the right lane trying to look for anything

Randall Stevens

out of the ordinary. He came over a slight hill and saw fluorescence orange warning cones that had not been there earlier. The cones were placed in the passing lane, at an angle, with a sign that indicated merge right. Over the crest of the next hill there was a yellow highway truck stopped by a median guardrail with its warning lights flashing. Sam pulled into the left lane in between the cones and parked in front of the highway truck. Two highway maintenance men stopped what they were doing and before Sam could get out, one of them waved at him.

"Yo, Amigo," the larger of the two hollered, "You can't stop here."

Sam exited the cab of his truck and smiled.

"I'm sorry. I just wanted to ask a question."

"Well you can't park that truck here. Park it over there on the right shoulder."

"OK, Sorry." Sam climbed back in his cab. He couldn't believe what he had just done. *'I really must be tired…not thinking straight'.*

After he parked the truck, he came back and explained his situation.

"We haven't seen anything unusual, except what was left on the highway from last night's storm," the taller one gestured to the debris that littered the road.

"Were there any accidents?" Sam asked. "You know, one car types, rollovers, anything like that?"

"Nope."

"Well," Sam said, frustrated as he looked down the road. He took a deep breath and added, "I'll be on my way then; Thanks."

Sheriff Earlee's squad pulled behind Sam's truck. The emergency blues came on. He got out and came over to Sam and the men.

"Sam," The sheriff nodded to the two men, "Manny, Jose."

He turned to Sam. "Found anything?"

"Nothing, I've gone twenty miles past Sonora and Ozona, twice. I was going to concentrate my search in this area, when I came upon these guys and decided to ask them if they'd seen anything."

The sheriff turned to the two with a questioning look in his eyes.

"Haven't seen anything sheriff and we're done after we fix this," Manny pointed to the damage on the guardrail.

"I don't remember hearing anything about an accident out here today," Sheriff Earlee said."

"This maybe happened yesterday," Manny said then added, "maybe Sunday."

"No," the sheriff shook his head reflectively, "I'd have heard."

"Maybe it happened last night during the storm." Sam added. He walked over to the damage that was on the eastern end of the guardrail and knelt down. The sun was getting low in the western horizon and cast darkened shadows on the dent. Sam looked closer and saw what appeared to be a few light colored paint specks. He couldn't make out the exact color against the shadows. He took out his key ring, unfolded the small penknife and scraped the paint chip off the metal. He let it fall into the palm of his hand. He stood and turned around not taking his eyes off the flake. "Light blue," he said as looked at the sheriff, "I passed here twice today, but I was concentrating more on the right side of the road. This could have come from Susan's car last night...storm coming through and all...she could have done this."

"That's possible," said the sheriff, "but the odds..."

Sam looked around for anything on the ground. There was nothing. He stopped and looked across the road to where his truck was parked. He went back to the sheriff and said excitedly, "She may have bounced off here and veered over across the road."

"Could be, could be" the sheriff said thoughtfully looking across the road. He felt Sam's excitement and looked back at him, "Let's go have a look," The sheriff turned back to the two men, "Thanks, Baya con dios amigos."

After they crossed the road the sheriff stopped and said to Sam, "Listen. Odds are that's not from your friend's car; we'll check it out. *But* we take it slow, OK?" Pause. "So we don't miss anything."

Sam nodded.

Twenty

Susan awoke to the sound of fists beating against the door. She was groggy, but managed to raise her head. The room began to spin, so she closed her eyes and held still a moment. She reopened them and saw a slender young woman beating frantically against the bedroom door.

"Let me out!! I've done nothing wrong!!" The young woman sobbed, her voice rising as she continued to slam her fists against the wooden door, **"I'm not a heretic!! I'm not!!**

Susan started to tell her to stop, but then she realized she was no longer tied to the bed. She threw off the bedspread, swung her legs over the side and tried to stand. The dizziness came back and she sat. She closed her eyes again. '*I could recover faster if it wasn't for that damned racket,*' she thought. She turned to face the woman.

"Would you please stop screaming?" Susan said in a soft voice, the kind she used to get a client's attention in court.

The woman stopped, but did not turn around.

"That's better," she said, "Thank you."

Susan looked at the woman standing at the door. She was dressed in a plain black skirt that fell almost to the floor, with a simple white long sleeved blouse and black leather shoes. She had on a white-lace bonnet that tied under her chin. The whole effect was almost Amish looking.

The woman slowly turned her head, keeping one side of her face against the door. She held fast to it, like someone on the ledge of a cliff, afraid to look down.

The woman turned her head back to face the door and screamed, "HELP ME…SHE'S AWAKE!"

"That's it!"

Susan stood up and directly moved toward the door.

The young woman's eyes widened and she beat on the door harder.

Susan grabbed her hands.

"You need to stop this. Now!" Susan firmly backed the young woman toward the other bed and sat her down. She looked into the scared woman's eye's, "Screaming and beating your hands on the door obviously aren't doing any good." She released the woman's wrist and stood.

"B'sides, I can't think with all that racket". She looked at the door and then back at the woman. "So you sit here and be quiet, all right?"

The woman nodded once in acknowledgement.

"Good," Susan turned and looked around the room. Her clothes were on the stuffed chair, cleaned and neatly folded. Her shoes had been cleaned and were under the chair.

Susan picked up her slacks, blouse and jacket expecting to find her under garments - none. She looked around the room. The good feeling vanished. She looked back at her clothes and let her robe drop to the floor, "*not much of an option.*"

As Susan sat on the bed to put on her shoes, she went over the events of the last day. *'I think you may need to trust people more.' Sam had told her at dinner Sunday night, 'It would be one way to start breaking down those defensive walls you've built around you. At the time it sounded like good advice. If she ever saw him again, she'd tell him a thing or two about trust. Not something you do with strangers, that was for sure'.*

There was a knock at the door followed by a key sound in the lock. Susan sat up on the side of her bed and the woman stood up.

"Get back!" A strong male voice commanded as the door opened.

The head of a young man looked around the edge of the door. His face was square and hard with dark, bushy eyebrows that made him look much older. His eyes searched the room carefully and then narrowed.

"You," he said to the woman, "sit down and do not speak."

The woman sat. She kept her eyes on the man as he walked to the ends of the beds and stood with his arms crossed.

"You may enter now, woman," he barked.

Mrs. Crowley entered the room carrying a tray with two bowls and cups along with a tall silver pitcher. She put the tray on the top of the dresser and left the room. The man followed her.

"I need to talk to Erik…" the woman stood up. "Legion Kliest, please! You know me, you can't believe --"

The young man raised his hand.

"Be silent," he backed out the door and locked it closed.

"Erik…? Erik Larsen?" Susan asked young the woman. "You know him?"

The young woman put her face in her hands.

"Answer me!" Susan commanded. "Do you know Erik Larsen?"

No response.

Susan stood and moved to the woman. She grabbed the woman's shoulders. She was tired of the charade and was going to shake an answer out of her. The woman began to scream hysterically. She leaned back shaking her head. Susan stood. The woman's legs shot straight out and kicked Susan's shins, toppling her to the floor. Susan clenched her teeth and grasped her shins in a fetal position. When the pain passed she focused on the short wooden legs of the chair. Under it was an assortment of dust bunnies. Suddenly, something caught Susan's attention. It was a support board that had broken off with one end resting on the floor. She crawled closer for a better look. She grabbed hold of the board. A sharp object cut her ring finger, piercing the fleshy skin opposite the nail. Susan yelped, as she pulled her hand back from the board. The dust bunnies scattered with the air currents. She saw a small trickle of blood and pressed her thumb firmly on the cut. She reached in with her other hand, being careful not to repeat the injury. She pulled on the board. It stayed securely fastened. Susan could move it up and down, but not sideways.

"This is bullshit," she huffed.

She got on her knees and pulled the chair forward then leaned it back against the wall. She grabbed the loose end and pulled on it. The nails creaked loudly. Susan stopped. *'If there's a guard outside the door he might hear it,'* she thought. *'I need a cover sound.'* She looked at her guest and struck onto an idea. Susan lowered the chair and moved in front of the woman, who was sitting again.

"Look," Susan said as she squatted down in front of the woman, "I need you to scream again, but when I tell you. Can you do that?"

The woman just looked straight ahead.

Frustrated, Susan looked down. She sat on the side of her bed. *'I have to try and reason with her,'* she thought. Susan took a second to regain her composure.

"My name's…Susan, "she paused. "I don't know your name; who you are, or where you come from, but I do know one thing about you." The woman's eyes squinted slightly. "You don't want to be in here any more than I do."

The woman said nothing, but Susan could sense she was listening.

"I've never been the kind of person that goes around and lets bad things happen to me if I can do something about it. I've seen what these…these people want to do to me and I'll be damned if I'm going to be that bastard's supper without a fight. Now, I would rather escape than try to fight a battle I know I have no chance of winning. You can sit there and do nothing, or you can help me. They have not responded to your previous screams for help. All I need..., " Susan emphasized, "am asking for ... is for you to do it one more time, so I can drown out the noise that board will make when I pull it off that chair. You don't have to speak to me, just nod if you will help me by screaming when I tell you to." Susan's eyes begged directly at the woman.

No response.

"Please," Susan pleaded.

The woman did not respond.

"OK," Susan said defiantly. "I'll do it without your help."

She went to the chair and positioned it. Then grabbed the board and placed her other hand where it provided the most resistance. She paused a moment to make sure all grips and leverages were correct. Then she took a deep breath and pulled.

At the same moment the nails made the loud wrenching sound, the woman let out a wailing scream.

Twenty-one

The nails released their grip with a screech almost as loud as the scream. The woman continued while she watched Susan place the chair back in its original position. Susan made a slashing signal across her neck and the woman stopped. She looked at her primitive weapon. It felt good to have control of something, even though she had no idea of where or when she was going to use it. There were a total of four nails in the three-inch wide board - two in each end. The two that held in last were bent outward by the force of the pull and extended like long spikes. The other two were still positioned perpendicular to the board's flat surface. Susan smiled.

"You did well." Susan said as she sat on her bed.

"So," looking up from the board in her hands. "How come you're stuck in here with me? What happened?"

The woman slowly raised her head. She looked at Susan with an incomprehensionable look. She took a deep breath and said, "My name is Karin. I've been accused of heresy against The Savior and …" she put her hands up to her face and wept softly. After a moment she put her hands down and still looking down said, "I've been told my husband turned me in because of these dreams I had." She rocked forward and shook her head from side to side, "But I don't believe it. He wouldn't do such a thing."

"Is your husband Erik… Erik Larsen?"

Karin stopped rocking and gave a slow nod without looking up.

'*How's that for irony*,' Susan thought and shook her head once, '*I'm imprisoned with the wife of the man who abducted me.*' She was speechless as she tried to grasp the events of the past day.

"I know Erik brought you here…" Karin said as she raised her head and looked at Susan with her moist eyes. "I'm so sorry. If there was anything I could do, I –"

There was the sudden rasp of the key in the door lock. Susan quickly looked for a hiding place for her weapon and slid it under the bed. Both women stood as the door opened.

Legion Kliest entered and moved over to the front of the dresser. Then Lord Lokan entered with the High Elder and another Elder following. Erik entered behind them and closed the door.

Lord Lokan stood in front of the women. He looked dispassionately at them.

"Sit down." he commanded.

Susan looked at him with contempt. She wanted to defy his command, but her body responded involuntarily. The women mirrored each other in unison, they looked at Lord Lokan. He nodded approval. The Elders moved the chair behind him and he sat. Upon sitting, he glanced at the cushion under him, paused, and then returned his attention to the women. He looked directly at Susan.

"I trust you are comfortable?" Lord Lokan asked.

Susan defiantly stared back. Her body was frozen in position. She felt a release in her jaw muscles, but remained silent.

"It is of no matter," Lord Lokan shrugged. He looked at Karin.

"It is you I have come to see. You have desecrated the name of The Savior. You have been possessed by demons that cannot be excised. Your soul has been contaminated. To prevent further infection of The Savior's flock you must be terminated. I therefore direct that you be called Blessing and brought before The Savior, with this other, at the end of this day."

Tears flowed down Karin's face as she moved her disbelieving eyes to Erik.

"Your husband has reported you and by the order of the sacrament you are guilty."

Erik stared straight ahead.

Lord Lokan raised his right hand above his head so that his arm was fully extended.

"So it has been commanded, so be it," then he lowered his hand and stood up. As he did, the chair was removed and replaced to its original spot. Erik turned, opened the door and held it open until they all exited. He turned to Karin and choked, "I'm...sorry...I." He lowered his head and left the room.

Susan turned and looked at Karin who continued to look at the door. Susan sat numbly; searching desperately for the right words to say - there were none.

Susan reflected on the horror she felt when she'd been told of her fate, '*but Karin...Christ...Karin is one of them...how she must feel; her own husband ... that bastard'*.

Karin turned her head and faced Susan. The tension bellowed between them. Karin wiped her face, sniffled and let her hand fall to her side. She spoke with a half cry and forced chuckle in her voice.

"Well...I guess that's...that." She let her eyes fall to the floor.

"I...I don't know what to say Karin ... I ..."

"You don't have to say anything," Karin said as she kept her eyes fixed on the floor. "I made a mistake." She shook her head slowly. "I should have ..." She raised her head again and looked quizzically at Susan, "I thought I was doing the right thing." She fell onto the bed, turned toward the wall and wept.

Susan felt a mild sting inside her chest. She looked down and placed her hand just above her bosom. Suddenly, she couldn't breathe! She opened her mouth and tried to inhale. Panic set in; she needed help; she needed Karin to help her. Susan looked at Karin and the moment she did her breathing returned. '*What was that?*' She thought, as the tingle of after-fear streamed down her spine. She looked at her chest again and the second she did, her lungs stopped. With questioned panic in her eyes, she looked up past Karin— no breath. Terror brought her to her feet.

Karin remained on the bed crying.

Susan grasped her neck as her eyes went to Karin again. Immediately her breathing started. "*What was going on? What was happening? Could this have something to do with her? ... It must.*' She looked above Karin; her breathing stopped. Quickly, she looked back and it restarted. She tried to make sense of what was happening as she sat again. '*I find myself in physical peril when I look away from her, why?*'

The mild sting in Susan's chest turned to an acute ache. She squinched forward keeping her eyes on Karin. Suddenly, she remembered feeling this before in her life. It was the same pain she felt when her mother died. Not the initial pain of loss, but the pain that mushroomed from that into *sympathy*. She felt this between the time of her mothers passing and the funeral; especially at the funeral. Everyone, it seemed, came up crying, weeping and sobbing as they bent to hug her. She could feel the wetness of their tears on her forehead and cheeks. As one of the neighbor ladies finished her hug and stood up, she smiled and stopped crying. She said, "There, that's better," and moved off. It came to Susan that the woman had just passed onto her the pain she was feeling. They were all doing it! They were passing on their pain to her! She didn't understand why. She wanted to leave, but her father made her stand by the casket with him and endure this hurt. She remembered the sting in her chest as they kept passing on their sympathy. The only thing she could do was close her eyes and turn away as the people approached her. It seemed to ease the pain. The more she turned away and tighter she closed her eyes the less it hurt.

Now the same pain resurfaced. Only this time she could not stop it by looking away. She couldn't close her eyes and ignore it. She was being forced to fully experience it. She suddenly remembered that she mentally chanted a phrase that helped and tried it, '*I don't want your pain…I don't want your pain…I don't want your pain …* it had no effect.

The vision of Karin laying there burned before her. Susan could not look away. The pain inside her chest elevated to a point where her body began to tremble. Suddenly, the pain and shaking stopped and she fell into a trance-like state. She couldn't move any part of her body. In her mind she went back to a time in her childhood. She was ten years old and spinning around in the kitchen holding her hand in pain. She had just burned her finger on the stove. She stopped spinning and saw a glass of iced tea on the counter.

Susan could feel the pain her child image was feeling.

She watched herself pull a cube from the glass and put it on the burn. The pain stopped – both pains. The scene fast-forwarded to a later time when her father came home. She told him what happened and that she felt the burn was really severe and she may have to go to the hospital, because when she tried to remove the ice, the pain came back. Her father looked at her hand. He placed it in his and with the other removed the ice. The pain returned. He looked at the finger then at her. *"Hold still,"* he said as he firmly held her hand and threw the ice cube into the sink.

Susan could not believe her father wanted her to experience this awful pain. She tried to pull her hand out of his and step toward the sink to get the ice, but her father held on and said, *"Wait a minute."* She hissed air through her clenched teeth as the pain increased. It kept climbing and finally reached its zenith; she thought she would not be able to stand it any longer…then…like magic the pain subsided. She looked at her dad and said, *"Where did the pain go?"*

"Your body absorbed it," he said. *"You have to let it run its course. All you did was postpone the pain with the ice… not prevent it.*

Susan came back to the moment and thought for a second, '*Could my heart do the same thing? Was all I was doing through the years was postponing sympathy's pain? Could other people's pain only hurt for a little while? Will my heart absorb it given enough time?'* She looked at Karin then looked at her own chest. Her breathing did not stop. She softly said, "Let it come." Then she looked back at Karin.

Karin raised her head slightly and asked with a half choking voice from sobbing, "What…what do you mean?"

The sympathy for Karin surrounded Susan's heart and stung it all at once. The pain pierced the surface. It lasted only a moment and then her heart did something it never did before; it absorbed the pain and relieved the hurt. Susan looked back at her chest and felt her heart do the job only a human heart can do…"*feel another human being's emotions.*"

Susan reacted to Karin's question by briefly shaking her head then focusing back to Karin, "I was…I was talking to myself, it's not important." Susan felt an overwhelming sense of cleansing; a feeling that comes when one shows compassion for another. It was like a transformation, a re-birth of her soul. Despite her predicament, Susan felt the hollowness in her fill. She raised the corners of her mouth slightly, "What can I do to help?"

Karin responded with a pleasingly surprised look on her face. She sat back up on the bed and said softly as she shook her head.

"There's nothing that can be done. Once Lord Lokan decrees something it becomes law and no one can reverse it."

Susan looked up at the tray on the dresser. "Maybe if you had something to drink you…"

"The water's the *only* thing safe on that tray," Karin said as she turned her head to watch Susan move to the dresser.

Susan stopped in her tracks and turned to Karin. "What do you mean?"

"I mean that anything else on that tray is made from The Savior's body and if you continue to eat it over time, you become one of us…them," and tilted her head to the door.

"I don't understand," Susan responded. "Frankly; I don't understand any of this;

there's a swamp in the Texas hill country; there's a thirties town in the twenty-first century; there's a leader that is transfixed on being a God of some sort; and … and there's a giant tree that turns into some kind of frickin' monster that devours people in a religious ceremony. It's…it's unbelievable. What kind of place is this? ... What kind of town?" Susan shrugged her shoulders, "What kind of people are you…?" She was now glaring at Karin.

Karin stared at Susan and then bowed.

Susan immediately had a resentful chill come over her. She felt she may have gone too far and shoved Karin back into a shell. She needed to do something and fast. Karin was the only one to supply her with answers. She silently cursed herself. *'Get a hold, Goddamn it, and calm down.'* Susan inhaled and held it a moment, "I'm sorry Karin, I…I…this whole thing…please Karin…I'm sorry."

Karin kept her head in the same position and said, "There's no need for apologies, you're right…" Then she raised her head again and said to Susan, "Please," she motioned to Susan's bed, "sit."

Twenty-two

Sam remembered that he hadn't called Susan's father. He opened the door to the truck. "Damn it!"

"What's the problem?" Sheriff Earlee asked.

"I forgot to turn my cell off. I don't have my car charger and I haven't called Susan's dad since *we* talked this morning. He's probably going nuts."

"Here, use mine," Sheriff Earlee unhooked the cell phone from his belt and tossed it to Sam.

"Thanks." Sam dialed.

"Hello?"

"Sir, this is Sam, sorry I haven't called, but I'm with the sheriff on the highway and I think we may have found something."

"What'd you find, Sam?!" Dr. Waythill asked excitedly.

"There's a damaged guardrail with some paint on it that's the same color as Susan's car." Sam didn't want to get into explaining the Lexus so used the term car.

"Do you think she was in an accident?"

"Sir, we don't even know if it was her car that left it. It's just what we have to go on at this point. We're looking for anything else that might give us a clue to where she went."

"Sam, I've decided to help you look for her. I can't just sit here."

"I think that's a bad idea, we'd be out of contact; it's going to be dark within a half hour." The last thing Sam needed was to be looking for him too. "But... I can't stop you." He wanted to add, '*If it were me, I'd do the same thing.*'

"Mrs. Reemer says I can go to the cell phone place on Highway10; they'd hook me up right away."

"If you're set on coming sir, do that; you got a pencil?" Sam gave him the cell number of the sheriff before he hung up.

"Thanks again," Sam said as he handed the phone back.

"What's wrong?"

"Her dad wants to come here and help. He's got a neighbor lady to watch his phone...he doesn't have a cell phone...he's going to go get one and travel out here. I tried to dissuade him, but...I can't stop him...actually...I'd do the same thing,"

Sheriff Earlee nodded in agreement.

Sam looked up at the sky, "Dark soon."

They both went to the front of the sheriff's cruiser and searched on either side of the shoulder. They eventually came upon what looked like skid marks made by wide tires. The sheriff knelt and carefully inspected the tracks. He looked to his left. Approximately five feet in front of where the plowed humps of stones ended, there were darkened marks on the edge of the asphalt. The marks looked like faded dashes of black tar that were used to cover cracks on black top. He stood up and moved over to the first one and knelt again.

"Sam, come here," the sheriff called.

Sam squatted beside him, "What do you have?"

"Look at this. It looks like tire rubber has been scraped off onto the side here." He scraped with his fingernail and raised it to his nose. "It's rubber all right; here."

He raised his finger under Sam's nose.

"What do you think it means?" Sam inquired.

Sheriff Earlee stood up and looked down the road. He moved away from the side of the road to where the shoulder gravel ended and grass of the land began. He paused, looked up the rise and then looked left to right. He walked east following the dash marks. Sam followed behind him not saying a word. They walked a little way more. The sheriff stopped.

"I'll tell you what I think this means," the sheriff said turning to Sam. "Mind you it's just a theory…but I can't for the life of me, think it could be anything else."

Sam looked anxiously at the sheriff.

"She's traveling east. Somehow she bangs into the guardrail up there. Could have been someone cut her off, animal ran in front of her and she swerved to avoid it, or it could have had something to do with the storm coming through here last night, which I believe fits. Anyway…she pulls to the shoulder and slams the brakes. She can't see in front of her vehicle…maybe her windshield is damaged, or the hail or rain was preventing her from seeing much. She can't see so she nurses the vehicle forward by feel of the front left tire rubbing against the road." He turned his head toward the east. "She must have noticed the overpass down there before this all happened and tried to get under it. I suspect these marks go all the way there. I suggest we drive down there and see if my theory holds water."

At the overpass they got out of their vehicles and inspected the edge of the road…no marks. Without saying a word the sheriff walked over to the other side of the overpass. Approximately thirty feet west, on the edge of the highway, was the last mark.

"It fits, Sam," the sheriff said.

Sam looked at the sheltered area provided by the overpass and followed the ground rise to the point where the girders met the roadway on top. He looked over at the highway on the other side then turned back to the sheriff. "You think she went on that road?"

"Don't know why…road don't go nowhere."

Sam was looking at the overpass and turned back to the sheriff with a questioned look on his face. "Excuse me?"

"It's just a bridge," the sheriff answered as he gazed up at the structure. "This was some brain surgeon's brilliant idea awhile back; build the bridges first…then connect the road." The sheriff went silent as he looked from one end of the bridge to the other. "There was supposed to be a road connecting 163 from Juno to Highway 10 so folks could get to Gondolba without having to go clear up to Sonora to get on, but the surveyors…planners, I don't rightly know which one, forgot about the smog swamp south of here."

"Smog swamp?"

"Yeah, I mentioned it to you back in my office…'member? It's just south of here. The access road up there separates from along side this highway for a mile or two just pass the overpass. It still runs parallel, but about a half mile away. Along the other side there's the swamp. It extends about fifteen miles east of here and about twenty-five miles wide. Back in 1900 a strong hurricane hit Galveston; killed a lot of people. It moved northwest and dumped a whole lot of rain in this area. Swamp down there formed for some reason. Some say the storm busted into a spring or somethin'' and the water stayed. Ain't no other explanation really; ain't exactly moist ground were standin' on."

"You think she could have gone in there…got lost or something?" Sam asked.

"I don't see how. The trees and shrubs around the perimeter are so thick you can't see in front of your face. I can't say for certain…I never been in there. But I know of a few that have tried to go in despite the warnings…you know…huntin' and all. They swear they went straight in, stayed in one direction and before they knew it they come out the same place they went in. We've even had choppers fly over the thing…flew to within ten feet of the fogged cover, thinkin' the wind from the blades would blow the fog, smog, whatever the hell it is, away so they could see the ground. That stuff kept bellowing up, but never did clear. That's where some say

Hell's servant has its lair. It's a strange place. Every now and then some state investigators come by with fancy equipment to see what's goin' on in there, but after awhile they pack up and leave; say they're goin' back to analyze the data. I think they're just frustrated. Anyway they put a fence around the whole area with warning signs sayin' possible radioactivity and to keep out, because of the explosion in 1932. Some type of meteor hit in there they said. Anyway it's not a good..."

"Unit one; central, over," The sheriff's belt radio, squawked.

"This is one; over."

"One; proceed code 3 to intersection 163 and 90, 10-81, two vehicles, injuries, ambulance in route; over."

"On my way: out. "

"Sorry pard gotta go; major car accident with injuries."

"What explosion?"

"I can't explain it now. I'll be back when I can, keep in touch!"

Sam watched the sheriff jump in his cruiser; slam the door; and scream the engine, lights, and siren to life. The cruiser's tires spun sending stones of different sizes and white dust shooting out from underneath the rear bumper. The sheriff cut the wheels hard to the left and squealed the tires like stuck sows caught in a wire fence across the roadway, turning the white graveled dust into a cloud of different shades of amethyst gray. The cruiser went airborne across the median and sailed around the center supports of the bridge. When it landed on the west bound lanes the sheriff turned his head and smiled at Sam as he sped off.

Sam waved and nodded saying with a low voice, "Loudest U-turn I ever saw; hope he makes it and doesn't become another 10-81."

Twenty-three

"Do you want some water?" Susan asked as she walked to the tray.

"No," Karin said softly.

Susan returned to her bed with a cup of water and sat.

"You're right," Karin began, "We're not normal. Everything today is as it was back in 1932…the time … the time The Savior appeared in the tree."

"The tree? How did the…"

"Please," Karin raised her hand, "I'll try to explain things to you."

"I'm sorry…it's my nature."

"It was 1932, just after midnight the 29th of February, the leap year. There was a great explosion outside our town. The blast shook the earth so strongly houses were damaged and several collapsed from the force. We all came running from our homes to find a tremendous crater had formed and there was a fire raging in the center of it. In the middle of the crater was this tree. It was burning like a giant torch. The rain and wind had no effect on it. The flames were burning straight up to the sky. The strange thing was that the flames were not consuming the tree.

It was growing. Suddenly the ground in front of the tree collapsed inward and loud echoes of screams came from within the gaping hole, like millions of voices crying out in pain. We were horrified at the sounds and ran back to the town. The screams continued all through the night. As morning came, they stopped. No one dared to leave their homes or look out their windows."

"Wait a minute, OK?" Susan said. You said we ran; as in you."

"Yes."

"Well you don't look a day over twenty. How can that be?"

"That's part of this whole thing here. I'll explain that in a minute."

Susan nodded with an understanding frown.

"Mid-day, the men put on their hats and coats and left their homes, their eyes vacant. What happened at the crater is in the secrets of the sacrament that Lord Lokan keeps in the Temple. That evening, the men returned to their homes and when they touched their women and children, all questions of what happened vanished from their minds. For some reason, I was not affected by my father's touch, but I knew better than to ask questions.

The next day everyone received a summons to go to the crater and that's when we met Lord Lokan. The crater became sacred ground. The tree that had been encased in flames was enormous and was deemed our Savior. All that was required was daily obedience to the three covenants of the sacrament: ingest the body, give thanks through worship and celebrate his coming every four years with a human sacrifice. For this the Savior protects, provides and pacifies us. And our reward is eternal life."

"You mean everyone is …?"

"Just the way they were in 1932," Karin finished.

Susan looked at the floor trying to comprehend all that Karin was telling her. She shot a look at Karin. "Wait, they already had a sacrifice. I saw it last night," Susan shook her head, "Why are we here?"

"This is the final ritual. The Savior will rise. Then begins a new world order

147

tomorrow; the *Evening Day."*

"I don't understand something. If you're imprisoned from the outside world, how do you survive? I mean what do you do in this…town?

"We have crop fields to tend, clothes to make, things to build. The Savior provides all…the seed, the cloth and any materials that are needed for any project that is directed by Lord Lokan."

Susan let out an unbelieving breath and returned her cup to the dresser.

"Who is this… this mystagogue Lokan that calls himself Lord?" Susan asked as she sat again.

"No one knows where he came from, but he interprets the teachings of the sacrament that he has written with the guidance of the Savior."

"So once every four years you kidnap and execute innocent people to that thing, in order to survive. Is that pretty much it?"

"I'm afraid so, yes. But the Blessings are not…as you say…kidnapped."

"Wait a minute!" Susan shot to her feet, "I was pulled out of my SUV, almost drowned in the swamp, tied up and gagged and thrown in the back of my SUV by Erik and some other goon. If that's not kidnapping, I don't know what is!"

Karin leaned back.

"No one is allowed to come to the bridge on Eternity Road by force and without escort of a Legion. The Blessing must come down that road on their own; no physical force used. The Legions are given certain powers that only last during their search; levitation is the only one I know of. This search is not without danger. The Legion must accomplish this task by midnight or a loved one will be sacrificed." Karin closed her eyes.

Susan thought about Erik's nervous banter at her protest, his pleading for her cooperation, his constant attention to the time. It all fit. And in reality, Susan realized she had come of her own free will.

"Now," Karin continued, as she looked directly into Susan's eyes, "I must tell you this. For the past three weeks, I have had this recurring dream. I awake in a dark pit. I can move nothing but my head. I look up at the only source of light. It does not light the hole, only me. It is a gray light and intermixed in it are letters circling and spinning in scattered directions. The more I look at them the faster they go. I can't make out all of them, because there are too many. I close my eyes and then open them. I find that the letters have slowed down, but begin to speed up again. As they do, they are rearranging themselves in another order. Each time I do this, they change to another position. I then wake up. I have tried each time to make sense of the letters, but can't. Then two nights ago I made out an 'N', and two oddly shaped 'S's. There were two others, two of them are shaped the same, but they were spinning too fast. I told Erik about the dream, but he said we should not mention it to anyone else. He wanted to pray on it. Last night as I waited for Eric to return, I had a vision of an old woman, and I heard myself speaking words I didn't understand. It was very strange.

Susan had that feeling of recognition come over her again when she heard what Karin's vision had said. The words were familiar or some of it at least. Then a word popped into her head and she felt a cold pain bouncing through her.

"Nidhogg," Susan whispered as she felt herself grow cold.

"Are you all right?" Karin asked as she watched Susan's face turn white.

"No, no I'm fine...please... continue." Susan felt a surge of apprehension, but fought it, trying to stay calm.

"When Erik brought me home, I told him what had happened to me. We decided not to say anything. Then today, two Elders came to our house and brought me to Lord Lokan's office. Until now I thought I was doomed. But it's going to be all right," Karin stood up, "because now I understand."

"What?" Susan looked at Karin's excited face.

"It's you!" Karin grabbed Susan's hands, "You're the one!! You're the one who's going to save us all!!!

Twenty-four

Sam looked at the top of the embankment and followed the slope down to the graveled edge of the road. He briefly knelt down and examined the small gravel stones. He walked to the middle of the underpass, staying on the shoulder. Everything looked normal as far as he could tell. He wished the sheriff were with him. Darkness was quickly approaching. The pale dusk air became colder as the sun lowered in the horizon. He went to his truck for his jacket and returned. He decided to physically examine the cement incline to the girders. Halfway he stopped to examine the area - nothing out of the ordinary. He continued to the top and had to squat when he reached the plateau. He sat down placing his feet on the slope and his forearms on his knees. "Nothing," he muttered to himself.

He started back down and something, some force, made him stop a third of the way and look at his truck. He stood fixated on it. There was nothing wrong or different about it, but he couldn't take his eyes off of it. Finally his eyes lowered and he saw what he was supposed to be focusing his attention on. It was in the foreground between him and the truck. The grass at the edge of the cement incline was pressed down in two areas about half way up from the bottom. As he got closer, he could see that the tracks continued to the top of the embankment on an oblique angle away from him.

'*She could have driven up this rise,* ' Sam thought.

Sam's excitement dashed when he reached the summit of the hill and saw the barbed wire fence. The tracks went right underneath. '*How could she have driven under…*' then a rationed thought shouted '*…must've been laid before the fence was put up.* ' He knelt down and put his hand on one the right tire impression. The grass was freshly bent. Sam raised himself to a squat and turned to look at the tracks going under the fence. '…but how? Darkness blanketed the ground; he needed his flashlight.

Sam returned moments later steering the funneled light on the tracks. He paused in front of the fence and raised the beam slowly against the barbed wire. There were tiny objects on the wires. Sam pointed the flashlight to the left and then to the right. He could see that the particles were only attached to the wires in two areas and those areas corresponded directly above the tracks on the ground. He pinched the substance off the wire and examined them. It was dried mud and grass. He let the substance fall and slid his fingers on the wire between the barbs. '*She pulled the fence down… and then drove over it?* ' Sam questioned to himself. '*And then put the fence back up?!*'

Sam moved to the nearest fence post and grabbed the top of it with his hand trying to move it from side to side - it didn't budge. He shook his head in disbelief. Sam placed the flashlight on the ground. This time he grabbed it with both hands and tried to move it - nothing. He tried in vain to pull the fence post straight out of the ground.

"This is fuckin' impossible," he said aloud.

He stormed over to the other post and got the same result. He moved back to the center. With the flashlight, he visually followed the tracks that led to the side of the access road.

"What's the Hell's going on here?" he muttered under his breath as he stared at the tracks.

Sam went back to his truck. He'd decided to get on the road beyond the fence. There was a message on his phone.

"Sam, Sheriff Earlee. This is a real mess; two dead and two injured. I don't know when I'll be able to get back to you, sorry. I'm going to turn this off for now, but will check it periodically for any messages. Good Luck".

Sam left a message telling the sheriff what he had discovered and what he intended to do. He turned it and let it drop to the seat beside him. He followed Sheriff Earlee's tracks across the median and back to Gondolba.

Twenty-five

"Don't you see? Karin exclaimed as Susan looked at her in amazement. "What the window reflection said...that's you! Your name said backwards as in a reflection or something ...*Nasus... Nasus, Susan!"*

Susan shook her head not believing what she was hearing.

"Nasus eno eht evas," Karin persisted, "The words are backwards. It's, Save the one, Susan!"

Susan stood up, shaking her head in denial.

"There's no way..."

"You can believe it or not," Karin continued, "but I believe you were brought here."

"Brought here?" Susan turned abruptly to face Karin, "You're goddamned right I was brought here, but not by some mystic vision thing! I was brought here by your husband."

"But something brought you to Erik..."

"I..."

"Hear me out," Karin said excitedly, as she stood up and came face to face with Susan. "Just…hear me out, OK? I started having these dreams three weeks ago. Something must have happened to you at the same time. Can you remember anything out of the ordinary, something you did or said?"

"I…I started to get a compulsion to buy a gun, but that was just within the last week," she answered thoughtfully "…a gun I didn't need."

"That might be it," Karen looked away and then back at Susan. "Was there anything else that happened, anything at all?"

Susan paused a moment and looked past Karin in thought.

"During the purchase I met the owner of the gun shop, Sam Masters. There was something about him. I could see it in his eyes. It was as if I knew him from somewhere in my past." Susan's eye's locked on Karin's. "I felt really comfortable with him." She furthered about Sam suggesting she trust people more and that's how she became involved with Eric.

"It's you," Karin said again, "You feel it don't you? You were sent here… or brought here," she softly smiled.

"But …" Susan paused reflectively.

Karin breathed in deeply in anxious anticipation that Susan believed what she was saying.

"No, No" Susan shook her head sternly. "I'm no special hero or anything. I admit that some things have happened to me recently, but they are all rational happenings, except this town and…"

"Susan, you're here for a reason," Karin moved a step closer. "Call it what you will, God or whatever, it is the good part that's within you that brought you here. All this," Karin spread her arms, "The town, the swamp, The Savior, it's all evil. Good is the only thing that can stop it! Good brought you here and through you we're being given a chance to be saved."

"Well…," Susan scoffed sarcastically, "I have that gun. And you're right in one respect, Karin. I'm going to fight to get out of here…and when I do, I'm running as

154

far and as fast as I can from here."

"You'll never make it through the swamp. You'll die."

"I'll take the road, the one I came in on."

"It's the only road and it's guarded; besides swamp water covers it when not in use." Karin reached out and gently took Susan's hands. "Susan, you asked before what kind of people we are? I'll tell you…we're prisoners, prisoners of our own ignorance and need. We and the *innocents* need help…" Karin raised her eyebrows and continued, "Your help…Please…"

"Wait a minute. Who are the innoc..."

They heard the familiar sound of a metal key turning the tumblers inside the lock. They both quickly sat on their beds and wait.

Twenty-six

The guard entered and was about to give his command, but ceased when he saw that Karin and Susan were already in position. The next to enter was Lord Lokan, then the two Elders who were there before. Erik was not in attendance. The Elders placed the chair in position and Lord Lokan sat, throne-like, upon it. He crossed his legs and said in a pleasant voice, "Good evening, Blessings."

The women did not say anything. Susan was shocked that the afternoon had past so quickly. There wasn't much time left.

"I was troubled by something during my last visit. This annoyance stayed within me all afternoon. It was like a gnat that kept flying around my head. It would not retreat no matter how many times I mentally swatted at it. After this afternoon's praise ceremony, I proceeded to my office in the Temple. I was going to rest before this evening's ceremony. Instead, I decided to sit in my chair and ponder what was troubling me. The revelation came to me the instant I sat down. There was something different about this room. I have been here many times and never felt this oddity before."

A sudden nervous chill came over Susan coupled with a floating sensation. She knew she was still sitting, but everything below her waist became buoyant.

"Do you want to know my discovery?" Lord Lokan sarcastically asked as he looked at Karin and then Susan. He bent forward and paused and said while pointing downward, "It's this very chair!" He glanced down at it then returned his attention to the ladies. "It doesn't have the normal feel." He stood up and paced a few steps ahead, passing between the women. He stopped and then turned around.

Susan and Karin both watched Lord Lokan pass between them and were looking up at him when he said, still quizzically staring directly at the chair, "I believe we should find out what the matter is with this piece of furniture." He nodded at the Elders.

The men grabbed the chair and turned it on its back and rear legs.

"Well, what have we here?" Lord Lokan asked rhetorically, moving directly to a position in between the women. He raised his head and spoke in a surprising voice at the Elders. "We seem to be missing a support from under the chair."
He cupped his left hand under his chin in a thoughtful pose. He took two steps towards it and turned around, "I wonder where it could be?" He turned around so he was facing the Elders again. "I know," as he pointed his left index finger at the Elders in an excited manner. "Maybe one of the Blessings knows what became of it? Let us ask them." He turned around once again.

Susan looked at the chair and then turned at Karin. She made a frustrated squint and abruptly stood. "You can stop the bullshit," she said with a stern voice as she made a step toward Lord Lokan and came to within inches of his face, "...your *Lordship*."

Lord Lokan was momentarily shocked at the sudden movement.

She sensed that for an instant she had an advantage over him again.

The High Elder made a move to subdue her. Lord Lokan mentally plunged back into the moment and commanded to the would-be rescuer, "Wait!" He did not remove his eyes from Susan's. Instead, he raised the corners of his mouth and then extended that into a full-blown grin - neither one blinked.

"You find something funny?" Susan pried.

Lord Lokan's grin disappeared from his face as his lips parted revealing his yellowish, aged, clenched teeth. "No... Blessing.*"*

"My name's Susan," she said, continuing her challenge.

He changed his facial expression once again, to one of being almost pleased.

"I find you a pleasant change to the normal frightened outsiders that are brought to me."

They maintained eye contact.

Susan thought, '*He backed down. I can't believe it. He's much too powerful and cautious to lose face in front of witnesses. Witnesses talk and he would lose the control...loose face. I may have gone too far, but I can't show weakness now...I just can't. No matter what happens I must maintain an appearance of strength.*'

"Normally, I would have struck you down for such insolence. But as I said, I find you refreshing and while I don't want actions such as yours to become common practice, I feel it should be both rewarded and punished. Therefore, I reward you by not exacting punishment. But the matter of implementing punishment for such actions must be enforced. This is indeed a quandary." He broke off the stare and switched his attention to Karin, "Ah, ha, solutions are always where one least expects to find them."

Susan turned and looked down at Karin. She returned her attention back to Lord Lokan.

Lord Lokan's eyes became slitted and produced red-orange fire within them. He changed his facial expression. His face became larger, as his jaw lowered. At the same time his skin became thick with billowy scales that secreted droplets of white paste-like puss under each one.

"Stand!" he commanded with a voice that sounded like it was coming from the depths of a bottomless pit. He raised his left hand and Susan flew onto the bed like she was a feather being blown by a wind. She felt herself become as stiff as a statue of stone lying on the bed. Susan could see fear in Karin's eyes as she slowly stood. The fear soon turned to terror at the sight of the demon that had just commanded her into that position. Karin's eyes widened with a fright that Susan had never seen in a face before. Her whole body shook to the point that her head looked as if it was in a huge vibrating machine. Her hair and clothes began to wave. Karin screamed as the now demon extended his right arm toward her. He slowly began to close his fingers one at a time, from the little one to the index finger. As they squeezed together Karin's body began to twist. Her feet were fastened to the floor as her waist began to turn to the left. With the ring finger closed, her upper chest began to turn to the right. Karin screamed to a point that Susan thought her eardrums were going to explode. The middle finger closed and Karin's neck began to twist in the direction of her waist. Her cries of pain became gargled as her head now turned in the opposite direction as the index finger closed. Then the demon's thumb, that was pointing straight up like he was hitchhiking. He looked down at Susan.

"I close this thumb, Blessing, and this one will be crushed to a pain that will last until taken to The Savior. "

Susan eyes were fixed on Karin's twisted tortured body. She was experiencing her own emotional pain as she witnessed the torture of her friend and could do nothing to stop it. Her heart was being squeezed by the demon's hand. The word *friend* struck her like a bolt of lightning. She instantly became cognizant that she felt Karin was her friend. Fullness entered her. Even as she witnessed Karin endure this unbelievable, monstrous pain…she thought of her as a friend - a friend she could not help.

Susan heard sounds coming from the demon, but did not realize they were meant for her. She suddenly found she could move her head as well as her mouth. She turned to face the hideous creature that controlled her and was inflicting unspeakable anguish upon her friend.

"Stop it!" Susan shouted. "You're killing her! Stop it."

"Cleanse yourself, Blessing, and I will release this one."

Susan did not know what he wanted. She looked at the thing with an expression of confusion. "What do you mean?" she asked.

"Cleanse yourself now!"

Susan's eyes went from Karin to the Elders, whose eyes were anchored on the horror before them. She looked back at the demon and shouted the only thing she could think of, "I'm sorry!"

Karin's body froze in the twisted position.

Susan looked at Karin then turned back and continued with an even louder shout "...I'M SORRY...FOR MY INSOLENCE!"

The demon held its posture and moved its tempered eyes in Susan's direction then lowered its arm back to its side. It began to retake the form of Lord Lokan as Karin fell to the floor.

Susan, her body now completely free of restraint, rolled off the bed and dropped to the floor, quickly moving to Karin. Susan placed her arms around Karin's shoulders and moved her into her lap.

"I'm sorry, Karin," Susan whispered as she placed her hand on Karin's face and brushed back the fallen hair from her brow. "I'm so sorry."

Karin briefly opened her eyes and strained them upward to meet Susan's. She gave a soft nod, then closed her eyes and collapsed like a rag doll.

Lord Lokan looked at Susan and asked, "Where is it?"

Susan gave him a contemptuous look.

"You should re-evaluate your silent insolence."

Susan's eyes fell halfway to the floor and then looked back at her friend. She answered with a sense of defeated defiance in her voice, "...under the mattress."

Lord Lokan nodded at the Elders. They immediately moved to the side of Susan's bed, sidestepping the women. They raised the mattress and one of them reached in and retrieved the support board. He turned and handed the board to Lord Lokan, who briefly examined it then waved it off with his left hand. The Elders lowered the mattress and then moved back to their original positions.

"Remove the chair," Lord Lokan commanded.

The Elders carried the chair out of the room as the guard held the door open. Lord Lokan moved to the spot where the chair had been. He turned around and placed his hands behind him. He looked down at the huddled women. He didn't say anything while he waited for the Elders to return. When they came back into the room he directed, "Place the one on its bed. You," he said to Susan, "back to your bed." The Elders removed Karin from Susan's lap and placed her on the bed. Susan stood up, all the while looking at Karin, as she returned to her spot on her bed.

Susan's felt the pain of her friend; the frustration of being controlled and simmering anger. She also felt a mild relieving sensation when a nebulous picture of her gun appeared to her. She thought about 'little lady'. *'That's my ace in the hole,'* she thought, *'I have to try and get to it, when and I get out of here.'* Her focus, back on Karin, jerked her back to reality.

When the Elders repositioned themselves behind Lord Lokan, he looked at Karin and spoke. "This one is not seriously disabled, bruised perhaps, but will recover before too long."

Susan looked at Lord Lokan careful to keep an indirect, placid expression.

"Before long you will be prepared for tonight's ceremony." He turned to go, then paused and turned back to Susan.

"Oh yes, there is one more thing. Today while men were inspecting your vehicle, they discovered something."

Susan's inside's experienced a deep chill. *'He found the gun!'* She held a detached look on her face. *'Don't show any surprise if he did find it.'* Susan's only weapon right now, if she could call it that, was to show no feeling of defeat. Another tactic carried out in the courtroom. Act as though there are no surprises as your opponent presence new evidence. That way no upper hand is shown either way. And this opponent gains superiority as he feeds off another's sense of hopelessness.

Lord Lokan raised his left hand. The High Elder stepped forward as he reached into his cloak pocket and brought out a small wrapped package. He placed it in Lord Lokan's palm. Lord Lokan unwrapped it while not breaking eye contact with Susan.

Susan watched his eyes grow wider with the anticipation of a disconsolate reaction.

He slowly unwrapped the last fold.

'Don't show any surprise,' Susan said to herself. *'Don't back down; don't show defeat; don't show any emotion,* she repeated, *'stay strong; **stay strong; STAY STRONG.'***

The last fold of cloth fell to the side. It revealed just what Susan had thought, the case that Sam had given her for her gun. She maintained her passive expression. She fought the compulsion to look at it with every emotional muscle in her arsenal.

Lord Lokan tried to break Susan's resistance with a push. "Little Lady," he said as he gazed deeper into Susan's eyes.

Hearing those words created an instant passionate fire inside her, like the flame from a gas stove exploding to life from the push of the pilot light, and she came close to expressing it.

Lord Lokan's eyelids closed slightly.

Susan could see he was not receiving anything from her. *'I'm not going to let you in, you bastard. You got the gun, but that's all you're getting'!*

Lord Lokan stood still for another moment. He raised the gun case so that it was directly in their line of sight.

"Is this your Little Lady?"

Susan pinpointed a focus on one of Lord Lokan's eyebrows, thereby blurring the case to a brown blob. She didn't say a word.

Lord Lokan lowered the case.

The High Elder took it; re-wrapped it; and placed it inside his cloak.

Lord Lokan gave an understanding nod with a sinister chuckle, and said, "You haven't won a thing." He turned and signaled for the door to be opened. Before he exited, he looked at Susan over his left shoulder. He slowly shook his head saying again, "...not a thing." He left the room followed by his entourage.

Lord Lokan stopped at the bottom of the stairwell just past the counter and turned to the two Elders. He raised his left hand and cradled his chin between his folded index finger and thumb as he looked down in a thoughtful pose.

"This one... I will audience with The Savior." He turned to the Elders. "Meanwhile, I think it wise to restrain *both* to the bed until preparation, see to it. Also have the old woman tend to the other and see that she is not too severely injured"

"Yes My Lord," they said simultaneously and nodded their heads.

"There is one other thing," he paused, "I think it wise to prevent any uninvited guest. Have Elder Ivarsson, take a Legion and open the Eternity Road. Alert the Fenfir for any misguided adventurers that may come seeking our," he lifted his eyes to the top of the stairs and continued, "...special Blessing upstairs."

"Yes My Lord, "High Elder Larson responded.

Twenty-seven

Sam returned to Gondolba and found an entrance to the highway's access road. It was at the south end of town and followed another road that wasn't much more than a wooded back road. He became inwardly driven. He did not hear a voice speaking to him through an echo chamber, or see ghostly visions through a haze of fog. He just had a feeling that one: Susan was still alive, two: she was in perilous trouble, and three: he was on the right trail… but, time was short.

Halfway to the access road Sam encountered a locked gate. The sign on the gate read, NO ENTRANCE PERMITTED, By order of the Gondolba Sheriff Department. Sam, normally a law abiding citizen, thought of going back to the Sheriff's department to get the key. He started backing up to find a turn around area. He slammed on the brakes, faced forward and stared at the gate. His left forearm was still resting on top of the steering wheel. Suddenly, a small reflection of light bounced off the crystal face of his watch and caught his attention. He stared at it a second, then back at the gate, then back at the watch. He then froze on the gate. A stern look of determination came across his face.

"Fuck It!"

With clenched his teeth, Sam slammed the gearshift in first and floored the gas pedal. The truck bulleted forward. Wood, wire, and the sign exploded off the front of the truck. He glanced in the rear view mirror and saw red reflections of gate debris falling to the ground. "I wonder what that's gonna cost?" Sam said to himself just above a whisper.

On the access road he proceeded in the direction of what he hoped were tracks made by Susan's SUV. Sam kept a close eye on his odometer. He had monitored the distance between the overpass and Gondolba. When he got close to the approximate distance, he turned on his flashers, moved the truck onto the shoulder of the oncoming lane and slowed to a crawl. He poked along with his window opened and his flashlight illuminating the bristly landscape. The whishing sounds from the traffic below mixed with the truck tire's popping sounds as they pinched the gravel underneath their weight. The bushes were already coated with dew droplets from the fast temperature decrease and reflected the luminescence from the flashlight. The odometer was nearing the mark. He saw a branch lying on the ground, then saw two dark marks perpendicularly etched on the asphalt. He stopped his truck, turned on the bright lights and got out to examine them. These were the tracks. The tire marks indicated a left turn and then faded away.

Twenty-eight

The Elders followed Lord Lokan down the hall. High Elder Larsen broke off and entered the dining area to look for Mrs. Crowley. He found her in the kitchen. She did not hear him come in. "His Lordship wants you to tend to the younger Blessing," he bawled loudly.

Mrs. Crowley dropped her utensils and gasped as she turned. "You gave me a fright", she paused, "Is she sick?"

"Injured, maybe... Get your things and come."

*****

Susan sat on Karin's bed after the door closed; her eyes filled with tears.

Karin turned onto her back and opened her eyes.

"I'm so very sorry," Susan choked.

Karin reached up and placed her hand on Susan's cheek.

"It's...OK." She closed her eyes and attempted a small smile.

166

Susan felt rage bubbles inside as she looked at her suffering friend. Her eyes dried and her face turned red as she thought about what had happened. She enclosed Karin's hand between hers and lowered it back to her side.

"Is there anything I can do? Is there anything broken? ...Do you feel ...?"

"Water," Karin whispered.

"Of course," Susan released Karin's hand and got the tray. She placed it on the small table between the beds. Susan put her hand under Karin's head for support and held the cup to Karin's lips.

"Slowly," she said as Karin sipped the water.

Susan gently laid Karin's head back on the pillow.

"I...don't feel there's...anything broken...just strained ...I guess," Karin said as she looked at the ceiling.

"That basta…"

Karin raised her hand and turned to look directly at Susan.

"Don't …you must," she coughed, "find a way out".

Susan leaned a little closer to Karin and said with authority, "If I find a way out, I'm going all the way out. You can count on that. And I'll be damned if I'm going to leave you here. You're coming with me."

"No, I can't; besides you're the only one that can do this." Karin raised her head despite the pain. *"It's your destiny!"*

Susan shook her head slowly from side to side as she said, "Nooo, I'm here by circumstance," she stilled her head. "Get that straight. I was not brought here by some outside force that decreed me a champion to defeat some monster and save everyone." She shook her head again in denial "I'm just a woman that stupidly gave her trust to someone and ended up here." Susan leaned closer, "I'm going to get out of here; one way or another and I'm… She straightened as the key clanged in the door and then turned back to look at Karin and whispered. "And I'm taking you with me!" Susan got up, placed the cup back on the tray and prepared herself.

High Elder Larsen entered the room with Mrs. Crowley. Susan awaited the appearance of the guard, but the Elder closed the door. She got a sudden rush when she realized two things at once: it was just this old woman and old man in here, *and* this was the man with who had the gun! She looked at his left chest area and saw a square bulge shadowing the cloth. *'Think of something, you're never going to get a better chance!'*

"Lay on your bed," the High Elder directed to Susan. He was holding rope straps.

Susan looked from side to side, desperately seeking something that would tell her what to do. She felt cold.

Mrs. Crowley went to Karin's bed and sat on the side.

"Lay on your bed," the High Elder demanded again.

'He's alone…the others are doing other things or they'd be here to help. He doesn't realize he still has the gun. He doesn't have any powers either, or he would have simply put me in the bed.'

Susan looked at the old woman with her attention focused on Karin.

'There's no time to think, do something…now!'

She bought a second or two as she bent at her knees to show a subservient curtsey to the High Elder. She remembered the silver plated pitcher on the tray behind her. When she felt she lowered herself enough, she took a quick look and caught a glimpse of the handle and began to grab for it…

Knock, knock, knock! A sound of bare knuckles hitting the wooden door stopped Susan. She straightened up.

The High Elder went to the door.

"His Lordship sent me to get the gun." A voice from the hallway pronounced.

'Damn It!' she shouted internally. As she did, she inadvertently made a frustrated sound of exhaled air.

The High Elder turned to Susan, looked quizzically as he handed the gun to the man. He locked the door and returned the key to his pocket.

Susan thought. *'The only thing that's changed is that he no longer has the gun.*

I'm in the same position and the pitcher is still there.

The High Elder moved in closer to Susan than he had before. He still had the straps and was separating them. He raised his head and demanded again, "Lay on your bed!"

Mrs. Crowley was looking at her; the time was now! Without looking behind her, Susan quickly reached for the pitcher.

Mrs. Crowley gasped.

The pitcher toppled over. Water splashed unto the side of Karin's bed and floor. Susan instinctively raised her other arm in a defensive posture.

He dropped the straps and grabbed at her arm with both hands.

The pitcher was still on the tray, lying on its side with the handle facing toward her. She grabbed the handle as he pulled her forward.

Mrs. Crowley, startled, quickly moved to the dresser.

Susan had the handle with her middle and ring finger as her body was jerked away with a tremendous force. She kept her defensive arm bent as much as possible. He was strong. Susan managed to get her thumb around the underside of the handle. She caught her balance by throwing her left leg out as fast and as far as she could. She brought the pitcher into a quarterback's passing arm position and froze it there for a micro-second to get a more secure grasp of the handle. She went with his pull. He was caught off balance and looked behind him. Susan threw her right hand forward with all the speed she could muster. His face was in the act of returning forward when Susan's silver pitcher came down upon his head like 'Maxwell's silver hammer.' The pitcher, positioned upside down, cut a gash below the left eye from the lip of the spout. The base struck his forehead with a deep clang. His head flipped to his right and sent blood spurting onto Mrs. Crowley's dress.

She screamed and then placed both hands over her mouth.

Susan felt a surge of adrenaline flow through her entire body as her victim released his grip and fell backwards, hitting his head against the wall. He slid down into a sitting position with his head tilted to the right, unconscious. The blood, mixed with the remaining water, sloshed onto his chest and lap.

Susan was bent over like a pitcher who just delivered his best fastball. She looked at the slumped body then straightened and turned to Mrs. Crowley, raising the pitcher over her shoulder in a threatening position.

Mrs. Crowley's eyes sprang in horror, She raised her arms above her head and screamed "No, no, no" shaking her head frantically from side to side.

"Miss Susan, don't!" Karin hoarsely shouted as she sat up.

Susan came back to the moment. She looked at Karin then back at Mrs. Crowley. "She'll get the same thing if she doesn't do exactly as I say," Susan instructed, not taking her eyes off Mrs. Crowley.

"Miss Susan, she won't do anything."

"Stay right there and don't move a muscle," Susan ordered.

"What about him?" Mrs. Crowley nervously asked as she nodded toward the unconscious High Elder.

"Let him be, you can look after him after we go." She turned to Karin and said, "Let's go."

"I can't… you know I can't… you go."

"Listen, I'm not going to leave you here; now get up."

"Miss Susan, I can't go with you…it's better for me to stay. I will tie her to the bed so it will look as if you did it. She will remain blameless. I will stay. I would just slow you down…besides…if you don't want that to happen to me…do something to *stop* it!"

"Not that again. I told you I'm getting out of here…all the way out of here! Now you can either come with me or stay here, it's up to you. There's no time to argue."

"I'm sorry Miss Susan; you'll have to go without me."

Susan stared at her with disbelief.

"Suit yourself."

Susan got the key from the High Elder's pocket then went to the door. She put her ear against it- silence. She unlocked and slowly opened it. She looked down the hallway. It was clear. Susan was halfway out and stopped. With one hand on the door's edge she looked inside.

"Last chance," she said to Karin.

"Go, and remember no one has ever been able to get through that swamp. If *they* don't get you, the swamp will."

"Wait!" Mrs. Crowley said. "He," she pointed to the unconscious High Elder, "mentioned that Elder Ivarsson and the guard went to open the road and set the trap." She looked at Karin and then back at Susan who had a quizzical look on her face.

"He must feel there is someone coming and is setting the bridge trap for them. It's the only reason he would open it," the old woman continued.

"What trap?" Susan said with a thought of her dad coming down that road.

"It's at the bridge... It's very dangerous for you to attempt any escape on that road," Mrs. Crowley added.

"I'll have to take the chance." Susan said knowing there was little time. She looked at Karin. She wanted to say something to change Karin's mind, but knew it was no use.

"Bye," she regretfully choked and disappeared behind the door.

Karin didn't say a word as the door closed.

Twenty-nine

"I don't think I should have left the house," remarked Legion Kliest.

"His Lordship personally directed it," Elder Ivarsson answered. He had already opened the road with the powers granted from Lord Lokan and they were traveling in the Blazer. They reached the bridge and stopped. Legion Kliest, who was driving, looked to the Elder expecting him to get out and open the gate. Elder Ivarsson sat still, staring out the front windshield. Legion Kliest got the message and reluctantly performed the task himself. They continued to the entrance off the access road and stopped just before the last turn.

"Keep it like this. After the gate trees begin to rise, turn it around," The Elder directed. He got out and walked to within twenty feet of the large twisted limbs that intertwined themselves across the entrance of Eternity Road.

The limbs lay on top of one another. Shadows created by the Blazer's headlights wrapped themselves around the bulk of contorted appendages. Elder Ivarsson motioned with his right arm. The giant limbs began to rustle and crack as if a large animal was traversing through the coiled maze, breaking and snapping the branches as it went. The limbs rose. The snared branches released and detonated the leaves like wrappings from an exploded firecracker. The two massive trees spread their limbs outward to form a cathedral entranceway. The Elder walked out to the access road inspecting the entrance.

The Blazer, now repositioned at the end on the road resembled a large creature with red eyes and hot breath patiently waiting to attack some unsuspecting prey. Elder Ivarsson smiled at the image and then started back. He scarcely got off the access road when lights from an approaching vehicle illuminated him. He ran to the Blazer. He opened the passenger door and said, "Let's go. There's someone coming. Turn off the lights and proceed slowly."

*****

Sam did a double take. He thought he saw something move in the far right reaches of his headlights.

"... the Hell was that?" he whispered.

He had been traveling slowly on the access road for nearly half an hour. He thought he'd seen all sorts of things in the half light, but this time it was different. He accelerated to where he thought the movement had been. *'Maybe it was a deer... or something'*. The thought vanished as he saw a break in the thick roadside brush. He stopped and looked through the passenger side window. He could make out a small mud tracked road going into the woods. He turned the truck so the lights could reveal the entrance. He set the emergency brake, turned on the four way flashers and got halfway out of the cab. With his flashlight held over the top of the cab, he directed the beam at the tops of the arched trees. If he hadn't known better, he would have sworn they were constructed by some theme park creator, making a spooky entrance into 'Scaryland'. Sam walked closer to the entranceway. The truck lights created ill-formed shadows across the road that seemed to move with the aid of the flashers methodical beat. *'The shadows were probably what I saw from the cab,'* he thought. He looked at the track lines that formed the road's entrance. The road had been used recently. Sam decided to enter the road on foot to at least the extent of the lights. When he got directly under the archway, he looked up. The limbs were massive and actually intertwined like huge braids. He ran the flashlight's beacon across the entire twisted canopy, turning his body as his eyes tracked the reflected light.

'*Amazing,*' he thought.

He walked along the track in the road and moved the flashlight from side to side as he went. The brush, thicket and cacti were clustered together so tightly it was difficult to see more than two feet off the sides of the road. He reached the first bend in the road and stood very still. He drank in the faint smell of exhaust hanging in the crisply chilled air.

"That nails it," he said faintly turning in a complete circle. *'Someone was here and, whomever it was, was standing on the access road when my lights hit him. He must have had a car waiting with the engine running...'*

*****

The two stood looking at Sam. "His Lordship was correct," Elder Ivarsson whispered to his accomplice. "Let's go set the trap."

Thirty

After Susan locked the door, she put the key in her pocket. The hallway was high and narrow, with the same wood trimmings and wallpaper as the room. There were three similar brass lamps suspended from the ceiling. The middle one, located directly over the stairwell landing, had one of the three display candles burnt out. Narrow partitions extended a foot and a half from the wall separating the two small hallways from the stair landing. Susan silently moved to the stairwell, wishing she had asked Karin about a rear exit.

From the landing she could see the top of the counter and part of the first floor. Susan's breathing quickened. Her heart pounded. The roots of her hair follicles began to soak with fine beads of perspiration. She placed one hand on the wooden rail and cautiously began to descended the stairs. The wooden steps objected with abnormally loud creaks. Susan was a third of the way down when the entrance bell rang. She could see the bottom part of the door wave over the floor and a blackened boot move against the black wool of a cloak bottom. Her throat dropped into her stomach. She quickly retreated up the stairs. The bell rang again, as the door slammed closed.

Susan hid behind the partition to her right. She got the key out and held it like a knife. The hope she had of the man staying downstairs dashed as she heard him climb the first stair. The patch over her eye absorbed the heavy sweat of that side of her brow. Salty overflow from her other eye brow dripped into her eye. Daring not to try and wipe it, she closed it for a moment then blinked as fast as she could to shake the stingy solution clear.

The man went straight to room seven and knocked. The muffled voices from the room flowed down the corridor.

"What?" the man shouted. "Where's the key?" There was another muffled sound. "… I'll get it."

The man raced back down the hall and took the stairs two at a time.

A chill passed through Susan's body.

The man came back up the stairs.

Susan peaked around the edge of the narrow partition and saw him insert the key.

'When he goes in… I'll have to run for it.' She wiped her brow with her left hand and put the key back in her pocket.

The man entered the room…

'Go!!!'

Susan sped around the partition. Her left hand was wet with the sweat of her brow. When she grabbed the rail, it slipped downward. She lost her balance and fell head first down the stairs. She used her right hand to break her fall. The heel of her hand hit the step and sent a bone jarring shock up her arm. Her shoulder snapped out of the socket. Susan couldn't hold the scream as she plummeted onto the staircase. She ended in a halfway sitting position with her head against the rails. The pain was intense and she was close to passing out. Panic slapped at her. *'Get up!... 'Get out!'... 'NOW!'* Susan leaned forward, but her injured arm screeched in torturous, electrifying pain, stopping her. It had to be immobilized. She pulled it tight to her side. The arm repeated its protest at the movement and she felt herself close to the brink of unconsciousness.

"I'll get her," a male voice shouted.

The voice snapped Susan back to the moment. She stumbled down the stairs and made a beeline for the front door, dragging her right side. She released her arm to grab the door handle. As she did, the weight of her injured arm pulled against her upper shoulder. It felt like her right side was being pulled to the floor. She opened the door so fast the bell tinged once as it circled the hanger completely and flew off bouncing on the top of the deacon's bench. The cold night air felt good against her sweating body. Susan screamed again as she bumped her shoulder on the door jamb. She bent over facing the stairs.

There was a violent yell from the top of the stairs. Susan looked up. The man, who she had avoided, came crashing down the stairs. She watched the falling mass bounce to the bottom. The man lay still on his chest, one arm spread to his side and the other arm underneath his midsection. One foot was resting on its instep on the second step. The leg that it was attached to was awkwardly bent at the knee - snapped. The other leg was on the floor, stretched like a wishbone.

Susan heard a noise and looked up. Karin was slowly and deliberately slumping her way down the stairs while holding on to the rail. She stopped when she could see Susan. She looked down at the twisted heap on the floor and then looked back at Susan. She let out a deep breath and held up the dented silver pitcher.

"Go..." Karin said barely above a whisper.

Susan didn't move.

"*Now!*" Karin shouted. She dropped the pitcher and desperately grabbed onto the rail with both hands.

Susan began to make a step towards Karin.

The metal container banged its way down the staircase eventually coming to rest on the man's back.

Karin, bent over the rail at the waist, turned towards Susan, anticipating her desire to help.

"NO!"

Susan stopped.

Karin lowered her head and brought it up again.

"I'll be OK…"

"But…"

"Please…GO…"

Susan debated whether to ignore or obey Karin's instructions.

"*NOW!*" Karin screamed as loud as she could.

A sudden transformation came over Susan as she stared frozenly into Karin's eyes. Her instinct came back to her with a bolt of intensity she never felt before. All at once she knew. Escaping this perdition was not her fate. Her destiny lay at the tree - The Savior Tree. She felt a surge of strength go through her body, like a fire hose expelling thousands of gallons of water to battle a raging inferno. Susan made an understanding nod to Karin, turned and left.

Karin watched Susan exit through the doorway. She again cast her eyes on the still body that lay six steps below her. She looked at her hands wrapped around the rail, perilously losing their strength. The stairs and hallway commenced a slow, methodical spin. Karin's shoulders slumped; her midsection deflated and legs folded beneath her. She lost her grip on the rail as her world turned to a black nothingness.

Susan looked both ways as she stood on the porch. The pain in her right arm returned to an increased level. It throbbed with each breath of the frigid night air. Then, like before in front of the gun shop in El Paso, something guided her to her right and she hurried down the walkway.

Thirty-one

Sam parked the truck on the side of the access road. He checked his cell for any messages - two. First one was from Dr. Waythill, *"Sam this is Dr.Waythill. My cell number is ...wait a minute, I'm driving and I have it on the seat..."* there was a click sound and rustling of paper, *"...here it is 210-555-2453. I am passing Leon Springs so I'm at least two hours away from you now. It's eight-thirty...I had some difficulty with...**break** ...sto.."*

Sam's phone was losing power. *"...there before you kn ...**break** ...call when you get this."* Sam checked his watch. It was later than he realized...nine twenty. He checked the other message. *"Sam this is Sheriff Earlee, call when you can."*

Sam looked at the display. The battery icon was blinking slowly; there was still enough charge to make calls.

"Dr. Waythill?" Sam asked.

"Sam, what's going on?"

"First of all, where are you?"

"'I just pasted Kerrville...I'm more than an hour away, yet"

179

"OK, I think I may have found something. It's an old dirt road off of the access road between Gondolba and Sonora. It's hard to describe where. I think the best thing for you to do is go to the sheriff's office when you get to Gondolba."

*"Sam you came in broken. Some… **break**- is phone. I think…**long break**…ona's …iff's…"*

Sam interpreted Dr. W's response that he would go to the sheriff's office. He gave an "OK," then disconnected.

Sam looked at the display again. The icon was flashing faster. It wasn't going to be long before he'd lose the charge. Before he called the sheriff, he got his thoughts together. He pressed the call button.

"Gondolba Sheriff's Office, how may I help you?"

He pressed the wrong call button.

"Listen, the power on my cell phone is going down. I am Sam Masters. I was in there earlier today with the sheriff…"

Then Sam thought, "Wait, is he there … the sheriff?"

"I'll connect you."

Sam let out a sigh of relief. *'He must have finished with the accident.'*

"Sheriff Earlee, how…"

"This is Sam, I don't have much power. I'm on the access road. There's a small dirt road going into the swamp."

"Sam …broken up."

"Sheriff, are you there?" Sam could not hear anything, He waited for a response - nothing. He tried again…same result. He looked at the phone; it was dead. Sam cursed to himself, *'Goddamn it!' and* threw the phone to the floorboard.

'What to do? He thought to himself. *'The first thing … calm down … can't make rational decisions when excited.'* He took a deep breath and exhaled slowly and then repeated it two more times. He was staring distantly into the hollowness of the dirt road. *'If I drive in there, the sheriff may not find this entrance. I wouldn't have seen it if my lights hadn't hit that moving shadow.'* He looked out the rear cab

window. '*However, if I leave the truck on the access road he would find it… if he got my message.*' He looked at the dirt road again, '*How far does that road go in?*'

"There's no time to find out … I'll have to roll the dice," he said a little above a whisper as he looked back at the access road, "He'll see the truck and drive in and pick me up. I'll have to bank on that."

Sam moved the truck closer to the entrance of the dirt road. He pulled an extra shirt from the bag he'd packed and put it on over the one he was wearing and then put on his jacket. He made sure he had everything he'd need; flashlight, a five foot long rope he got from under the seat, (he didn't know if he'd need it, but his philosophy had always been, *I'd rather have it and not need it, than need it and not have it)*, his Astro's baseball cap, and his gun. Sam shut off the truck engine and the interior lights. He stepped out of the cab and closed the door, paused and opened it again. He reached in and turned on the flashers. The yellow-orange lights splashed their methodical glare on the harsh landscape and vegetation in front of the truck while the red halo of light did the same in the rear. Sam closed the door and locked it and put the keys into his inside jacket pocket with the rope and began his walk on the dirt road. When he reached the bend in the road, he stopped and looked back at his truck lights flashing at the entrance. The brush was so thick on either side of the road that he could only see the amber and red glows above the trees. He turned on his flashlight and walked.

Thirty-two

Karin collapsed on the stairs.

High Elder Larsen came stumbling out of the room holding a blood soaked cloth on the side of his face. In his other hand he clutched his hat. When he got to the top of the stairs, he stopped and looked at the two bodies sprawled below. Mrs. Crowley came to his side. She gasped. High Elder Larsen positioned himself on the step beside Karin. He let his hat fall, placed his hand below Karin's jaw and gently lifted.

"Is she... dead?" Mrs. Crowley whispered.

"No, tend to her while I check the other." He placed his hand on the man's lower leg and moved it slightly - there was no reaction - dead.

"She needs to be put back in bed," Mrs. Crowley said.

"I'll tend to it," the High Elder said, "You go the Temple and tell his Lordship what happened."

"Sir, I'm sorry..," She said with a frightened look in her eyes, "... I cannot go out. I'm not allowed."

He sighed.

"Sir, can you help me carry...?" she nodded her head towards Karin.

"Wait." He placed his hand on the man's back and moved the body to the side of the hall by the counter. He positioned him flat on his back with his hands folded across his chest.

*****

Senior Elder Larsen entered the Temple and stood silently in the vestibule. He removed his hat and the blood soaked cloth from his face to see if the bleeding had stopped - it had not. He repositioned it.

The main worship hall was decorated with blackened windows, paintings and statues of The Savior in different stages of its metamorphosis. Twisted branches grew out of the walls in different lengths and cradled large balls of fire from their twigged ends without being frittered away by the flames. Arbitrarily scattered throughout the hall were standing branches that seemed to have grown from the floor and glowed fire like the wall branches. In the front of the worship hall was a two step platform with a lectern in the middle. Behind the lectern was a wide, scaled down, tree-fall altar that was very similar to the one that stood outside. Atop of the altar was a flat surface displaying a large opened book. On either side it was lit brownish candles that secreted white pustule drippings, similar to the discharge from The Savior Tree's scales. The altar was attached to a large replica of The Savior Tree with the Serpent fully emerged from its barked sanctuary. The statue was made from magnificently carved wood. The Serpent was posed as a Cobra ready to strike. Its large glassy eye was fully opened and reflected all the fire lights inside the lyceum. The two limbed arms stretched out, hands opened, to just above the first few pews. The spiney claws pointed downward as if ready to pluck worshipers at its will. Other limbs protruded from the trunk and spread out into the walls. Two of the limbs were bent down into the floor, like big wooden pipes. The ends of the limbs resurfaced out of the main floor to form the backless pews.

"High Elder Larsen," a voice spoke from behind him. "What are you doing here?"

Startled, he turned about and was face to face with Lord Lokan.

Lord Lokan saw the blood soaked cloth. He squinted his eyes. "What happened?"

"There was trouble with the Blessings, My Lord. Mrs. Crowley and I were caught off guard and attacked by the outsider."

"Where was Legion Kliest, the guard?"

"He must have gone with the Elder Ivarsson, My Lord." He looked at the floor. "There's more … the outsider Blessing has escaped and Legion Harrison is dead."

Lord Lokan's eyes formed into the reddish-orange slits. His face started to expand and his jaw lowered.

High Elder Larsen's eyes widened in horror. He dropped his hat and released the cloth from his face as his arm fell to his side. Blood seeped from the opened flesh.

Suddenly, the demon-like creature ceased its metamorphosis and turned back to the shape of Lord Lokan.

"There is no time for this now. I will settle with you later. Go and prepare the other for the ceremony."

High Elder Larsen bent and picked up his hat and cloth from the floor, "Yes, My Lord."

Lord Lokan turned and swiftly exited through the front door. He proceeded to the large lectern in front of The Savior Tree while the High Elder made his way back to the Inn.

Lord Lokan climbed the ten steps of the lectern. He removed his hat and placed it on the flat surface. On the two sides of the lectern were identical vertical handles. Lord Lokan grabbed each one tightly, closed his eyes and bowed. After a moment the bark of The Savoir Tree began pulsating to life. Lord Lokan raised his head and opened his eyes. This time his eyes were solid white. As he spoke, his words echoed in the minds of all the Elders and Legions in the town.

'*The Savior seeks your aid. The Blessing has escaped. It needs to be found immediately. He craves it and will not be denied. Seek the entire perimeter and bring it directly to the Temple."* He closed his eyes and bowed - the tree became still.

Thirty-three

Susan made her way down the first alleyway that led into a larger alley. The pain in her shoulder was becoming unbearable. With every step it pulled against her shoulder muscles. She began to feel floaty like when first coming off a boat after hours on wavy water. She hid in the dark shadow of a doorway and kept her back and head pasted to the door. She grimaced from the excruciating pain.

This had happened to her once before when she was eleven years old. She had fallen out of the oak tree in her back yard. Her father was in the garage when she fell and heard her scream. He rushed to her aid. He knew how to knock it back into the socket and helped her do it on the fence before he took her to the emergency room.

She had to knock it back into place again. It was painful to do, but knew it had to be done. Susan hissed in pain as she lifted her arm so that the ball of the bone was parallel to the shoulder socket. Using the door jam as a brace she slammed the arm back into place. It took two agonizing tries. Pained tears rushed down her face as she concentrated on not crying out. There was a mild sense of relief when it snapped in, but almost immediately a new pain surfaced. She looked around on the ground for anything that she could possibly use as a sling. It was very hard to see anything in the blackness. What became frighteningly distinguishable was the misty cloud of air being exhaled from her mouth. Coldness crept over her. All she had on was her shoes, black linen pants and beige silk blouse. In her rush to escape she had forgotten to take her jacket.

Susan's breathing became erratic. "Calm down," she whispered to herself as she placed the back of her head on the door. She closed her eyes, inhaled and let the heated air back out in a prolonged methodical manner. *'Relax... Think... Think... ...what can you use?'* She took another deep, slow breath. A thought struck her, *'Blouse'* she looked at it in doubt... *it will have to do.'*

Susan stepped away from the door. She unbuttoned her blouse, slid it off her left shoulder and let it fall off her arm. She grabbed her right wrist. Despite the stinging ache she slowly and gently bent the arm at the elbow and brought her right forearm in front of her stomach. The arm was stiff and fought the move with torturous agony. She pushed the right hand into her waistband of her pants. Before putting the blouse on she turned the right sleeve inside out to prevent it from flopping as she moved. She finally managed to get the blouse buttoned. The arm was now stabilized - as much as she could get it.

Susan moved to through the alley. She was at the end of the town. There was fifty yards of open field before the wooded brush that ran along one side of the road. To her left, was the back entrance to the town and small cabins beyond it. The chimneys lazily sent their smoky umbilical cords into the fogged ceiling above. To her right was a black wall that led into the swamp. She listened for any movement...silence. She took a deep breath and then raced across the opening. She reached the first of the oak trees and quickly hid behind one. The jarring movement didn't make her arm feel any better. She looked back at the town. It looked so peaceful and quiet, just the kind of serene landscapes Susan had seen in the past. *'Looks can be so deceiving,'* she thought. She moved further into the woods.

Susan got to the small chapel and made her way around behind it. From the road in front came a noise. The sound of the footsteps was accompanied by heavy breathing. Whoever was coming down the hill from the site was moving in a hurry. She moved away from the chapel and stumbled on a rock. She caught herself on the trunk of a tree. "Oooof," sounded from her as she landed against it.

The footsteps on the road stopped.

Susan turned against the trunk and leaned her back on it. She closed her eyes, tilted her head against the trunk and clenched her teeth. She hit her right arm as she fell and the electric stings pulsated ferociously up her arm. She held her breath and fought to be as silent as possible. The pain subsided a little. She opened her eyes as the person from the road shouted.

"Who's there?"

Susan shuddered at the recognition of the voice. It was the Elder she had hit and knocked out when she made her escape.

"I say, who's there?"

Susan's lungs ached to release the air inside them. The Elder was no more than twenty feet away. Despite the coldness of the night air she began to perspire again. It was impossible to hold her breath any longer. She bent her face down and exhaled slow repeated breaths.

"Who's there?" the voice asked again as it came closer.

She let out the remaining air against the sound and took another gasp. Susan remembered the key in her pocket. Thinking of it as a weapon, she made a quiet, gradual move to retrieve it.

"I know you're in there…the other is dead," High Elder Larsen said with quiet, deliberate modulation as he inched his way down the middle of the clearing.

Without thinking, Susan brought the key out and threw it towards the woods behind the chapel. It hit another tree about fifteen feet away then bounced through a bush.

"*Stop!*" he commanded and ran to the back of the chapel.

At the same time, Susan turned and ran into the woods towards the site.

"She's in here!"

Susan veered to her right and ascended deeper into the woods. She made her way down the other side and squatted by the base of a tree. Her breaths were fast and heavy. She knew she was close to the sacred area.

'The other is dead,' he said…*'Not Karin,'* Susan thought to herself. She repositioned her body from squatting to sitting with her back against the tree and knees bent upward so her heels were nestled under her buttocks. She placed her good elbow on her knee and cradled her forehead in her hand. *'He couldn't have meant her. It must be the man Karin knocked down the stairs…he wasn't moving.'* Susan's eyes were shut as she replayed the scene in the stairwell. *'She was standing there.'* She raised her head and looked forward into blackness. *'Did she fall?'*

"Goddamn it, I knew I should have gone to her," she cursed with a silent whisper. Susan wiped her eyes. *'It can't be her.'* She stiffened and demanded of herself, *'Think logically, he said that to make you think Karin was dead, it was an attempt to defeat you mentally… you would have done the same. Go with the thought, the Legion is dead, not Karin.'*

Susan's sense of presence restored her attention and she began to look around. Her breathing returned to normal and she noticed she was beginning to chill again. *'I've got to keep moving until I can find some kind of shelter,'* she thought as she got back to her feet.

Thirty Four

"Let us leave here and go back to the town to aid in the search," Elder Ivarsson said.

"Shouldn't we stay and see that the trap works?" asked Legion Kliest.

"No. We are needed back there, besides; the road should be closed as soon as possible."

*****

Sam had walked on the road for twenty minutes. The ruts were muddy in some areas and bone dry in others. The branches hung out over the road and swept at his shoulders like bony fingers of a blind night creature. Sam had to duck beneath and side step them. He avoided the long center grass and stayed on the tracks. He was beginning to think that this walk wasn't such a great idea. There was a path that opened on his right. It looked as if someone had recently traveled it. Sam hesitated and then decided to go in a little way to see where it went.

*****

Sheriff Earlee spun the cruiser's tires, which sent pebbles flying through the night air like snowflakes in a blizzard. The cruiser's lights and siren blasted their alerts as the cruiser fishtailed onto the street. Code three through the town and under Highway Ten's bridge. Then onto the back road as Sam had done. The sheriff stopped abruptly at the shattered gate. He turned off the lights, siren. "What the …?" he cursed under his breath. As the cruiser nursed through the opening, he surveyed the damage. "He's gonna pay for that!" he said louder and continued to the access road.

When the sheriff came upon Sam's truck, he parked behind it. He turned on his blue emergency lights and got out to investigate. The mixture of the red, blue and amber flashing lights rebounded in all directions through the black background of the night. It created a light show any rock band would envy. The sheriff cautiously moved to the driver's side of the cab and shined his flashlight in the bed area then through the rear window, no Sam. He pointed his light at the road that led into the swamp. He took in the haunted archway. The hair on the back of his neck stood. He pulled his weapon and, with caution, approached the entrance. He had traveled the access road many times and knew one thing for certain – this road never existed. He thought, *'He went in there alone?… on foot?! What the Hell was he thinking?'*

The sheriff went back to his cruiser to call in his location.

*****

Ten feet onto the path, the night's quiet echo suddenly caught Sam's attention. He stopped, held his breath and turned his head very slowly. He tried to pick up the least little sound from any nocturnal creature- nothing. A sheet of aloneness blanketed him. *'One cricket making a mating sound with its legs',* he thought, *'that's all. You probably don't hear anything because they're too smart to be out here. Keep focused!'* The path made several aimless turns and bends.

Ten minutes later a faint, deep, whirred sound caught Sam's attention. The tall brush made it impossible to tell the direction, but he knew it could only be coming from the main road. "Gotta be the sheriff." Sam turned to make his way back to the road.

*****

The cruiser did not handle the road's turns and bumps as well as a truck or SUV. The Sheriff bounced around inside like a bingo ball in an air tunnel The branches slapped at the sides of the cruiser like the hands and arms of an angry mob. Despite these difficulties, he kept the cruiser under control.

*****

The motor sound got louder. Sam moved down the path at a faster pace. He hoped he could intercept the sheriff in time. He began to run. The light from his flashlight splashed up and down against the vegetation. The path seemed longer and had more turns than he remembered. The branches seemed longer too. They almost appeared to be growing as he went. They scraped at his head and shoulders. The engine sounds were getting closer.

'*After the next turn,*' he thought.

"Whrrr…thud…"

Sam was breathing harder as he passed what he thought was the last turn…the path continued. '*Up there then.*'

'*Thud thump thump…whrrr…*'

The sound was closer; he turned a corner… the path continued.

'*One more turn.*'

He ran passed it…the path continued…He stopped, looked around in disbelief. He turned his head back…'*one more turn.*' He raced toward it.

'***Thump whrrr thud…***' the car sounded like it was right in front of him…why couldn't he see it?

'**THUD…WHRRR…THUMP…**' He came around what he thought was the last turn…the path continued.

'**WHRRR…**'

He sprinted to the next turn…the path continued.

'**THUMP…WHRRR…**' next turn.

'**WHRRR…**'

Just as he felt he was going to break through…

'**WHRRR…THUMP** THUD… *WHrrrrrrrrrrrrrrrrr*'

…the engine noise whisked by and the path came to a dead end!

*****

The road narrowed as the cruiser tumbled through the deepen ruts. Then, to the farthest extent of the headlight's appeared a tall structure. He stopped. The sheriff turned on his emergency lights and slowed his advanced toward the object. It was an old bridge with a closed gate. It had an entranceway made of three logs. On the right support log was a rectangular sign. The blue lights were interfering with his ability to read the sign. He killed the flashers and lit the sign with the remote spotlight.

HELEN

'We count

' our blessings.'

"Humpf," he sounded as he reached for his mike.

"Central this is one over."

"Hissssssssssssss," was all that came out of his speaker.

"Central this is One, OVER."

"Hissssssssssssss."

"CENTRAL THIS IS ONE…OVER," he shouted into his mike.

"Hissssssssssssss"

*"*She'd better have a God damned good excuse for not being on the desk," he muttered.

He re-spiked the emergency blues and sat for a moment. He was going to take a closer look. He unbuckled his seatbelt and pulled against the door handle. It didn't budge. He pulled harder on it – no give.

"What the Hell's going on here?"

He leaned to his right to get a better perspective on the door. He turned on the interior lights and tried again, this time with both hands – nothing. A puzzled look crossed his face as he stared at the door. He turned to the passenger door and tried in vain the same procedure.

"This is bullshit!" He exclaimed as he looked around the interior.

The rear doors could only be opened from the outside. He straightened in his seat and tried to figure out what was wrong. He looked back at his door handle.

All at once, it moved!

"What the …!" he shouted. Both front doors clicked open at the same time. He looked at the passenger door and before he could look back, both front doors tore off their hinges. The sheriff threw himself back in his seat. Then the rear doors crashed open. As the sheriff reached for his gun. From his right a large spiked tentacle sliced the air and quickly wrapped around his neck. "Arrrrg!" he screamed in agony. He grabbed at tentacle. Blood spurted from beneath the elastic limb and spewed down his shoulders in a waterfall of red liquid. It pulled the sheriff's upper torso down to his right. At the same time another spiked tentacle from the left latched around the sheriff's legs. It's spikes sank into the shin bones. The pain was unbearable. The sheriff fought for his life. The tentacles pulled in opposite directions adhering him tightly on his right side to the car seat. The windshield smashed inward as a huge slime pasted, forked tongue with small hooked spikes slammed inward. The green slime dripped and splashed off the surface as it lashed out and snatched at the sheriff's waist. He was raised off the seat like two hands raising a cob of corn off of a plate. The sheriff could see past the tongue. The bridge opened like a monstrous mouth and the tongue was coming out of the hollow. He reached for his gun. The tongue immediately wrapped its clawed surface around his middle. It pinned his hand on the gun butt. The tiny claws tore through the sheriff's skin ripping and shredding all to pieces. His screams rang out as blood scattered and gushed in all directions. His hand was ripped off his arm and his intestines popped out of the shredded skin. The tongue lashed again and crushed the ribs and backbone like twigs. The blood belched out of the sheriff's mouth, nostrils, and ears. His eyes bulged to the size of golf balls. They popped and splattered a milky stringed substance like exploding lava. The tentacles that had the sheriff by the head and legs released their hold and the tongue quickly pulled its meal back out through the windshield.

The car violently rocked from side to side. The road opened into a giant watery crevasse and swallowed. The cruiser disappeared and a huge bubble rose to the surface. It boiled and then concaved its shape into a whirlpool. The road closed and the bridge lowered back into place.

*****

"Hear that?" Elder Ivarsson asked the Legion as they stood beside the vehicle parked at the edge of the town. The sounds of water splashing and screams pierced through the night air.

"It's done?" asked the Legion.

"It's done."

HELLN, TEXAS

The Elder raised his right hand and lowered it. The swamp water spilled over the sides of the road. Wet thicket and brush surfaced to replace what had been the road.

Thirty-five

Susan heard the muffled voices of searchers echo through the woods as she moved toward the site. She rested by a tree and tilted her head back with eyes closed. An image of her father came to her. He was driving in the night. She could see a concerned look on his face as opposing lights lit up the shiny highlights of his creased brow. Feelings surfaced like flashcards in her mind: fear, pain, powerlessness.

"Oh Dad," Susan softly whispered.

After a moment of grief filled silence she opened and wiped her moisten eyes. She knew she had to quell the thoughts of her dad and push on to the sacred area. A thought of surrender entered her mind. She quickly dispensed it stood and made her way to her destination.

The ground leveled as Susan drew nearer the site. She emerged from the dark woods into an open area between two large buildings. Corn cobs scattered around the ground told her that they were probably storage barns. Large chains across the doors told her they were locked. A smaller shed was partially hidden between the barns. She looked in both directions and listened for any sound. She crept to the shed and hoped against hope that *it* wasn't locked.

Her movements were quick and silent as she moved to the rear of the shed. Susan leaned her back against the wall and looked over both shoulders. She crouched and crept around the corner and squatted just past the door. She took a quick look around, then reached up for the doorknob. She turned it and gave a little push. The door moved a little, then resisted.

"Shit," she said under her breath as she looked up. Above the knob was a hasp with a lock on it. Instinctively, she grabbed the lock and pulled...it didn't open. In frustration, she released the lock. It made a *'thump'* sound against the door. She cringed low against the wooden surface. She was about to return to the wooded brush and try to figure something out when she heard a noise from the direction of the other building. She could see someone move in the shadows. Her heart dropped into her stomach. There was no time to get to the woods. Beside her was stack of boxes and a rain barrel. She squeezed in between the small space. The boxes wobbled, so she leaned away placing the trembling weight of her right side on the barrel. The shoulder pain shot into her like a lightning bolt. She bit down on the tip of her tongue to keep from screams inside.

The searcher moved to the fence between the front of the buildings. After he shook the gate he continued walking along the fence line to the shed.

Susan was shaking in terror. She felt the barrel move slightly as the searcher looked behind it. Her breath was stilled, her legs were numb and the shoulder pain was growing unbearable. She prepared to jump out at the man. There was his boot. It was go time!

"You find anything?" a voice suddenly said from the rear of the shed.

Susan froze. Then an additional fear struck as she realized who just spoke. It was Erik!

"No, I don't think *she* would be stupid enough to hide around here." the searcher replied, his leg no more than two feet in front of Susan.

"I have the keys to this shed and the two others. Go help the others. I'll finish here".

The searcher turned without a word and left.

A raged range of emotions rose within Susan. Fear of discovery, revenge, flight or fight, all shuddered through her as she watched Erik. Her heart pounded so fast and hard she thought it would explode. She was about to jump out of her skin.

Then she heard the key inserted into the lock. She readied herself to get back into the woods when Erik went into the shed. The door opened. Susan leaned forward.

"Quick, in here," Erik said in a voice just above a whisper.

Susan froze with a questioned look. *'Who is he talking to? Is there someone with him?'* She held her breath.

"Miss Susan; get in here." Erik walked around the boxes and reached for her.

She was paralyzed with fear and didn't move.

"Please," Erik whispered.

Susan raised and locked eyes with Erik. She couldn't feel her hand as it extended. She gasped as Erik closed his fingers around hers and gently pulled her toward him. She lost her balance and fell into his arms.

"Can't feel my legs," she gasped.

"Come on," Erik said. He pulled Susan into the small shed. The inside was illuminated by striped light coming through the board spacing from the outside torches.

Erik moved and sat her on a small bench.

"What...?" Susan said as she reached with her good arm and rubbed her legs, trying to get the circulation going.

"Shhhh, not now", Erik whispered. He turned and started for the door.

Susan eyes followed Erik as he walked away. The fire-lined vertical stripes flickered across his body. Her contempt for him festered inside; her eyes slitted with anger. Panicked filled her as she watched him go out the door.

'He's going to lock me in here!'

Erik reappeared in the doorway placing his hat on his head just as Susan rushed full force into him. He straightened up just as Susan's good fist connected squarely on his jaw. Erik quickly grabbed at her arm and held it away.

Susan fought for her life. She tore her arm free of his grasp and went for his throat. Her fingers and thumb locked on his neck.

Erik grabbed her and choked out, "Damn it, I'm trying to help!" He managed to peel back her fingers, grab her wrist, turn and slam her to the ground. He was on top of her. He still controlled her arm. With his other hand he pressed her face to the side. He leaned down so his face was close to her ear. "I'm on your side, Goddamn it!" He said with his teeth clenched. "Calm down!"

Susan stopped her fighting. Her makeshift slung arm was screeching in pain. Puffs of dirt swirled from in front her face as she exhaled. He had her pinned. She couldn't move or fight anymore.

"OK," Susan breathed out dejectedly.

"You gonna stop fighting?" Erik asked quietly.

"Yes," she choked through the dirt in her mouth.

"Keep your voice down. I'm going to let you up, but you have to be quiet …OK?"

Susan made a quick nod.

Erik let her up and they stumbled back into the cabin.

Erik closed the door and came over to Susan on the bench.

"I hope no one heard us".

Susan held her throbbing arm and grimaced.

"What happened to your arm?" Erik whispered.

"Fuck you!" she answered and look at him with gritted teeth.

"Look, I know you're mad as Hell. I don't blame you one bit. And I know it won't help, but I'm sorry …" Erik said in a low voice as he wiped blood from his mouth. He looked around and swept his free arm, "for all this."

Susan stood up. "You're sorry?! She leaned into his face. "You son of a bitch. Is that supposed to make every thing OK?"

"Listen," he said with his hands raised. "I know you're pissed, but something happened to me."

"What the Hell *do* you mean; happened?" She voiced louder then bent over, coughing, "you fucking bastard."

"Quiet!' Erik looked around. "You have to keep it down. You don't understand..."

"I understand just fine," Susan stood back up and interrupted in a softer, but still firm voice. She grimaced at the pain again, then looked back at him, "You lured me here to feed me to that fucking thing out there and when you found that wasn't enough, you added your own *wife!"* The bandage over her eye flipped down over her eye. She tore it off.

"I didn't do that..." Erik denied.

"What...?" Susan elevated her voice again. "You..."

"Wait a minute," Erik said. 'Keep your voice down and let me explain."
Susan snorted.

"I admit I used you, OK?" He looked straight into her eyes and leaned in. "But I did not sacrifice Karin, you must believe that."

"I believe I want to kill you; that's what I believe."

"I don't blame you. But listen, ask yourself a question...'why did I stop that Legion out there from finding you and then bring you in here?' I could have let him find you, ...or turned you in myself." He slowly shook his head as he spoke, "I didn't mean for Karin to get where she is. It was a total surprise to me when Lord Lokan decreed that this afternoon."

"And what about me, do you deny...?"

Erik lowered his head and said, "Unfortunately ...you, I did." He looked up, "...but that was before I knew."

"Knew what?"

"I found out," he took a deep breath, "that you were brought here through me … to end all this."

Susan didn't say anything. She stared at him for a long minute. "Karin mentioned something similar to me earlier," Susan said in a softer, thoughtful tone as she looked away.

"What did she say?"

She exhaled deeply. "I'm supposed to be some type of rescuer, sent here by some mystical power or something. She said she saw it in a vision."

"That's right!" Erik exclaimed.

"Right?" she quizzed.

"I went to the Inn as instructed. Then Lord Lokan and my dad and the other…"

"Your dad!?" Susan interrupted.

"Yes, he's one of the two Elders that assist Lord Lokan."

"Which one is he?"

"He always stands to Lord Lokan's left."

Her stomach sickened when she thought about Karin's torture. *'She's his daughter-in-law and he did nothing to stop it. These fuckin' people…'* She felt a little pleasure in replaying her escape.

"Lord Lokan told me to join them and that's how I was in the room when he decreed that Karin be sacrificed. I couldn't believe what happened. I wanted to run back and get her out, but knew it was impossible. I went back to our home and just sat."

"Couldn't your dad…?" Susan began to question.

Erik shook his head.

"What, he couldn't do anything?"

"He's not been my father for a long time. Not since he sacrificed my mother."

Susan raised her shocked eyebrows and gasped.

"The next town will be his. He will have all the powers Lord Lokan has and will command with the next Savior."

"Where's that going to be?"

"I don't know," Eric shook his head.

"While I was at home I had the same vision that Karin had. Only it was an old man and it told me one word; *"Nasus"*. After the vision left the room spun around me. I got dizzy. I must have passed out. I woke up on the floor. When I opened my eyes, it came to me; I don't know how or why; it just did. *'Nasus'!* That's you. For some reason I'm supposed to help *you*! There was also this thing, not a voice, not a vision or anything like that, just… like … a memory… an understanding. I'm part of a plan that involves you and … I was ordained to bring you here … to Helen. It's what I was supposed to do all along. It's like I was commanded to do what I did and not by Lord Lokan - by something else. I have this powerful feeling that helping you will in someway rescue Karin. An urge came over me to get the keys to this shed and open it at half past ten tonight. So that's how I got here. I want to save Karin and if that means helping you do whatever…I'll do it…so…how can I help?*"

Susan didn't want to tell him that Karin might already be dead. If he heard that, he might figure it's too late and save himself by turning her in.

Erik's face questioned.

"I'm not sure," she answered with anxiety in her voice, "I have no idea what I'm supposed to do." She paused, "Look, I don't even know why I'm talking to you. For all I know this is just another scheme of yours to … to … I don't know what. But I'll be damned if I'm going to ever trust you again."

"Doesn't this prove anything?" he paused. "Listen, I have to try and rescue Karin. I'm going to do it with or without your help."

"Why should I trust you? I did once and look where it got me. You're going to have to prove yourself before I ever put any faith in you again."

Erik thought for a moment, "How about if I get you a gun?"

Susan was taken aback. "If you can do that …," She said with hesitation, *"…*I'd have no other choice."

Erik nodded. He pointed to Susan's right side. "What happened?"

"I dislocated it," she grimaced as she looked at it. "I don't suppose you can bring a doctor back?"

"We don't have one. No need for one, The Savior heals us…with water from the well."

"What well?"

"It's in the Temple. The water from it heals anything."

"Bring a cup of that back."

"It wouldn't do any good." Erik countered. "You don't drink it; And ... Lord Lokan has to apply it."

"Naturally," she said with disgust.

"Unless you want me to bring him back with me?" Erik grinned.

Susan grinned in spite of herself, "No, thank you."

Erik froze; a blank look on his face.

"What is it?"

"Lord Lokan," Erik responded.

"He's coming?" Susan panicked.

"No," he replied as he reached out and steadied Susan by placing his hand on her shoulder. "He just summoned everyone to the town for a house to house search. He also said…" Erik paused.

"Erik…" she brushed his hand off of her shoulder and stepped closer to him, "…Said what?"

"He said the one who was searching for the Blessing has been eliminated on the Eternity Road."

Susan had a sinking feeling in her stomach. The only one that she could imagine coming for her was her father. Tears immediately filled her eyes.

"Who was it… how?"

"He didn't say."

Susan turned away. She clenched her left hand into a fist and pressed it against her forehead.

"Oh Dad," she softly said as she wept.

"It was your Dad? Are you sure?" Erik asked.

Erik's concerned questions brought Susan back to the reality and severity of her predicament. She lowered her arm stiffly, maintaining the fist. She sucked air between her clenched teeth and turned to face Erik. She spoke slowly, soft and deliberate as she locked eyes with him, "He's the only one who knew where I was before I met you." She raised her voice a couple of octaves, "*...just before I laid my eyes on you,*" she closed the distance between them. Susan put her face an inch from his as he stiffened his back against a center support beam of the shed. She reached up and put her hand around Erik's throat, but did not squeeze. Erik placed both of his hands on her wrist. She said with clenched teeth "*...Just before...*" Susan stiffened in mid sentence. The *voice* inside her head came to her.

'Stop; this is not the time; no good can come of this; listen to me. The most important thing is to get the gun!

She stopped, paused, and said, "Get the fucking gun," she snapped as she released her hold and stepped back.

"I can't right now... I have to go. Lord Lokan's summoned us. If I don't go, he'll know something is wrong."

Susan thought for a moment. "Tell me where it is...I'll get it myself."

Erik shook his head, "You can't, it's too dangerous."

"Dangerous!" Susan could not believe what he said. "God damn it Erik, this has been one danger after another. Tell me; there's no time to lose...tell me!"

"It's in the Temple," Erik reluctantly said, "Behind the altar is a kind of storage shelf. Under the first shelf there is a small drawer, you can't see it unless you squat down. Push it in slightly and then it will open. Be very careful, if you push too hard it won't open, then only Lord Lokan can get it opened."

Susan asked with determination, "How do I get in?"

Thirty six

After Erik left Susan waited a few minutes and was about to leave when she heard a loud sound, crash, coming from outside the front of the shed. She went over to the wall and knelt on the bench. She looked through an elongated separation between the boards. There, beyond the other side of the circular road, lay a lighted torch that had fallen from its post holder. Susan gasped loudly as she saw part of a leg coming into her limited view. The leg stopped. She leaned to the opposite side to gain a better look. At the same time, the figure took a cautious step forward and stopped again.

It was Lord Lokan!

Susan backed away from the spacing. The thought of another setup at the hands of Erik crossed her mind. She heard deliberate footfalls. They were getting louder. He was coming towards the shed. She ducked behind the center pole. The bottoms of Lord Lokan's boots crackled the pebbles on the cobblestones. Susan quickly scanned her surroundings. She needed a place to hide. She crawled under the bench she had been sitting on.

Randall Stevens

Several flickered lines disappeared across the floor as Lord Lokan approached. He looked into the shed through the same hole Susan looked through a moment before.

The keys Erik had given her squeezed against her thigh from the pocket of her stretch pants. Fright sharpened its blade and swiftly cut through her body with a cold swing, as she envisioned the hasp on the door with the lock hanging open.

"Humpf," she heard. His shadow began to fade away. The fire lines extended from the back wall to the front.

Susan moved cautiously from under the bench and looked through the space.

Lord Lokan walked to the torch and picked it up.

Susan was shocked at what she saw.

He had picked up the torch from the fiery end and replaced the torch in its cradle. The fire's translucent rings of orange, yellow and red encased his hand and forearm. When he pulled his arm back there was no sign of any burning…not even a whiff of smoldering smoke rose from his sleeve.

What she saw was shocking enough, but what she saw next was beyond belief. He walked to the trunk of The Savior Tree and stood. His face and body only inches from it. He placed his hands between two massive chunks of bark. His arms disappeared up to his elbows. He murmured softly and the bark of the entire tree began to pulsate. He raised his head and then stepped forward into the tree like walking through a stage curtain.

Susan leaned back from the opening and sat in stunned silence trying to sort out the events. *Fire doesn't faze him? ... and the tree ... the tree? That must be where he gets his power! Destroy the tree and he'll go with it…but how? Fire doesn't seem to harm it or him. Think Susan think!!! Karin said that The Savior Tree burned and grew larger when it appeared years ago. She also said it was a windy, rainy evening…'* Susan tried to envision that night as one of the townspeople watching the horrific sight. *'The tree was burning. The cold night wind and pelting rain had no effect on the flames.'* Susan had the feeling she was close to the answer. *'Its right here, damn it'* Susan was chastising her subconscious to tell her the answer, *'Show me…show me…'*

Suddenly, she replayed the sacrifice she saw the night before. They were standing right next to one of the torches and she was shivering cold. It never occurred to her at the time, but she should have felt some heat coming from the flames. It was certainly a large enough fire to have produced some heat. *That's it, the fire is an illusion!* She turned and looked through the space again. A smile came across her face. *'Burn the tree with real fire … it and Lokan will be destroyed!'*

An image of the Temple appeared before her.

Thirty-seven

Susan left the shed and placed the lock back on the hasp. She tossed the keys in the water barrel and made her way to the front of the Temple. She was careful to stay in the shadows. The front doors were fashioned from the huge pieces of bark that had apparently been taken off The Savior Tree. The handles on the doors were small crooked branches. She pulled one of the doors open and entered. Wide-eyed she walked through the dark hallway. When she got halfway, the door slammed shut. She gasped and put her back to the wall. She froze for a minute – no one there. '*It must have been the wind*'. Then the wooden brace fell down across the door. She went back to the door and lifted the log. It was heavy, but came out of the brackets. She let it fall back into place. '*I should have done that in the first place.*'

Susan walked with a fast pace to the end of the hallway and paused; she couldn't believe the haunted ambience of the worship area. The immediate object that caught her eye was the lifelike carved replica of The Savior Tree and the snake-serpent it housed. Susan walked through the center of the chamber staring at the eye of the serpent. It captivated her more with every step. Images began to race through her mind, too fast to recognize. Susan wanted to turn and run, but the force that had directed her in the past was now pulling her forward. The toes of her foot made contact with the fascia of the first step of the stage. She stopped and looked down. As she raised her eyes from the step, they crossed over one of the roots. She blinked and a scene flashed before her. The view was from the air. It appeared she was in something that was going to crash into the back of the head of a giant snake gnawing on a large tree root. Somehow there were flames to the side of her face. She had hold of a burning branch with her mouth. She could actually feel the heat of the splashing flames. The head of the giant snake turned as she plunged closer. It opened its mouth and sprung forward and violently slashed its elongated forked-tongue at her.

The image vanished as fast as it came. Susan fell to her knees. She steadied herself with her good hand and slowly looked up at the snake-serpent. Her anxious eyes locked on the serpent's eye. Her mind screamed, *"How do I know you?"*

The tree began a soft steady throb. Susan, still on her knees, looked at the trunk and leaned back. The thump sounded like a heart beat. A deep extended noise cracked from behind the tree's trunk. Susan quickened to her feet and walked around the altar. She kept her eyes focused on the pulsation of the trunk. When she got around the tree a large section of the bark, the size of a normal door, pushed forward. As it did, powerful swords of yellow-white light shot out from the opening. The bark slid to one side of the tree trunk like the opening of an airliner door. The light became one brilliant glow of bouncing crystals.

Susan shielded her eyes against the powerful light. She tilted her head and bent forward to see inside. Somehow she felt a deep, familiar comfort surround her. She straightened and moved in closer. The light became softer and more tolerable to her eyes. Her attention was transfixed on the illumination from inside the hollow of the tree. The opening revealed a circular stone wall about four feet high.

"The Well!" Susan whispered in astonishment.

The light changed its color to a soft blue, almost as a response to Susan's voice.

The light above the well changed its hue and brightened again. Then just as it had appeared to her twenty-five years ago, the image of her mother floated out of the light!

"Mother!" Susan choked as she reached out. Her eyes watered with delight.

"*Susie,*" her mother smiled in a calm voice.

"Oh, how I missed you!" Susan cried. She stepped closer.

"*I have been with you since last we talked,*" her mother said with a soft smile. "*Do you remember?*"

The memory of all that her mother had told her came back to her.

"Yes..., yes I do," she wiped her eyes and furthered. "I've come through the test, haven't I? Trusting Erik and Karin has guided me here?"

Her Mother smiled. "*Yes, Now it is time for you to use your ability, but the decision will not be an easy one.*"

Susan's heart swelled with a mixture of fear, apprehension and excitement. Her mind unlocked the vaulted memories that had once been her life. A tornado of purpose, protection and power swirled within her to give her an unbridled confidence. With this internal transformation, Susan stepped forward and spoke, "I am prepared."

Thirty-eight

"I am your Mother Freda, and you are my daughter Arindis. You are a part of a historical time. A time when God's of both good and evil filled all of creation. Worlds then were divided and spawned deceptive battles for dominance of all. Different forms of life, from dwarfs, to humans, to giants, to Gods grew. All with the desire to rule.

"Your Father, Odin, was ruler of all. And although most powerful, he was in constant fear that there would come a time when the world and all he protected would be destroyed. Your Father and I decided that there was need to have an ally that no one would know about. That would have abilities protect and strike if necessary, in a time of need. To this end we decided to have another child , but to keep it hidden. That child is you. You are the youngest of the child of Odin the Wise. You are Arindis, 'Eagle Guardian' When the time came you were transformed into an eagle to live in and protect the tree of Life, the tree called Yggdrasil. You were also tasked with guarding the magic Mirmir Well beside the tree".

"The tree out there; it's the Yggdrasil, that's why I feel I know it?" Susan said

212

with a shocked introspection. "And this well is..."

"*Yes, it is*".

"I remember now... Lokan is the 'God Loki'. ***That's*** why he recognized me.

"Yes, he has three children. Of the three, the worst is his daughter Hel. She was so evil Odin cast her to the underworld 'Nifilheim'. There she rules the dead. She hates all life, embraces death. She and her brother, Fenfir, have vowed to one day to return and destroy all that your father created. This day has been deemed the 'Evening Day,' by Loki. There is only one way for Hel to rise from Nifilheim and that is to destroy the Tree of Life. And there is only one creature capable of that task and that is the snake serpent Nidhogg."

"That's the snake serpent, the thing Lord Lokan has been worshipping," Susan whispered, "It recognized me also."

"You have fought and defeated The Nidhogg many times. Should the Nidhogg ever truly succeed in chewing through the roots of Yggdrasil, then the end of the gods will finally come, the 'Ragnarok'".

"For many centuries, all was quiet."

"The time has come again, Arindis. The Nidhogg has risen and seeks to finally destroy the Tree. Therein, the passage will be created for Hel's destruction of all things living. You must stop them both."

"But I'm not an eagle," Susan protested, "Even if I could become one, my arm is injured."

"The arm is of no consequence. Time is growing short. I believe that you will decide on the side of selfless logic and prevent the ending of all things."

"If I decide to do this, how..."

"The Well of Mirmir. It has the power to give magic, wisdom and knowledge to those who ask. Beware, it will ask a price for that granting. Your father gave an eye to gain the wisdom he possesses." Freya smiled gently, *"I must go now. You have proven your worth. Carry the trust that is now in your heart."*

"But I have so many more questions..." Susan watched as Freya's form faded into the light.

Susan turned her head in both directions then paused. Her voice lowered, "What do I do now?"

"Is that a question you would have answered?" A voice resonated from the depths of the Mirmir Well.

Susan moved, with caution, closer to the well and studied it a moment.

"Time is short. Is that the question you would have answered?" the voice repeated.

"Yes," Susan responded.

"I want to walk the earth as a mortal." The voice replied, *"Your human form is the price for the answer".*

Susan protested, "I can't defeat the Nidhogg without a body."

"I will grant you the body you have worn many times before. But you will remain that form, for now and always. Do you still wish to ask your questions?"

Susan looked up from the well. Thoughts of Sam raced through her mind. Could she give up any chance of a life with him? She knew what he would do. In fact, both he and Karin, the people she had grown closest to, would both do it without hesitation. They would give up everything to save others. Could she do any less? Sam would always be in her heart, no matter what happened. She was only sorry that she hadn't gotten the chance to know her father better. She turned to the well.

"I will make the trade," Susan said.

"Ask your question."

"First, I need to know about Sam. Show me Sam".

Susan watched as the surface of the water boiled then quieted to a mirror-like stillness. She choked a laugh of relief as she saw Sam through her moisten eyes. He was alive and running through the swamp. He was scared and bloodied, but he was alive. The scene quickly changed. Sam was sitting on the bridge rail, scrunched up, shaking with cold. Her view was from above him. He looked up. She could see fear and apprehension in his eyes.

"There is no more time, Arindis."

Susan looked away and suddenly envisioned Karin being lifted up and torn in half. Her mind filled with the images of people dying, flames, death on a global scale. She shivered.

"What do I have to do to defeat Nidhogg?"

"Break a branch from Yggdrasil and carry it into Nifilheim. Gather the fire from the lake of fire and return to the base of the tree. Next is very important. Prior to the insertion of the sacrifice you must cast the branch into the boiling pit of the tree. Nidhogg will be driven back and Hel will be sucked back into the earth."

Susan took a deep breath.

"There is one more thing. The normal path you took into Nifilheim, the one through the Nidhogg's lair has been closed off. You must fly through the high gates."

"Those gates are never opened …?" Susan stopped before she asked another question and had to trade something else for the answer.

Fortunately the well continued.

"Hel is going to have to pass through the gates. This will afford you the opportunity."

Susan stepped forward and said, "Let's do it."

"Get the chalice in the corner; dip it in the water and drink."

Susan got the chalice and before she came back retrieved gun from the podium. She checked it and tucked it in her sling. She walked to the edge of the well.

"Hold it!" a strong male voice challenged from behind her.

Thirty-nine

The icy water rose fast. It had swelled over the tops of Sam's boots. He was already soaked. The water sheeted around him like an icy suit. The tips of his ears and fingers pierced with the stinging pain of frost. His nose revolted in pain when he instinctively wiped it with his wet jacket sleeve. He put his wet gloves in his coat pocket and placed his hands inside under his armpits. The Wisconsinite had never felt a cold like this before in his life; it cut to the bone.

Mystified at how he got trapped on the trail, he searched his mind for answers. He knew he couldn't have been more than ten feet from the sheriff's car when it passed. Even though palm bushes had blocked the path to the road, he should have seen something – lights, reflections …something. The sense of his surroundings returned. Was it his imagination or was the vegetation closing in on him? There was no wind to move them? He looked around in a panic. Sounds of the milky shedding of a snakeskin caught his attention. It was all around him. The branches in front of his face were moving, growing. The ends split off in different directions. They began to grab and pull at his clothing. He pulled the nearest ones away. Others took their place. The more he pulled, the more there were. One fingered its way under his collar, while another slid quickly down his back. His hat was pulled off his head. He made an instinctive grab for it as it sailed away on the tops of the brush like a person in a mosh pit. As he pulled his arm back, the branches tentacled around it and held on. He pulled; they resisted. Without hesitation, he pulled his gun and fired three shots into the brush. The loud report had a momentary shock effect. The space opened up around him as the branches retreated. Sam pulled his arm free. He needed to move and move quick.

The water was now above his knees. His boots cemented in the mud. His feet felt like spongy anchors that pulled away from his ankles at the slightest attempt to move them. He fired two more shots to keep the brush in its suspended animation then put the gun in his jacket pocket. He unfolded his knife, reached below the water and cut the laces. His fingertips were getting numb. His feet had dulled to fat weights. As he pulled the boot flaps apart, the branch ends re-attacked with a fury. He straightened. They grabbed the wrist of the knife hand as it came out of the water. Before he could get hold of the knife with his other hand, they pulled his fingers apart and it fell into the water. Sam broke the twigs back off his knife hand, as his ears, and nose were penetrated. The others wickedly slashed across his exposed skin. He slapped them away, but more came.

He tried to lift one leg – no luck. He tried the other; it gave. His knee came up and he leaned toward the palm plants. He got hold of one of the branches. His only chance was to use the pulling action of the branch to help get him free. The spindly twigs continued stabbing and slashing. Suddenly, he felt resistance with his free leg. His foot was on solid ground or a large rock. His hair was being pulled from his scalp. He pushed for all he was worth. Sam closed his eyes and violently turned his head from side to side. Warm trickles of blood splattered from the cuts on his face. As the droplets splashed away, the twigs sprung after them, like frog tongues capturing a fly. The bigger arms of branches began to encircle his body and pull downward. He was being turned. He heard a splash and knew his gun had fallen out of his pocket. He was in a death struggle. His only lifeline was the palm branch. Sam held on for his life. The branches pulled harder. He lost his grip and went under the water. The attackers swarmed on him like frenzied piranha. He pulled at the branches around his waist. His other foot broke free. He turned, twisted and pushed. His head popped above the water and he gasped for air. He was next to the palm. He got hold of it. He pushed and pulled for all he was worth. He worked himself between the palms. The attackers retreated. He gave momentary thought of retrieving his boots. No sooner the thought entered when the palmed leaves quickly attached themselves to him like huge white blood cells. Sam flailed and thrashed again. He broke out the other side. Another few seconds and he would not have been able to move.

Sam found himself in a narrow stream. It was the road submerged under water. He continued in the direction he was going. He couldn't go far with bare hands and feet, but thought he might run into the sheriff and a warm dry car. Sam followed the river road through two more turns then came upon the bridge whose platform was above the water. Sam moved as fast as he could to reach it. The first thing he did was take off his jacket and one of his shirts. He re-donned his jacket and sat on the side rail. It was wide enough so he could bring his feet up and brace his back against one of the supports. Sam wrung out his shirt as dry as he could get it. He wrapped it around his feet and began to massage them. He had his knees up to his chest and bent his head between them. Suddenly, he felt comforting warmth surround him. He looked skyward. He felt someone was watching him. Then…as fast as it came, the feeling vanished.

Forty

In one quick move, Susan dropped the chalice, pulled the gun out of her makeshift holster, turned and fired. The bullet tore a hole through the right shoulder of an Elder. He turned and bent over from the force of the bullet.

"Get up!" Susan said with a stern voice while holding the gun at chest level.

His face grimaced with pain.

"What happened?" the Well voice asked.

"I shot one of the Elders…" Susan responded without taking her eyes off her target.

"He's here for the ceremony book, the one on the altar".

"Take off your hat; coat and boots." Susan commanded.

The Elder hesitated.

"Now, you bastard, or I swear, I'll take them off your dead body."

He nervously complied.

"Wrap the boots and hat inside the coat," Susan directed. "Tie the sleeves …hurry."

The Elder grimaced as he stood and placed hand over his wound.

"Pick up the chalice," Susan motioned with her gun.

"What now?" she asked the Well.

"Dip it in the water," the Well said. The mirrors turned to a hazel-blue liquid.

"Do it," Susan commanded the Elder as she pointed the gun toward the Well. The Elder dipped the chalice in the water and held it above the Well.

"Now first pour it on your shoulder."

Susan nodded at the Elder. She raised the gun to his head and said, "Don't try anything stupid."

With a shaky hand he poured the water on Susan's shoulder.

"Put the chalice on the floor and back up."

Susan's shoulder crackled from within. Her arm socket snapped as the arm bone went back into position. She could also feel her shoulder muscles as they pulled and tendons constricted back into place. She slid her hand from the waistband and straightened her arm to her side. It was still inside her blouse, but it felt back to normal.

"Come back here," She directed the Elder.

She signaled him to stop when he got in front of her.

"Pick up the Chalice and raise it to my lips."

She drank the rest of the liquid.

"What do I do now?" She asked the well.

"Nothing," the Well responded. *"I will do the rest."*

"Get in there," Susan directed The Elder inside the tree cavity, "all the way behind it."

Suddenly there were crashes against the Temple doors.

"They must've heard the shot. There's no time…we must hurry."

"Do it now!" Susan said.

The Well glowed with a rainbow of sparkled colors. Deep humming sounds surfaced from its bottom. At the same time The Elder became transfixed on what was happening before his eyes.

Susan's arms spread out to her sides and hundreds of long flowing feathers sprouted from under them. The gun dropped to the floor. Her upper body swelled outward and then transformed into a muscular heart shape with large legs and claws with huge sharp talons. Susan's head became the focal point of this beautiful eagle.

She stood bigger than her human form. She was Arindis the Eagle, Protector of the Yggdrasil. Her sharp steel eyes poignantly spoke with the knowledge of her mission.

The brace holding the doors of the Temple suddenly rose from the brackets and the doors flew open. The Elders and Legions raced to the hall.

Arindis let out an earthshaking "SCHREEEEEECH" that shook the walls of the Temple. The floor moved as if hit by an earthquake. The Elders and Legions grabbed hold of what they could to steady themselves, others tumbled to the floor like bowling pins.

Arindis grabbed the gun with her claw and put it on top of the black bundle. With its other talon, it clutched the package.

The intruders regained their nerve and advanced.

Arindis spread her massive wings and with a powerful downward motion took flight. She circled just below the domed ceiling and landed on the clawed arm of the carved Savior Tree. The men froze in their tracks.

"Close the doors!" one of them shouted.

The eagle leaped toward the ceiling.

A powerful 'SCHREEEEEEEECH' reverberated inside the skulls of the men, sending them to their knees as they covered their ears.

Arindis exploded through the ceiling as if it was made of paper. Everything came crashing down. The men attempted to flee as the massive debris rained down upon them. Splintered branches dove down like spears and stabbed through shoulders, heads and crouching backs. Some were pinned to the floor of the Temple like insects on a science display board.

Forty-one

The door to Karin's room opened and three Elders entered. Mrs. Crowley was sitting on the edge of the bed tending to Karin.

"It is time," one of the Elders said.

"Yes," Mrs. Crowley replied. She looked at Karin one more time.

Karin slowly opened her eyes. She lifted her hand, placed it on the old woman's cheek. Mrs. Crowley put her hand on Karin's, and gave a gentle squeeze. She slowly removed it from her cheek and placed it to Karin's side. She left the room.

Two of the Elders helped Karin sit on the side of the bed and gave Karin a cup and said, "Drink."

Karin swallowed its contents and handed the cup back.

They escorted her out of the room securely holding her upper arms.

Out front of the hotel was a wooden wagon, the type used to parade the condemned on the way to the gallows. Eight Legions, four on each side of the wagon's tongue, stood ready to pull the cart to the ceremonial area. Four Elders lifted Karin onto the platform of the cart; two others tied her to the post.

Lord Lokan led the way out of town, followed by the Elders, the cart and the Legions.

Erik was just behind the cart. He watched helplessly as his wife was tied to the post. He hoped beyond dreams that he had done enough to aid Susan and help her find the way to rescue Karin. He kept his moistened eyes focused on the heads of the Legions pulling the wagon.

Just as they started to move, a report of three muffled gunshots rebounded through the main street from the direction of the swamp road. The procession halted. Two more shots were heard. Lord Lokan called for Elder Ivarsson who quickly presented himself.

"I thought you eliminated the searcher?" Lord Lokan asked in a low suspicious voice.

"Tha…that is correct…M…My Lord," Elder Ivarsson replied.

Lord Lokan leaned in closer, "Then you can explain the gunshots that befell my ears just now?"

Elder Ivarsson looked back at the swamp and turned back to face him. His eyes were wide with fright and his jaw shook.

"We heard the…"

"Heard?" Lord Lokan interrupted. "You did not witness the elimination?"

He bowed his head, "No, My Lord."

Lord Lokan called for High Elder Larsen. He appeared when called. His right eye was almost swollen shut. Dried scabs had formed from the cut below the eye and he had a bump on his forehead that made his hat not fit evenly.

"You will go to the road. Anyone you find will die and you will watch." Lord Lokan hissed, "Take Legion Kliest with you. And no more mistakes." He turned to Elder Ivarsson. "You will be dealt with later."

The procession continued. When they arrived at The Savior Altar, two Elders untied Karin and lowered her to the four Elders on the ground. Erik resisted the impulse to grab her and run. He kept telling himself to *trust* in what he had been told by the entity. The Elders and Karin ascended the stairs when another gunshot rang out.

Every head except Karin's turned in the direction of the Temple.

Lord Lokan fiercely pointed to the Temple. "The Blessing's in the Temple".

The men charged ahead. Erik lagged. By the time they were all at the Temple, he was at the rear and positioned near the bottom steps.

The men pushed against the doors.

Lord Lokan pushed himself through the mob on the stairs and shouted, "Cease!" He raised his right hand and the doors flew open. The men moved around him into the Temple.

Lord Lokan stood at the Temple doors and stiffened at the sound of the eagle's SCREECH.

Erik was standing alone at the bottom of the stairway. He looked up at Lord Lokan. A look of suspicion came back to him. Erik was about to say something, when the second SCREECH rang out.

Lord Lokan turned away and disappeared inside. As he went in the ceiling of the Temple's main hall came crashing down. He heard the cries of pain and yells that echoed from the cavernous main hall. He moved to the entrance and stood. Men were felled and moaning in pain throughout the hall. He made a step forward and as he did he made a sweeping motion with his powerful hand. The fallen debris was blown into the sides of the Temple walls as if a great wind had blown through the chamber. One Temple wall gave way from the force and exploded outward.

Darkened dust and smoke mixed with painful cries rose from the carnage. The Temple's hall resembled the aftermath of an aerial bombardment. Some of the men had javelin branches that had pierced through their shoulders and backs. Others lay beneath large support logs; many weren't moving. The right wall was a scattered log pile. The carved Savior Tree remained intact, except for the clawed arms that collapsed from the ceiling debris.

Lord Lokan strode into the ceiling-less hall. He approached the nearest Legion, who was on his knees with a branch sticking out of the back of his shoulder. Red splinters displayed like flowering spines around the wound. Lord Lokan grabbed the branch with both hands, put his foot on the man's back and pulled it out. The Legion screamed as the blood came gushing out of the extraction. He stood and blood was forming fast all over his chest.

Lord Lokan grabbed the Legion's hat and pushed it over the chest wound. "Hold that!" he commanded.

The Legion reached up in pain and did as directed. Knowing he was bleeding from his back as well.

"Go and tell Elder Cartwright to prepare the sacrifice. I will be there directly."

The Legion looked at him with disbelief.

"NOW!"

The contorted Legion stumbled his way out of the Temple.

Lord Lokan surveyed the remains. He sneered with contempt and anger. So as not to appear defeated to those still able to watch him, he positioned himself like a conquering general about to receive an honor from his king and walked to the front of the Temple. As he walked, he cleared a path to the altar. The logs, pews and wreckage flew in all directions. Lord Lokan totally disregarded where anything was tossed. His eyes remained glued to the tree's trunk.

Outside, the waste of the Temple thrashed hundreds of feet in the air and crashed down on some of the surrounding structures. The Legions and Elders that formed the sacrifice ceremony had to duck out of the way of the flying wooden shrapnel. Some of the bodies, that were lying crushed and bloodied under the logs, came with them. The mid-air mixtures of body fluids, reflected by the torch fires, displayed hauntingly beautiful liquid rainbows.

Lord Lokan saw the ceremony book with its pages splayed open. Telekinetically, he put it under his arm. When he got to the rear of the tree, he stopped and commanded it to open. There was nothing inside but the dead body of an Elder. Lord Lokan's body stiffened and then shook with an exasperated fury. The book dropped to the floor as he arched his back. His head flew backward and he raised his hands skyward. The frustrated wail of a thousand voices echoed violently throughout what remained of the building.

Forty-two

The tremendous power of Arindis's wings propelled her quickly to the fogged ceiling. She circled once to view the ceremonial area. Karin was staked on the altar and an Elder was ascending the steps. She glanced to the Temple and saw Erik. She wanted desperately to interfere with what was going on, but knew she couldn't... there was something she had to do first. She straightened her flight and headed directly for the town. As she flew, she could hear what sounded like rumbling after-shocks coming from the direction of the Temple.

*****

Sam's shaken body was huddled on the rail of the bridge. He started to feel some tingling around his ankle sides and instep.

Suddenly, there were deep rumbles reverberating through the swamp. The sound wasn't loud when it reached him, but he felt that at the source it must have been. He couldn't imagine what it was.

*****

High Elder Larsen and Legion Kliest heard the sudden crash from the direction of the sacred area.

"Should we go back?" Legion Kliest asked.

"We're going to do what we were told to do."

*****

Two figures that walked the town's main road heading towards the swamp caught Arindis's attention. She suspected they were going to intercept Sam. The road's entrance was obscured by the tops of the trees. It was going to make it difficult to find the bridge. She flew in a large circular pattern, scanning the treetops for any sign of separation that would reveal the road. Time was running short. The Temple ceiling brought some time, but not much.

As she began her final pass, the tops of the trees began to shrink like flowers closing their pedals as the days sun disappears. The road appeared and she could see the bridge. She dove toward it. All at once she saw him. Sam had jumped off the rail and looked in her direction.

A lover's warmth filled her. She wanted to cry out his name. She was no more than twenty-feet away when the shock of Sam's reaction hit her.

He did not recognize her. Sam raised his arms in a defensive position and cowered down.

She dropped the bundle on the bridge and flew straight up.

*****

The treetops started to move as if a strong wind gusted through them. Sam gazed at the trees and the foliage around him. It was all moving. The trees and brush were reforming in ways that were so lifelike, Sam thought there were people inside them. Tree branches and bushes crackled as they had before, only this time they were spreading apart. The water was receding from the sides of the bridge.

Sam jumped off the bridge rail. Painful needles stung his feet. All the movement in the swamp abruptly ceased, silent, hollow, cold. Sam's eyes caught a black movement in the gap at the tops of the trees. At first he thought it was stubborn clumps of tree branches pulling apart. No, it was some kind of large bird headed straight for him. He looked in all directions… no weapon, no shield, totally exposed. Sam looked back at the bird, horrified. Its eyes were furled to the center and focused directly on him; and it had something in its claws! He raised his arms in shelter, moved closer to the rail and crouched.

The blast of air pushed him to his knees. Sam braced himself from being completely flattened by the squall. There was a thump, like the first sack of laundry hitting a basement floor. He raised his head and saw the bird flying away over the treetops. He expected it to come back for another sweep. He turned and faced the night sky where it had originally appeared and waited - nothing happened.

He cautiously moved over to where the object laid. It was a cloth bundle and there was a metal object on top; it was a gun. Sam picked it up. A chill ran through his entire body. His attention went from the gun to the bundle; he knelt.

"A coat!?" Sam exclaimed. "My luck's finally changing."

He picked up the garment by the shoulders. Pants, a pair of boots and a wide brimmed hat fell out. Sam didn't even notice the moist darkened hole in the shoulder as he threw the coat over him like a shawl. He was just grateful for the immediate warmth it provided. Sam put his arms through the sleeves. His index finger caught in the hole. He looked at his finger tip protruding through it and knew immediately recognized what had caused it.

''There's no time to question this,' he thought.

He put the hat on and grabbed the boots, then moved to the rail and put them on. They were about one size too big, but it didn't matter to him.

Sam moved back to where the gun lay and picked it up. He ejected the clip. There were rounds in it. He quickly slid the rounds out and found it was one short. He replaced the bullets and slammed the clip back in the receiver. He held the barrel up to his nose. Burnt gun powder, it had recently been fired.

'*It probably produced the hole in the coat,*' he thought.

He was about to lower the gun when he caught a glimpse of the serial number. He read it again. He drew a harsh breath. He knew the number…it was Susan's gun…'*Little Lady.*'

Forty-three

Arindis headed back to the ceremony site with a hope she hadn't jeopardized her mission. The two men she had seen earlier were about to enter the swamp road. She felt better that Sam would be prepared if he ran into them, provided he hadn't been too shaken to open the package.

Arindis flew back to the site. She landed in the tree and selected a branch long enough to carry a flame back from Nifilheim. It snapped off easily with the power of her talons. She took to the air. The tunnel to Hel's domain began at the hole at the tree's base. When the proper height was attained she turned and began her dive. She broke through the heavy clouds like an inbound missile targeting the base of the tree.

*****

Lord Lokan walked back through the rubble in the hall to the front doors. There, he came across Erik who was on the platform entrance.

"You had something to do with this travesty," Lord Lokan accused.

Erik stood silent, guilt etched on his face.

He pointed his finger at Erik, "Betrayer!" he shouted. "You have desecrated The Savior's sacrament and spat upon his favor." He then growled. "This transgression must be punish…"

Lord Lokan's words were interrupted by a loud snap in the tree. He looked up. His eye's instantly widened with rage.

"Arindis!" he screamed.

Erik turned and watched a large eagle disappear into the cloud ceiling.

With his finger still pointed at Erik he turned to the gathered men, **"Take this one. He is no longer worthy of The Savior's grace!"** he shouted.

The Elders were almost on Erik when Arindis exploded down through the clouds.

Erik, sensing the eagle was the sign he was waiting for, smiled. Something was wrong immediately. The eagle started to spin out of control. Peripherally, Erik seen Lord Lokan's arm raised and pointed in the eagle's direction.

"Nooo!" Erik cried out as he grabbed Lord Lokan's wrist with both hands. He turned him backwards with the rush. But Lord Lokan brought his other arm across his body and struck Erik's back with a powerful downward blow. Erik hit the floor hard. He lay paralyzed.

*****

Arindis was out of control, in a total spin. She was going to crash if she didn't do something quick. She tried to slow her spinning descent, but couldn't expand her wings. With an unexpected freedom, the force that had bound her released. She expanded her wings which stopped the spin, but did nothing for the fall. The only thing left was the branch in her talons. *'There might be enough twigs and small branches at the end to act as a cushion'.* At the last second, she pointed the end directly beneath her. The branch hit. She released it and turned her body so her back would take most of the impact. She bounced off and went rolling off to the side. She was dazed. She shook her head, grabbed the branch and blazed a trail back into the clouds.

'Lord Lokan had to have something to do with missing the mark,' she thought. *'He would be waiting for me to return try at the entrance hole. How am I going to get by him? How was she going to stop the horror that was below'?*

Forty-four

Sam put the gun in his coat pocket. The warmth of the pocket felt so good he kept his hand wrapped around the handle. He picked up the muddy wet shirt he had had wrapped around his feet and threw it over the side. When it hit the water, a deep and monstrous growl reverberated from underneath. The bridge shook. Sam turned and ran to the nearest off side, which happened to be toward the town. He wasn't quite off the surface when the bridge lifted up behind him and the force sent him tumbling to the road. He regained his balance and started running away. The volume of the growl diminished as he went. When he thought he was at a safe distance, he stopped and looked back over his shoulder. Nothing was chasing him. But what he saw at the bridge sent stabbing pins of horror up and down his back.

The bridge platform was completely raised opened from the other side. There was a yellowish, red glow from beneath it. The shrubbery on the opening side of the bridge was waving violently back and forth. Something large and long was slashing through the air. It was a tongue! Like a snakes tongue with a split at the end. It snapped like a whip. The light reflected off the hundreds of shiny hooks on the tongue's surface. Some hooks had pieces of swamp debris hanging from them. Sam thought most of it was leaves, long dark sticks or weeds. But when he took a closer look a sicken reality set inside his guts. There was no darken sticks or weeds. What was entangled on several of the spikes was ripped clothes. An a belt...a leather belt with a triangular object at the end; a black holster...with a hand attached, snapped off just above the wrist!

Sam closed his eyes a second. *'Maybe an illusion',* He thought. But it was soon discarded when he took another look.

"Son-of-a Bitch!" he said. His anger flared when memories of Sheriff Earlee flashed in front of him. He wanted to charge the thing and empty his pistol at it.

The tongue then disappeared and the bridge fell closed.

Sam ran bent over. He covered his mouth to prevent from gagging as he ran. He felt clammy. He looked back at the turn in the road. A shiver of fear went through him when he became aware that if he had not gone down the path, he would have met the same fate as the sheriff.

He then heard noise coming from the opposite direction. A feared sweat came over him when he heard voices.

'Friendly or not,' he thought. *'Almost everything he encountered in the swamp tried to kill him; why should he expect anything different from whomever was approaching? Whoever they were, they were coming quick'.*

Sam lay down behind the brush along the edge of the road. Two men, one older and taller than the other, raced by. They were dressed in the same garb he was in. When the men went around the bend, Sam got up and crept to the turn. He knelt and peered around the bush. They were standing at the base of the bridge. One of the two said something to the other but Sam could not make out what it was. They looked under the bridge. The tall one said two words that escalated Sam's fear level, "*...missed him.*"

Sam secured the handle of *'Little Lady.'*

"Somehow he got by here," the tall one continued as he looked around. "We must've passed him in our haste. We'll search the sides back to town."

Sam evaluated the situation - the men behind, but what lay ahead? One thing he did know for sure…Susan was ahead of him…somewhere.

Sam moved down the road, staying on the grassy center. He came around a turn. The road emptied into a clearing; just beyond that, buildings. Sam, breathing heavily, looked over his shoulder then back at the town. He felt trapped. He thought to hide and maybe capture one of them as they came by. He looked down at his clothes and a realization popped into his mind.

'The one they're searching for wouldn't have these clothes on!'

Sam moved to the end of the road and stood in the center facing the swamp. He pulled the brim of his hat down and put his hands in his coat pockets - one holding *'Little Lady'*.

They were very close.

Sam's mind was racing – second guess - eyes blinking rapidly - sweat beads stung at his face cuts. Rustling of the bushes. He was beginning to panic,

'What the Hell are you doing?' He looked all around him. No place to hide! *Run...Run…! Before it's too late…**Run…NOW!**'*

… too late.

When the men came around the corner they stopped abruptly.

Stilled silence filled the air, the kind that exists between two gamblers when one sends a bluffed challenge across the table. Only this time, the stakes were much high.

Forty-five

Arindis glided over the clouds in a dread. *'What was he to do? She would have to chance another attempt and soon".* She was about to go into her descent when she heard a voice in her mind.

"There is another way," it was her mother's voice.

"Where?"

"It is located under the bridge in the swamp. The spiked tongue in Fenfir's mouth guards it."

'But?'

"Go quickly!"

The tongue was out again. It lazily slid from side to side.

Arindis thought as she circled above the bridge, 'two things were going for her, speed and surprise. She waited until the tongue was on the this side and retreating to the other. She hugged her wings to her body, extended the branch to the rear and dove for the unoccupied side of the bridge.

The Serpent Wolf's keen auditory sense alerted it. The tongue slashed through the air on course with Arindis's approach.

Surprise gone, she changed her route in a split second and sprinted to the other side.

None too soon for the tip of the tongue nipped the end of the branch. The tongue made a hasty retreat to the other side, but Arindis had already entered the abyss.

Because of the hole's immense blackness, Arindis had to fly through it using the feel of her feathers. She soon smelled the distinct odor of rotting flesh as she neared her destination. The smell gnawed through her throat and lungs. Suddenly she saw the circled opening. It was outlined with shredded flesh, which was snagged on the edges, from the inward stream of the wind. Blood splattered off the ragged shreds and spun in a circular motion with no sign of any gravitational pull.

Arindis fruitlessly tried to avoid the droplets. She closed her eyes. When she no longer felt the drops hit her, she knew she was through.

Hel's domicile lay before her eyes. The gates to The Lake of Fire were decorated with human skeletal remains, torn flesh, and blood stained clothes. Off to one side was Nidhogg's cavernous lair. The memories of this horrid place came rushing back. Arindis flew to the nearby blood-darkened shoreline of the great water that surrounded Helheim. Mounds of bodies, in different stages of decomposition lay on the sand. Malodorous vapors hung above the piles like poisonous clouds of gas. On the reddish-brown sands were various sized boulders, all mosaically pasted with mangled body parts the high tide waves hammered against them. These were the carcasses of the truly evil people to be devoured by The Nidhogg.

Hel's gates opened.

Arindis flew behind two huge boulders. She positioned herself so she could see. Standing, centered in the opening, silhouetted by the radiance of the burning death hues inside, stood Hel. She embodied evil. Her vile facial features, extenuated by the downward cast shadows of the red-orange light, featured hollow white eyes.

They followed the slanted brows to the center of her face. Two protruding horns grew out above her eyebrows and circled tightly along the sides of her head. Ram horns, they finished in upward points on both sides of her neck.

At her feet were her hideous troll-servants. They numbered in the hundreds and huddled around her attentively. They were small with pale green scales over a good portion of their bodies. Two fins protruded from the center of their forehead just above the eyes, forming a 'V'. They continued around the sides of their head and became ears. The fins could rise into a sharp blade. Slender slits sufficed for eyes. Inside the slits, were yellowish goo-like bulbs that glistened florescent rays of light. An odd shaped hole in the center of their face with a cartilaged bone above it, displayed as a nose. Because their lips came together like steel cutting blades, their mouths were absent any teeth. Like humans, they had two arm and leg appendages. Additionally, they had a pointy tail that slid on the ground as they walked. Three fingers with sharp talons and a huge opposing thumb composed theirs hands. Their legs and feet resembled the hind legs and hooves of a horse.

Hel stared at the loathsome sky, waiting to begin her reign of terror on the world above.

Once she started to move, it meant that Nidhogg had fully appeared and begun to focus on the sacrifice…Karin.

Forty-six

Arindis anxiously waited behind the rocks. Sirens wailed abruptly, so loud that the ground shook like hit by a massive earthquake. The brownish seawater frizzled as bodies toppled from atop the mounds. The branch fell loose from her grip. She dove and pinned it against the granite surface. She froze for a moment hoping she did not expose herself. Carefully she worked herself back so she could see.

Hel was moving from side to side like an anxious caged animal. Her head billowed and horns circled like explosive pinwheels. The haunted sky colors reflected the tones of her robes and skin. The sirens stopped. It became as quite as an empty cathedral. Hel stared at the entrance hole that led to the tree. She extended her arms upward. A wind began blowing in from the sea. It began to build strength and swirl in an upward motion from the water's edge. Hel's robe splayed from her feet as the sirens fired another ear shattering salvo. The wind became a stationary horizontal hurricane. The vortex sent everything in its path skyward.

Arindis held on for all she was worth, but there was no use in fighting the air current. She extended her wings and glided with it. She hoped to find a place to spin out.

Strips of flesh ripped from their moorings and sent hurling skyward. Eyeballs, clumps of scalp, intestines, bones and other assorted appendages soon followed, as well as the unattached torsos.

Arindis spun from the vortex just as Hel made her move toward the hole. Arindis dove toward the gates. The trolls, seeing her approach, scattered like fire ants as she sped past. She followed the road that led to the Lake of Fires. Towering walls of sharp black rocks bordered the road.

Arindis reached the lake faster than she could ever remember. The flames on the water exploded skyward like fire on the sun. Arindis flew parallel to the shore, turned on her side, and stuck the branch into the flames. The dried ends caught fire immediately and she soared back.

As she exited the cliffs, Arindis was met with an obstacle she had not anticipated. The trolls were amassed in front of the opened gates with spears and catapults filled with burning coals. There was no time to hesitate. She had to get through. The first catapult was released and hundreds of red-hot coals burst into the air. She avoided the shot. '*These little bastards are not going stop me,*' she vowed. Arindis flew right at them. Without a second thought, she dove toward the center mass of the trolls. She folded her wings tightly against her body and dropped below the flying coals. The trolls threw their spears, but not one struck her as she shot through the gates.

The tunnel Hel had taken was the shortest route back, but Arindis did not want to encounter Hel until it was time to send her and her pet back here – where they belong. She soared into the bridge tunnel with the flames fluttering behind her like explosive exhaust from a powerful jet engine.

Forty-seven

"Prepare for the coming," Lord Lokan shouted from the Temple's platform.

The men immediately turned their attention from Erik's motionless body and moved to their formations.

Lord Lokan retrieved the book and took his position at the podium. He surveyed the formations and directed his attention to Karin. "Lectum avarveal somtom!" he ordered.

The tree came to life.

The Nidhogg appeared in a colossal show of dominance as it broadened its wide head. It acknowledged Lord Lokan then surveyed the site. When its eye fell upon the smoldering wreckage of the Temple it stopped.

Lord Lokan's maintained a stern presence.

The Nidhogg's eye pierced him with its gaze.

Lord Lokan's fingers nervously twitched on the top of the podium. His head started to shake.

The Nidhogg bent closer to the Dark Lord of Helen, Texas. Its eye bulged outwards as it positioned itself directly over Lord Lokan's head. His hat blew away as he bent his head backwards.

"NO, NO, NO," he cried.

The wind stopped and silence befell the area. Suddenly, one of the limbed arms violently knocked Lord Lokan and the podium into the air.

The Elders and Legions gasped.

The Nidhogg snapped upright and turned its attention to the Elders. They immediately dropped to their knees and bowed.

"Yes My Lord," Elder Cartwright spoke as he stood. The Elder pointed in the direction of Lord Lokan.

"Stand and secure this Blessing for sacrifice!" he commanded.

The men stood, but froze; the command was beyond their belief.

"NOW!" the Elder roared with a voice that reverberated through the site.

The men, slapped back in the moment, recovered the unconscious body of Lord Lokan and carried him to the base of the altar.

Two Legions were directed to release Karin. They brought her down off the altar and helped her make her way to the bottom of the Temple steps.

The Elders secured Lord Lokan and his arms to the stake and left.

Elder Cartwright intently walked up the altar steps.

The Nidhogg followed the procedure with great interest.

Lord Lokan's slung head slowly began to roll from side to side. He gained consciousness and immediately became aware of his predicament. He saw the Nidhogg ogling him. The corners of its giant eye elevated ever so slightly.

"What have you DONE?" Lord Lokan questioned with a defiant sneer to the Elder.

The Nidhogg leaned forward.

Lord Lokan's jaw dropped open. "My daughter?" he shouted. "How could she betray me like this?" he asked himself in a lower voice as he looked down.

He raised his head as he received another message from the Nidhogg.

"We were going to rule as one... not part of... Lord Lokan stopped his sentence. He stared blindly into space as he came to the realization that The Nidhogg had made a deal with Hel. His eyes mentally searched for a way out. He stared into the eye of the beast. *"Listen to me. She will betray you too!"* He let the thought float into the giant's mind then continued. *"You will not be the benefactor of any side of a bargain, no matter what it is!"*

The Nidhogg apparently had had enough. It turned to the Elder and signaled that he could begin the final sacrifice.

Elder Cartwright raised his right hand and shouted, *"Hovall thin saval!"*

The lava popped anxiously as it prepared for its meal. The wind once again forcefully swirled.

"NO...NO, WAIT!" shouted Lord Lokan as the voices of the formations continuously moaned louder.

The Elder drew his knife.

Lord Lokan tried in vain to pull his right arm from his side. The chain held.

Elder Cartwright removed Lord Lokan's boots. He slashed the bottoms of the dark figure's feet and allowed a good portion of his blood to fill the boots. He stood, walked to the front of the altar and raised them in praise to the Nidhogg - then hurled them into the pit.

Lord Lokan regained his movement and screamed in pain as the Elder made a hasty retreat.

No sooner had the he left the stand when the tree's limbs came from both sides of Lord Lokan. The tree's the right claw snapped at his head then closed its talons on his upper torso keeping his arms pressed to his sides. The other clamped onto the legs.

"NO, NO!" he shouted.

The chain fell and he was lifted up. Lord Lokan was fighting and screaming like a frightened child. The claws turned and readied him for the feast.

Forty-eight

"Did you find them?" A voice from inside Sam shouted. The words came out before he knew he'd done it.

"We followed him here. You did not see him?" High Elder Larsen replied as they made their first step towards Sam.

Sam didn't say a word.

The men stopped when they didn't hear an answer.

"No," the voice within Sam answered. He didn't know what was going on.

They advanced. The smaller of the two continued inspecting the bushes. High Elder Larsen maintained eye contact. "It must be near time to begin?" he questioned.

"I was sent to get you." The voice replied.

Sam was at a loss. Something or someone else was in control. What was it doing? Luring them closer, why? - What was next?

"He's not here;" the smaller man said "…what are we going to do?"

"Nothing," High Elder Larsen responded, "…because he's right…"

"Freeze!" Sam said, this time on his own, as he firmly pulled the gun from his pocket.

The men stopped.

"Get your hands in the air."

"As you wish," High Elder Larsen said with a sinister smile.

Just then an enormous sound of a windstorm rebounded off the buildings from behind Sam. He didn't turn around.

"Stay right as you are," Sam cautiously stepped around behind them. "Don't move a muscle." Sam saw the multicolored flashes over the horizon. It reminded him of nighttime bomb explosions.

"The building to your right," Sam said, "Move to its shadow when I say. Do you understand?"

The men nodded.

"I haven't slept for two days. In that time I've been through a lot of shit so don't try anything stupid, because my temper is rather short. Move!"

Sam stopped them in the shadow. "Don't turn around." He moved closer to the men's backs.

"OK," his said just above a whisper. "This is the way we're going to dance at this ball. I ask; you answer. I don't like the answer; one of you two is going have to leave...understand?"

They both nodded.

"I've been following a good friend of mine and I know she's here, or been here. She's tall, slender, dark red hair, where is she?"

"We don't have such a woman." High Elder Larsen answered.

"Wrong answer," Sam clicked the hammer back.

"No," the Legion sparked in an excited, but controlled voice. He turned his head to emphasize his protest. "He's telling the truth. She was here...but she escaped. We were looking for her when Lord..."

"Shut up," High Elder Larsen demanded.

Sam stuck the barrel of the gun in the back of High Elder Larsen and said, "You shut up. Now," Sam stepped back. "Let's try this again. Lord? You've got a guy here you call Lord?"

"He is the Mayor," The high Elder corrected, "Mayor Lord."

The Legion turned his head with a questioned look.

"I told you not to move."

He turned his head back as the High Elder continued his tale. "The one you're looking for escaped from our jail. She committed a crime and was awaiting the magistrate. He's due to arrive tomorrow. We were trying to find her. She killed the sheriff in her escape...she had a gun..."

Fury rose within Sam and he knocked the High Elder out with the butt of the gun. Sam placed the barrel of the gun on the right cheek of the Legion. With his other hand he slapped him in the back of the head and the Legion's hat flew off. Sam put his face inches from the young Legion's.

"I ain't buying any of this bullshit my friend," He pressed the barrel harder into the bone of the right cheek, "Tell me what's going on."

The Legion winced with pain.

"It's true...the part that she escaped that is...not the killing. We were looking for her when Lord Lokan...he's our leader, directed us to find the disturbance in the swamp."

"Me?"

"Yes sir...that's right. We thought *you* were Lord Lokan when we came down the road. You sure sounded like him."

"What's going on up there?" Sam made a quick motion with the gun.

The Legion didn't say anything.

Sam kidney punched the Legion. The Legion concaved his back from the blow. Sam grabbed hold of his collar and slammed his face into the side of the building.

"Look, I'm really losing it here. You bastards want to play this the hard way?" He put the barrel back into the Legion's cheek. "One more time...what's going on

247

up there?"

"It's the sacrifice," he answered without hesitation.

"Sacrifice? What kind of crazy shi…?" He pulled back on the Legion's collar. "Come on… show me."

They started to the rear of the building.

"What about him?" the Legion asked.

"He'll keep." Sam said as he pushed the Legion forward.

A low muffled sound caught their attention and Sam pulled back on the Legion's collar.

"Hold it."

The rumbled noise was coming from the swamp road. The sound would shut down and then be intermissioned by the sound of a bump or thud, then race back to its original volume. Whatever it was, it was getting closer.

"That's a truck," Sam spoke rhetorically. He turned to face his prisoner, "Who's that coming?"

"I…I…don't know."

Sam pushed him against the building again.

"Really…no one here owns a truck…or car?"

Quick white flashes glittered through the spaces between the vegetation. The truck lights lit them up for a second as it came around the last bend in the road.

"Really; it's not ours," The Legion offered.

The truck accelerated as if it were going to enter on a ramp. Suddenly, the truck made a nose diving stop. A cloud of dust sailed past it. A painful chill ran up Sam's spine as the dirt cloud settled. His jaw dropped open …it was his truck! He pushed the Legion toward the truck. "Move!" he commanded.

The passenger window began to lower.

"Excuse me sirs, but…"

"Get the fuck out of my truck," Sam shouted over the voice.

"Sam?" the voice elevated.

"That right," Sam tilted his head to get a better look at the shadowy figure still keeping his gun pointed directly at his hostage. "Who are you?"

"Doctor Waythill, Sam I…"

"Susan's dad?"

"That's right; I've been looking for you and…"

"Shut up!" Sam shouted. "Shut off the motor."

Just then a thunder blast exploded from the horizon.

"Sam, there's no time. Get in…we must go to save Susan…she's involved in that up there."

Sam turned his head back to the cab. He quickly glanced back at the swamp and back to the cab.

"How'd you…the bridge…how'd you get past that?"

"I closed it."

"Closed it? How?"

"I'll explain everything Sam…please … get in…now."

Sam directed his hostage, "Get in." He raised the weapon at the man's face. "If you try anything stupid; you die." Sam opened the passenger door and pushed him in. The truck bolted forward as Sam jumped in.

"Damn, let me get in will you?"

"Sorry…I'm better with automatics." Dr. Waythill said as he kept alternating his attention between the road and his hand on the floor shift.

"Here…let me drive."

Dr. Waythill shifted into second and the truck smoothly accelerated.

"There… it's getting it started I have the most difficulty with."

"What's this all about?"

"Well," he shifted to third gear. "Susan is involved in preventing a disaster of Biblical proportion."

Both Sam and the Legion's jaws dropped.

Forty-nine

Volcanic horror festered through the earth's crust as Lord Lokan was devoured by the Nidhogg.

A geyser of blood spewed from the hole at the base of tree. The swill jetted into the clouds turning the grays to crimson. They swirled in whirlpools around the top of the tree as its rhythmic beats resonated throughout the site. The wind increased, and bent the top limbs and branches of all the trees into a curling pose. The fountain's spew turned to long yellowish vapors. From this, ghostly bodies separated and floated in all directions like lava lamp billows. Their forms varied in shape and density as they swam through the air intertwining around each other. Their shredded skin hung on their bodies like the gooey tentacles of jellyfish. They drifted to the formations of the Legions and Elders and skimmed amidst their stiffened bodies.

Cavernous echoes emanated under the ground as if the earth were moving a mountain beneath its surface. The men looked down at the parcels of soil they were standing on. Rings of dirt spread outward from their feet and became small circle waves of muck water. The rings grew larger until the entire surface of the site was rocking in three-foot ground swells. All the men sank into the sea of brown. The growing waves crashed violently into the trees and structures sending bursts of stones and rocks into the air. The sky rained its granite shrapnel upon the exposed heads of the men - many knocked unconscious. The wicked undertow sucked them into their dirt-watered graves. The others swam to the stairs, clamoring with some difficulty to climb to the top.

Karin, in terrified quickness, had ascended to the top when the earth rumblings began.

The ground in front of the tree, not affected by the waves, swelled and became a large dune, rising in height equal to the opened pit of the tree. The wind, clouds and water thrashed in wild frenzy as the dune jaggedly split open and a light of reddish yellow speared out from within. Suddenly, there was blackness as Hel filled the opening. She rose from it as if standing on a stage lift. She opened her death-hollow eyes and spread her arms out to her sides. She stood as a solid statue while the elements danced demonically around her flailing robe. Her white eyeballs became fireballs of reflective glass.

The Elders and Legions held tight to the rails of the stairs. Karin had been pushed back into the Temple's entrance. She stood with her back against one of the damaged doors and held on to its bracket. Her hair flapped against the sides of her face as the wind hollowed through the gutted hallway. In the wind she heard a faint, moan-like, sound. It was difficult to see anything against the wind. She heard the moan again. She placed her hand just above her eyes to re-direct some of the wind's currents. On the floor, ten feet away, she saw two legs of a man sticking out from behind the bottom half of a partition. She crawled to him. The man was lying on his stomach with his face turned toward the wall.

"Erik!" she cried as she knelt to his side.

"Karin," he muffled.

She hugged her chest on his back and placed her cheek on the side of his face.

"What happened, are you hurt?"

Erik raised his head. "Yes, I tried to save… you Karin. I didn't mean…"

"I know … I know…" she shouted and then added, "I saw it in your eyes."

Erik placed his hands on the floor under his shoulders and raised his upper body. Karin helped him turn over. She positioned him so that his head and shoulders were behind the half wall. Karin turned to look at the site then back to Erik.

"What's going on out there?" Erik shouted.

"Everything's changing…there's no control; Lord Lokan was sacrificed instead of me."

He bent a little smile.

"The land has become a sea…it's all changed. The men…some were pulled under the ground… the ones that survived are up here on the stairs…they're scared. I don't know… no one knows."

The wind intensified.

Erik motioned for her to put her ear close to his mouth, she did, "Karin, listen I…I helped Miss Susan, I…saw the vision."

Karin looked around quickly then back to Erik.

"Miss Susan, where is she?" Karin mouthed.

He motioned for her ear again; "I left her in the shed."

Karin backed up as if to get to her feet and go to her.

"No, wait," Erik cried and grabbed her arm.

Karin stopped. Erik wanted to speak again. She put her ear down.

"She said she was going to come here in the Temple… said the answer lay in here somewhere. Lord Lokan crashed the Temple to the ground after he saw the hole in the roof. I came up the stairs and he was standing at the altar. He accused me of causing all this."

"What caused the hole in the roof?" Karin asked and then replaced her ear in front of Erik's mouth.

Erik explained, "The Eagle crashed through it."

Karin backed away and then asked with exaggerated mouth expressions, "What eagle?"

Erik's eyes diverted past Karin's face. He raised his arm and pointed.

"THAT EAGLE!"

Fifty

The grayish light of the tunnel opening appeared, but something felt wrong. It was shrinking - closing fast! Arindis streamlined her body to full extent. The hole turned to complete black. There was no time to think, she continued and shot through the opening. The night shadows of the bridge caused the hole to turn black seconds before the final closure.

Arindis crashed into the swamp. But maintained the branch above the water. She ended on her back against the tall shore weeds. She shook off the effects. Immediately she saw why the bridge had closed. There was a vehicle going across it. She caught a glimpse of the tail lights as it exited the bridge.

Arindis screamed out of the swamp like a fiery guided missile toward the site. Without second thought she sailed through the swirling clouds. Against the fierce wind she had difficulty, but finally secured a hold on one of the thicker limbs of the Yggdrasil Tree.

Her heart fell deep in her chest when she saw that Hel was already there… *'I'm late,'* she thought to herself. *'Everything's lost…I failed.'* She was devastated. …

'*KARIN!*' She stared blankly at Hel.

The Nidhogg and Hel turned their attention to *her*.

Arindis saw immediately that they were starring at the fire branch! Fear was in their eyes. '*Can this fire still defeat her?*' she thought. '*Maybe the Well was wrong and I can still...*'
Two fireballs shot out of Hel's eyes and headed directly at her.

Arindis sprang from the branch and banked. One fireball exploded the branch she had just left and the other hit one behind it. Arindis dove then reversed her direction. One of the Tree's arms came violently whistling by her, missing by inches. The air current sent her into a spin. She saw the other arm coming and dove. The claw swooped above. They were no match for her speed. Hel shot two more fireballs into the clouds. They let loose with a thunderous rain of red. The drops formed wind-sheets of crimson that zinged horizontally. She had all she could do to dodge the red blades and the tree's swinging arms. The wind stopped and the rain fell straight down. Arindis spread her wings and pointed the flame of the branch straight under her. The flames climbed quickly. Hel made a smug smile. Suddenly, one limbed claw knocked the branch out of Arindis' grip. The strength of the blow turned her into an uncontrollable spin. She crashed into the top branches of an adjacent tree. The fire-branch plummeted toward the murky ground waves. It landed with the heaviest portion first so the fire remained above the waves; it was sinking fast.

Arindis was entangled in the branches of the tree. The fire was growing smaller; it was going out - there was no time to get to it ... it would soon be over. Both tree claws were coming straight at her.

The rain beat on the flames. Four flames ... three flames ... two ... an arm passed over the two remaining flames and splashed into the brown water beneath. Like a submarine rising from the ocean's depths, the branch was suddenly lifted by a small hand ... it was Karin's hand.

Karin had not known the significance of the fiery branch, only that it was the object of the battle and she felt compelled to rescue it. She swam back to the stairs, holding it above the waves. She had to get it under the shelter of the stairs.

Arindis sprang away from the tree's first claw at the last second and landed on top of it. She dug her talons around one of its scales and held on. The other claw reached over, but she used the same tactic and landed on it. She cast a gaze to where the branch had been. To her amazement it was lit and moving towards the Temple's stairs. She dove down.

Hel saw where she was headed.

Karin reached the bottom step and went around behind the staircase.

Fireballs exploded as they hit the stairs sending the woodened steps and some of the men scattering in all different directions. The force of the first shots did not affect Karin. The second shots would.

As Hel was preparing to let off two more fireballs, three gunshots rang out and her attention was diverted in the opposite direction.

*****

The truck slid sideways to a halt at the apex of the crater. Sam swung open his door and got out. The Legion came out and stood beside him. His attention was centered on the scene below. Dr. Waythill came around the front of the truck. It was raining on them. But the red rain was only falling in the site area. They saw the eagle being hit and a fiery branch sailing downward to the dark moving ground.

"What the Hell?" Sam exclaimed.

"Exactly," Dr. Waythill confirmed, looking straight ahead.

Sam looked at him and then back at the surreal action before him. They witnessed the fireballs being shot.

"Sam, shoot at her," Dr. Waythill yelled.

"What?"

The Legion was frozen.

"Trust me Sam; I know what I'm talking about. Shoot now while I get ready."

"Get ready?"

Sam turned to him and was momentarily stunned at what he saw. Dr. Waythill was looking right at him. This was the first time Sam could see his full face. He had no left eye. It wasn't just missing with an eyelid closed over the socket. He had no left eyebrow, eye, or anything over on that side of his face - just skin.

"DAMN IT SAM, PLEASE!"

Sam turned and fired three shot. The rounds fell harmlessly short of their mark. Sam looked questionably at the barrel of the gun. He knew the target was in range, yet the bullets fell like they had no force behind them. He looked back at the horned woman.

Two flashes darted from her face.

"OH SHIT!" Sam shouted out as he dove for the ground.

One fireball flew over his head. The other hit the Legion in the chest and sent him flying back on fire into the side of Sam's truck. The truck exploded and sent it rolling as a fireball into the trees. Sam looked back at his burning truck then looked at what had been Dr. Waythill. There, in his place stood a god-like figure. Arrayed in golden body armor holding a large golden sword in his left hand, he had white hair that extended passed his shoulders and a long white beard. He was a more imposing and powerful figure than Sam had ever seen, even with his left eye gone. He raised the sword vertically and with the other hand pointed down toward the horned woman.

Sam turned back and saw her shoot another salvo of fireballs. The fireballs were harmlessly absorbed into the sword of the former Dr Waythill.

*****

Karin moved the branch further back. It was barely aglow. She turned it so the flames would catch onto other portions. She was physically spent; treading water on pure adrenaline.

As Arindis got closer she suddenly realized who was holding the branch …KARIN. Her heart filled with relief and joy. She grabbed the branch with one claw and Karin's arm with the other. With all the force she could extract from her wings, she raised both out of the murky cesspool. Arindis rose and navigated to the spot where she last saw Erik. He was still there. She gently released Karin beside him.

Arindis turned her attention to the tree and saw that Nidhogg and Hel were still turned around. She flew at them. Nidhogg noticed her approach. Both of its arms swiped at her, but she dodged through them. Only a few specks of fire still ate at the bark. She released the branch over the pit and watched.

The branch fell on target. Suddenly, the webbed hand of Hel snatched the branch out of the air. She was about to bring her hand back to her and extinguish the flame forever when eight steel sharp talons suddenly stung into her wrist. Arindis thrashed onto Hel's wrist with all the force she could gain. Her hand opened from the attack and the branch dropped, finding its mark in the blistering lava of the tree.

The last few sparkles of flames disappeared in the lava. It quickly leveled its boil and turned into a blackened, tar-like substance that pasted itself lifeless in the hole. The hole at the base of the tree started a vacuum force. The ghostlike demons, which were still around the site, were caught in the hole's suction. The ground became frozen solid in its wavy posture and the rain ceased.

Arindis was still attached to Hel's wrist and watched her reaction as the fiery belly of the tree went dark. Arindis released her grip and flew to a tree on the crest of the crater.

Hel looked at the two on the site's rim who had diverted her attention. Her eyes slitted with defiance.

"Hel, daughter of Loki, you have desecrated my good will and returned!" Odin shouted as he pointed his accusing index finger.

Hel pointed back in defiance. ***"I vowed I would one day destroy those who*** *would not have me,"* she retorted.

"This is not your world and never shall be. You will return to your domain."

A deepened rumbling sound resonated from the cavity in the tree. Soon it grew to a level of earthquake proportions. The Nidhogg's eye closed and as it did, it vanished. The ribboned end of its tongue vibrated as it sounded a loud squall. It stiffened and was forcibly tugged back into the earth. The arms turned back into limbs.

Hel watched helplessly as her accomplice vanished and then turned her attention back to Odin. She saw Arindis and shot a barrage of fireballs at her. Arindis flew off the tree. The fireballs hit the tree and ignited it. Hel continued to fire more at her, lighting up the night like tracer rounds of artillery guns. Odin's hand diverted the fireballs. They landed in the treetops; the flames engulfing them.

Hel ceased her attack when the ground below her trembled. She looked down. A crack in the ground started from the Temple stairs and jaggedly cut toward the dune - widening as it lengthened. Similar cracks originated from the outside of the site toward the dune. When the breaks met, the dune shook and sank into the earth.

"This is not the end. I shall one day destroy this earth. You've simply delayed the inevitable!" she shouted as she sank into the earth. The ground of the cratered surface fell away, like broken ice affected by a spring thaw.

Fifty-one

Giant flames exploded from the bottoms of ever-deepening crevices. The sacrificial altar broke apart. The surrounding buildings buckled. The trees wavered and toppled like dominoes. The Temple stairs and platform were going to be the next to go.

Arindis suddenly remembered Erik and Karin.

A Legion saw Arindis approach and shouted, *"The eagle is coming to save us!"*

The men began pushing toward the direction of her approach. Fighting ensued. In the chaos many were knocked off the structure. Their screams echoed the pain of being cooked on the way down. What was left of the complex began to fall apart. The men stopped their fighting and grasped for anything they could

Karin and Erik grasped onto the wall's edge.

Arindis perched on the top edge of the wall just above them. She kept her wings spread and stared at Erik. He got the message.

"She's come to rescue us."

"She can't possibly take both of us," Karin said over the screams in the air, "…

you go."

The floor angled violently beneath them. They looked down.

"We go together or perish together." Erik shouted.

Arindis flapped her wings and let out a powerful "SCREECH".
They both looked at her.

She raised her right claw.

Karin lost her grip as the floor collapsed. Erik grabbed her upper arm. His grip weakened and their hands clasp together.

Arindis dove and wrapped her talons around the coupling of their hands.

The floor gave way and sank.

Arindis pumped her wings as hard as she could. The weight resisted like an anchor caught on coral.

They descended despite Arindis's best effort.

"She can't do it!" Erik shouted looking at the flames growing closer. "We're going down!"

Karin looked up. "Trust her Erik! …She can do it! …Trust her!"

Hearing the words of faith swelled a power within Arindis so great she flapped her wings as if they were motorized and set on super high; they all began to rise. Karin and Erik held on to one another with their free arms.

Arindis flew over to Odin and Sam; she hovered above them.

"He's hurt," Karin shouted.

Sam wrapped his arms around Erik's waist and gently lowered him to the ground. Karin knelt at his side. She lifted his head and shoulders on her lap and kissed him.

Arindis landed aside Odin.

"That's the bird that brought me these clothes," Sam said.

"Her name is Arindis," Odin said. He faced her, "she's my daughter."

"Wait a minute, where's…" Sam turned to look at Karin and Erik. He quickly returned his questioning eyes to Odin. "Where's Susan?"

Odin stepped closer to Arindis and gently placed the blade of his sword on her head.

"Right here," he whispered.

Odin raised his sword above their heads.

"You have fulfilled my *trust*." He raised his face to the heavens.

A circle of stared lights began spinning above their heads. They looked into each others eyes as the circle lowered over them. Their figures melded with the swirls.

Sam, Karin, and Erik had to shield their eyes from the brightness. The light spun to a pillar of blue-white. A soft tone filled the air. The pillar faded its brilliance and its rotation slowed to reveal two differently shaped figures. Dr. Waythill and Susan were posed exactly like they were before the light stars encircled them. They fell into each other expressing sighs of relief.

"It's over dear," her father comforted.

Susan muffled, "I... I know

Sam was looking on in disbelief. "Susan?" Sam questioned aloud.

Susan lifted her face from her father's chest and turned to look at Sam.

"Yes, Sam, it's me," Susan said. She smiled nervously at him and sensed the conflict within as he appeared frozen and unsure of his thoughts.

"Go to him," her father quietly urged.

Susan broke from her father's arms.

Sam's eyes smiled with joy and relief as Susan came to him. They embraced. They looked into each other's eyes.

Susan touched his face with her hand and slowly ran her fingers along some of the scratches. "You're injured."

"I fell in the swamp."

Susan's eyes went from the scratches back to his eyes with a questioned expression.

"Several times," Sam added.

Susan smiled.

Sam paused then kissed her.

A weakness of surrender cascaded throughout her body. She melted against him. Sam released his kiss. He stared deeply into Susan's eyes.

"I love you, *Little Lady*."

"I love you too," she sighed.

Fifty-two

The ground trembled and shook. The crater exploded. The air filled with fire burning the clouds away to reveal a starry night sky. As fast as the fire came, it extinguished and everything quieted in the site. The cracks and crevices mended without a trace of ever having existed. Everything was gone. It resembled a large dried up lake-bottom.

"Look!" Karin cried.

On the edge of the crater was the smoldering Ceremony Book, lying open faced. Susan looked for anything to smother it before flames ignited. She whipped off the coat Sam had put around her shoulders and threw it over the book, patting it gently.

Sam knelt beside her.

"What is it?" he asked.

"Answers, hopefully," she said as she pulled the coat off the book.

"Answers?" Sam said automatically.

Susan turned to him, "You don't have any questions about what you were just a part?"

Sam nodded with a bowed head. "Sorry, I spoke before thought."

"That huge tree was the Yggdrasil, the *life* tree. If it dies, all life dies. It was destroyed, yet we're still here! Why?"

"It's a good thing it was blown out of there," Dr. Waythill said as he leaned down for a closer look, "It looks like some of the pages were charred."

"Get up and put your hands on your head," a rough voice sounded behind them. The man stepped from the shadows. It was the High Elder Larsen. He was standing with a rifle pointed at those around the book. He looked like a man that had been beaten once too often. He was a little bent over without his hat. His hair was bloody and there was blood oozing down his face.

"Dad ...no!" Erik cried out from the resting lap of his wife.

He looked down at the two.

"Erik what are you ...Karin?" he said in a bewildered voice

"Don't Dad, it's all over."

"Nothing's over." He stepped toward Erik. and wiped at his bloody eye.

"They're all gone: Lord Lokan, The Savior, everything."

"Impossible."

"Look for yourself." Erik motioned toward the site.

He moved to within ten feet of the ridge, stopped and looked. He turned and cast his eyes on the book at Susan's feet. Then looked at her. "You... you're the cause of all this."

He pointed his rifle directly at her face.

"DAD, DON"T! Erik raised and shouted.

Sam made a move.

The High Elder redirected the gun at him and Sam froze.

"DAD STOP!" Erik shouted again.

The High Elder paused in thought, staring at Sam.

"You're the one with the gun," he finally said. "Where is it?"

Sam cautiously moved his gun hand from his head.

"Stop," the High Elder ordered. "Take it out with your other hand, using the thumb and one finger."

Sam did as directed.

"Toss it over here; carefully."

It landed midway between them. About five feet from Karin and Erik.

He motioned the rifle toward the smoldering pile of metal that was once Sam's truck. "All of you, over there and face toward the truck."

The High Elder looked at Erik. "Our time has come," he said with vaulted excitement in his voice.

"What do you mean?" Erik asked softly.

"We have the book; we can resurrect the Savior within the other tree and continue its work." We can bring *HER* back. She will be grateful … I will be Lord and you will be at my side as High Elder."

"No," he said shaking his head, "It has to stop". He looked into Karin's eyes then at his father. "This can't go on anymore. Don't you see? The Savior, the immortality, the innocents, all of this," he raised his head, "This…it's all wrong." He looked at his Father with a pleading in his eyes.

"You're forgetting what's in that book." The High Elder picked it up. "It is our destiny to serve The Savior and bring *HER* radiance and glory to the entire world."

"You don't know what you're saying," Susan said. She and the others were still faced away.

"Silence!"

"She's not coming to rule; she's coming to destroy," Susan shouted back, "you, me, the whole world!"

"You're wrong. It is written, that *SHE* shall rule the lands that once banished her."

"Hel!" Dr. Waythill said. Then he turned to face the High Elder. The others turned also.

The High Elder looked at him.

"The ruler of the Land of Nifilheim," "Hel, she's the daughter of the God Loki."

All stood silenced.

Dr Waythill continued, "You're right; she was banished from all the lands and sent to rule her likenesses in Nifilheim. And she vowed, she and her brother Fenfir..." he paused and said to he group, "That's the Serpent/Wolf under the bridge by the way". He turned back to face the Elder, "They vowed to return one day, but not to rule, they vowed to come back and destroy all – the whole world."

"He's right. The Savior killed Lord Lokan," Karin added. "He was sacrificed instead of me."

The High Elder raised the gun and fired.

"SHUT UP!"

They cowered.

"You're all lying."

He looked at Erik and with a cold voice said, "You have to decide. Come with me or stay with these others ... and join them in their fate."

Eric didn't move.

After a pause The High Elder sneered, "Very well, it's apparent that you no longer belong to the order. Thereby you are just one of them and no longer exist ... my son, and his wife, are dead. Both of you, move over to the others"

"I can't walk," Erik said.

The High Elder turned to the others, "You, old man. Help her move him over there."

Dr Waythill nodded and moved to the couple.

"I'll take the shoulders, you take his feet," he instructed.

Dr. Waythill gently lifted Erik by his back. Karin lifted Erik's feet by the ankles.

Karin made a few steps backward, stumbled and fell.

"Watch it!" The High Elder warned.

She got up brushed her robe, then continued her task.

When in place The High Elder moved and positioned himself about ten feet from them, like a sergeant facing his squad formation.

Karin was to his far left supporting Erik's head in her lap. To their left was Dr. Waythill, to his left Sam and then Susan.

He looked at Susan with disdain.

"If it weren't for you, none of this would have happened."

Susan's face was etched in fear.

He pointed the rifle barrel at her face. "Enjoy Hell…." The trigger gave way under the pressure of the index finger.

Sam lunged forward to grab the barrel. His fingers landed on the bluing steel too late and the gun fired.

The shot hit the side of the head and traveled through the skull, shattering the rear wall of bone into a thousand splinters. Hair, gray matter and blood splattered like a sledgehammer hitting a stuffed bag of tomatoes.

No one was more startled than Susan when High Elder Larsen fell. Everyone looked to their right and saw a zephyr of smoke rising from the end of the pistol barrel Erik was holding.

Fifty-three

Erik's father lay on his side still holding the rifle. His dead eyes stared at Susan. Susan knelt in front of Erik and Karin.

"I'm so sorry."

Erik shook his head.

"I lost him years ago," Erik whispered. He looked at Susan. "I hope you *trust* me now."

While this had played out something else was happening. The fire in the trees had spread. Their branches cried with pops and crackles. A large limb crashed to the ground just on the other side of Sam's truck.

"The fire will spread to town." Karin said. "The people won't come out of their homes; they'll be burnt alive. We must warn them."

Sam went to Erik and put him on his back in the Fireman carry.

Dr. Waythill picked up the book.

Flames from the tops of the trees spread across the road, igniting the trees on the other side.

Karin and Susan led the way, each carrying a weapon. Dr. Waythill brought up the rear. When they reached the town they dispersed.

Sam put Erik on the first porch.

"There," he said as he lowered him. He straightened and began to stretch. "I should have done this before I picked you..." he stopped before completing the sentence.

"What?" Erik asked.

"Your...your...err...face, it's... different somehow," Sam looked over both his shoulders and then looked back at Erik. "It must be the light of the fire, or these old street lamps."

"What do you mean different?"

"It's nothing. I thought you were younger that's all."

Erik looked down at the backs of his hands. His knuckles were more pronounced. His fingers started to twitch into an arthritic curl. He raised them to his face and felt the deepening cornrows of skin on his forehead.

"Please," Erik said in a weaken voice. "Get a mirror, or something."

Sam took off to the other side of the street and went around the side of the building. Dr. Waythill was coming. Sam ran up to him.

"You better come," Sam said.

"What's the ...?"

"It's Erik."

They both returned to Eric.

Dr. Waythill looked at Erik's eyes set deep in their sockets with pulpy lids that only opened halfway. His pointy jaw quivered as the muscles strained to hold it closed.

"Karrr ..," Erik mouthed out from his cracked lips.

"Quiet now," Dr. Waythill said. "Sam, help me get his back supported against this post."

"Dad! Sam!" Susan's voice shouted from a distance.

Randall Stevens

"Go see what the matter is." Dr. Waythill said. "I'll stay here."

Sam saw Susan helping Karin walk.

"It's awful Sam," Susan gasped.

Sam lifted Karin in his arms. She was weak and frail.

"What happened?"

"She's growing old. Everyone is! They…they were turning old before my eyes, sitting in chairs, lying on the floors, wrinkles forming, hair and teeth falling out, their bodies would shrink and bend. There were decayed bodies…skin fallen off…their insides leaked out through their clothes…it was awful."

"There's something with Erik too," Sam said. "He asked for her."

Sam could feel Karin's weight disappearing as he jogged. He gently placed Karin on the porch aside Erik.

"Karin," Erik whispered. He reached to her face, but didn't have the strength to hold it there. Karin grabbed his hand with both of hers and placed it on her cheek. She formed a smile. Tears dripped from the corners of her wrinkled eyes and followed the age lines down her weathered face.

"You're…"

"Shhhhh," Karin pursed with her lips. "I know."

Erik nodded and closed his eyes.

"Miss Susan," Erik barely mouthed.

Susan leaned in.

"I…mmm sor…sorry."

Susan grinned and blinked quickly to prevent her tears from falling.

Erik moved his eyes back to Karin and said, "love…" then closed his eyes for the last time.

Karin squeezed his hand one more time and carefully placed it on his chest.

A loud roar of rotor blades suddenly filled the air. They looked up and saw a helicopter in the dawn's sky.

"Go," Karin said, "I'll stay. Take the book and find a way, save them."

"But," Susan said.

"You can't get caught here. Go, now, your car is in the back alley shed."

"She's right," Dr. Waythill said.

"They'll wave off babble from an old lady. I'll live long enough. Now go!"

Susan hesitated.

"Please... go. And remember to save the innocents."

"Innocents?" Susan questioned.

"I trust you," Karin said as she leaned back and closed her eyes.

Susan slowly bent down to kiss Karin on the cheek.

*****

"Look's better than the day I picked it up," Susan lightened after they opened the shed door.

Sam tore away the headliner hanging around Susan's head.

"You all right Dad?" Susan asked.

"Fine, just go. I want to go through this book."

Sam looked out the side rear windows as Susan kept her attention focused on the swamp road.

"Damn." Sam said, "Look at that!"

"Sam, I can't," Susan rebounded.

"The swamp ... it's disappearing as we go by," Sam said.

Dr. Waythill looked up as Susan hit the brakes.

Everything behind them had turned to flat prairie land with cacti, mesas, and light brown sand. The Texas sun was spreading long shadows across a flattened landscape.

"Where's the town? ... the fire? ... the fricking road?" Susan asked.

"Everything has gone back," Dr Waythill said.

They were silent for a moment.

"Susan, I want to ask you something. Karin mentioned a name, Lord Lokan, said he was sacrificed"

"Yes," Susan responded. "He was in charge of the town, had magical powers and controlled everything."

"That answers some questions"

"What do you mean?"

"I mean Lord Lokan was in fact the Evil God Loki. And I doubt very much if he was destroyed. He has the power to turn himself into anything. Your brother Thor and I searched for him after he managed to get Balder killed. We found him in a mountain stream as a Salmon. There's no telling what he manifested himself into before the body he was using was sacrificed. That whole thing back there was a family project. Loki, and his oldest son Fenfir, the wolf serpent, were all involved in summoning Hel to once again wreak havoc on the world. Loki must have thought he could control her on earth, but somehow she managed to attempt to betray him with the help of the Nidhogg."

"Nidhogg?" Sam spurted out. "What is all this?"

"That giant snake in the tree, Nidhogg. It's the main serpent in the Land of Nifilheim or generally known as Hell."

"It had an eye," Sam said. "I saw it."

"Actually that's Dad's eye," Susan added casually.

"What!?"

"Sam, it's all explained in the Norse Mythology. Odin, the God I reincarnated from, sacrificed his eye in the Mirmir Well for the power of wisdom and magic. The Mirmir Well was captured by the Nidhogg and that's how he got the eye."

"That's right," Susan said. "It was in the Temple. Mother showed me in a vision. It turned me into Arindis the eagle so I could battle the Nidhogg and Hel and protect the Yggdrasil."

Sam's face was one big question mark.

"Sam," Dr. Waythill said. "The Yggdrasil Tree is the tree of all life. Without it all dies. Its root reaches down into Nifilheim. The Nidhogg's task was to gnaw through it roots. In order to keep that from happening Odin turned Susan into the eagle so she could fly into Nifilheim and drive the Nidhogg away with Hell's fires."

"The battle went on for eons," Susan said. "Finally the Nidhogg prevailed. The Mirmir Well, located at the base of the Yggdrasil, wanted to save the tree. So it turned me into human form to reincarnate and one day be brought back and fight it again."

"It could turn you back to the eagle, but only I could turn you back to my daughter," Dr. Waythill added.

"What about the tree?" Sam asked. "It was destroyed."

"There must be another and I think the Mirmir Well might know something about that. I saw my eye disappear from the Nidhogg before it was sucked into the earth."

"I remember that!" Sam confirmed.

"This book will tell us more. For now I think we should get out of here. Even though "here" is going away."

Susan turned back and continued on the road.

Sam didn't say a word.

They came to the bridge and Susan stopped the SUV. Without a word she put the gearshift in park and got out.

"What's she doing?" Sam asked.

"I don't know," answered Dr. Waythill as they watched her cross the bridge.

"By the way," Sam turned. "How'd you find us? ... the road? ... the town? ... the truck?" He raised his voice an octave, "And how do I fit in all this?"

Dr.Waythill smiled a slightly. "I got the directions from the sheriff's office. He called in his location and they were kind enough to show me on the map. When I found the truck I assumed it was yours. I knew my caddy wouldn't make it down the road so I took your truck; simple."

"It was locked."

"I got to thinking what kind of guy you were. You seemed like the kind that, for the most part, liked to have a back up." Dr. Waythill reached into his pocket and brought out a small metal case. "I found this." Marked on the metal case were the words Hide-A-Key.

Sam smiled.

"One thing you have to know Sam. The power to do all that we did was carried in us in case the world was ever in danger of destruction. It's over now and so are the powers we carried. Susan and I are mere mortals," he smiled. "We're back to normal."

"And me and her, does she know that?"

"Of course, about you and her. When you first met was there an attraction of some kind. You know an unexplainable magnetism?"

Sam turned to look at Susan. "Yes, there was something between us. I don't know about her, but I sure felt it."

Dr. Waythill smiled.

"What?" Sam said.

"For now Sam, let's just say in a former life you knew each other." He put a hand on Sam's and furthered, "You were very, very close." He removed the hand and went back to the book.

Susan stood silent on the other side of the bridge. She mentally replayed all that had happened to her. She looked over to the sign. Welcome; 'We count our Blessings'. A small part of the third board had been broken off. She looked down and saw a small piece of wood sticking out from under a bush. She picked it up and turned it over. There was the word, *on* inscribed on it. She held it on the sign to the place from where it had broken. The sign now read, 'Welcome, We count '*on*' our Blessings. '*What a difference one small word can make*,' she thought. Susan pulled the wood piece back and cupped it in her palm. She took off the coat and not wanting to have any reminders of her ordeal, let it drop on the bridge.

Susan pulled the SUV onto the asphalt of the service road and parked. As they walked back to the Cadillac, Sam remarked, "Even the entranceway has vanished."

The trees were still appropriately positioned with brush and cacti spattered around, but the road; swamp and fog had all melted into thin air.

"Sam there is one thing I've learned through all this," Susan said.

"What's that?'

"If you trust the right people, they'll do the right thing."

They smiled and embraced.

"Arindis vs. Hel"

by Randall Stevens

HELLN, TEXAS